"You offered to pay anything for my services. Or have you forgotten?"

Grasping her arms, Damien pulled her onto the bed. Her hair spread across his pillow.

"I haven't forgotten. How much do you want?"

"Money isn't what I want from you, Jenna," he said. He dipped his head, inhaling the delicate scent that rose from her throat. "No, I have enough money."

Her breathing quickened. "What *do* you want?"

"A trade. That would be fair, wouldn't it?"

"I'm not negotiating any deal while I'm lying in your bed."

"Ah, but, Jenna," Damien whispered, his hand gently caressing her face. "A bed is the perfect place to negotiate this particular deal."

Dear Reader,

Whether or not it's back to school—for you *or* the kids—Special Edition this month is the place to return to for romance!

Our THAT SPECIAL WOMAN!, Serena Fanon, is heading straight for a Montana wedding in Jackie Merritt's *Montana Passion*, the second title in Jackie's MADE IN MONTANA miniseries. But that's not the only wedding this month—in Christine Flynn's *The Black Sheep's Bride*, another blushing bride joins the family in the latest installment of THE WHITAKER BRIDES. And three little matchmakers scheme to bring their unsuspecting parents back together again in *Daddy of the House*, book one of Diana Whitney's new miniseries, PARENTHOOD.

This month, the special cross-line miniseries DADDY KNOWS LAST comes to Special Edition. In *Married... With Twins!*, Jennifer Mikels tells the tale of a couple on the brink of a breakup—that is, until they become instant parents to two adorable girls. September brings two Silhouette authors to the Special Edition family for the first time. Shirley Larson's *A Cowboy Is Forever* is a reunion ranch story not to be missed, and in Ingrid Weaver's latest, *The Wolf and the Woman's Touch*, a sexy loner agrees to help a woman find her missing niece—but only if she'll give him one night of passion.

I hope you enjoy each and every story to come!

Sincerely,

Tara Gavin,
Senior Editor

Please address questions and book requests to:
Silhouette Reader Service
U.S.: 3010 Walden Ave., P.O. Box 1325, Buffalo, NY 14269
Canadian: P.O. Box 609, Fort Erie, Ont. L2A 5X3

INGRID WEAVER

THE WOLF AND THE WOMAN'S TOUCH

Published by Silhouette Books
America's Publisher of Contemporary Romance

To Ella Susi, with love. Thanks, Mom.

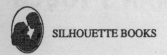

SILHOUETTE BOOKS

ISBN 0-373-24056-2

THE WOLF AND THE WOMAN'S TOUCH

Copyright © 1996 by Ingrid Caris

This edition published by arrangement with Harlequin Books S.A.

Printed in U.S.A.

INGRID WEAVER

admits to being a compulsive reader who loves a book that can make her cry. A former teacher, now a homemaker and mother, she delights in creating stories that reflect the wonder and adventure of falling in love. When she isn't writing or reading, she enjoys old "Star Trek" reruns, going on sweater-knitting binges, taking long walks with her husband and waking up early to canoe after camera-shy loons.

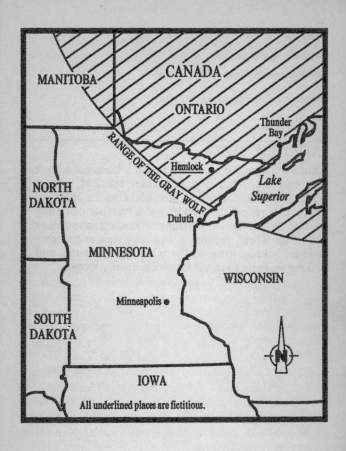

MANITOBA

CANADA

ONTARIO

Thunder
Bay

RANGE OF THE GRAY WOLF

Hemlock

NORTH
DAKOTA

Lake
Superior

Duluth

MINNESOTA

WISCONSIN

Minneapolis ●

SOUTH
DAKOTA

N

IOWA

All underlined places are fictitious.

Prologue

It was in that timeless, suspended, vulnerable moment before sleep, when weariness dissolves the body's defenses and wariness finally seeps from the mind, that Damien sensed the woman's cry. Wordless, formless, soundless, the soul-tearing anguish seared through his brain.

His response was instant and unthinking. Help. He had to help her. Whoever she was, wherever she was, she needed him. He rolled from the bed and stumbled over his discarded clothes, weaving past the heavy furniture by feel. Even now the echoes of her plea vibrated through the air he breathed, infusing him with her urgency and frustration and desperate hope.

Cold tiles numbed his feet, frigid air whispered over his naked skin when he reached the main room. His tall, lean body gleamed bronze in the light of the dying fire, his raven black hair fell in sleep-tangled waves to his shoulders. He crossed the floor and fumbled with the latch on the front door, his fingers tingling, clumsy with the un-controlled spurt of adrenaline that pounded through his blood.

She had called him. She needed him. He had to help.

The latch gave. He braced one heel against the frame and pulled, straining to crack the rim of frost that sealed the door shut. A gust of wind wrenched the knob from his hand, sending the door slamming against the wall, whirl-ing a blast of snow into the cabin. Beyond the shelter of the porch roof the night writhed with shades of black and gray. The storm that had swept in at dusk shrouded the stars, the pines that stood sentinel beside the lane, the granite outcrop that guarded his front yard, everything. There was no light, no hint of movement that didn't be-long, no clue to the woman whose plaintive cry still trem-bled through his mind.

"Where are you?"

His shout was swallowed by the wail of the wind past the eaves.

"Is anyone there?"

A stinging sheet of snow swirled across the threshold and lashed his bare legs, bringing him brutally, com-pletely awake.

He listened, his knuckles white where he gripped the doorframe, each nerve pulsing with sudden awareness, each sense stretching to the limits of human perception. He shouted again. And waited. And shouted again.

Nothing. Only the hiss of smooth-sloped, deepening drifts and the ceaseless scream of the wind.

Not until his voice was hoarse and cold air burned his lungs did Damien finally accept the obvious. Even if she were mere yards away, she wouldn't be able to hear him over the fury of the storm. And he couldn't have heard anyone. Not through the sturdy walls of the cabin, not through the keening in the eaves. No one was there. Of course, no one was there. He had no neighbors, he had no visitors. The nearest road was two miles of steep, twisting hillside away.

It must have been a dream, that was all. A dream.

From the rug on the hearth, Smoke raised his head, eyes glowing yellow in the light of the fire, an inquisitive whine rumbling from his throat.

Damien glanced over his shoulder at the wolf. Yes, it must have been a dream. If the woman's cry had been real, Smoke would have been on his feet and howling at the door. The animal's senses were more acute than his own.

So he couldn't have heard it.

No, he couldn't have *heard* it, but he could have...

"No!"

A dream, that was all it was. That's all it could have been.

A shudder racked his body. Another blast of freezing air shot into the cabin before he caught the edge of the door and swung it shut. He leaned his forehead against the varnished wood, his breath coming in short, sharp pants as he struggled to regain control.

The woman's cry had been a dream, a hell of a vivid dream that had almost compelled him to walk nude into a snowstorm, but that didn't mean anything. No, that didn't mean the nightmare was coming back.

But it had been so real. Just the way it used to be. Slipping past his defenses. Calling him. Drawing him. Wordless, formless, soundless...

Soundless?

No. All that was over. Dead and buried. It wasn't starting again. He'd made his peace.

But it had been so real.

"*No!*" He smashed his fist into the door, sending shafts of pain through bones already stiff with cold. He hit it again, then raised his hand to his mouth, tasting the blood that welled from his split knuckles. His nostrils flared, bringing him the tang of woodsmoke and the subtle bite of snowflakes melting on his skin. Touch, taste, smell. Lungs heaving, he turned around. Flames danced behind the steel-mesh curtain and flared in the draft up the chimney as the fire feasted on the fresh air. A log popped, sparks crackled. Sight, hearing. Senses everyone shared. Senses he could understand and accept. Yes. Reality.

"I didn't hear her," he said. "I didn't hear anything."

The shaking started then. Long, racking shivers that traveled from the top of his spine to the soles of his feet. Damien crossed his arms and moved toward the fireplace, rubbing the chill from his skin. He tugged his grandmother's quilt from the back of the couch and wrapped it around his shoulders before he sank cross-legged to the cushions, clenching his jaw in an effort to keep his teeth from chattering.

He rubbed his face, hearing the rasp of week-old whiskers, feeling the rough scrape against his palms. He'd been asleep, that was all. He'd been working twenty-hour days for the past week and he'd been asleep. Dreams happened to everyone. Even him. He looked toward the shadowed archway of the bedroom and his muscles tightened. The darkness had held monsters when he'd been a child. The unknown had sent him screaming through empty corridors, looking for comfort that no one could give.

Damien had stopped seeking comfort long ago. Just as he'd learned to face the monsters in his own darkness. No, it wasn't starting again. There was no woman. No voice in his head. No one.

With a muttered curse he rose from the couch and stalked to the hearth. Holding the quilt together with his throbbing fist, he picked up the poker and jabbed at the fire until the logs broke apart, then threw more wood on top of the glowing embers. In the sudden flare of light, Smoke pushed onto his haunches and yawned, casually displaying a deadly array of gleaming teeth before he turned around and settled himself farther away from the fire, huffing crankily over being disturbed.

Damien stood motionless, soaking up the heat until his shaking stopped. Gradually the panic eased. He listened to the storm batter the cabin in one vicious gust after another and felt a twinge of satisfaction at the added guarantee of isolation the snow would bring. The road would be impassable for days. Until he was ready to take his work to town, he wouldn't need to see anyone, wouldn't need to risk the contact with all those minds—

No. It was impossible. He hadn't had so much as a twinge of his gift—his curse—for years. He was fine, now. Safe. Normal.

Slowly he turned to face the door. What if it *was* coming back? What if the woman's voice in his head hadn't been a dream? What if, against all the odds, there really was someone out there in the blizzard, calling for his help, needing him?

It would be simple to check. Put on his clothes, grab a flashlight and go outside to look around the property. Just in case... in case the impossible really was happening.

While he was denying her reality, *because* he was denying her reality, she could be dying.

But if he accepted the possibility that the voice in his head might have been real, then he would be admitting what he had spent five years trying to deny. He would have to face the monsters again.

It *couldn't* be coming back. It *couldn't* be starting over. Because if it was...

"Damn," he whispered, rubbing his forehead. He pulled his hands in front of him and stared. His fingers had started to shake again. "Damn."

Chapter One

It couldn't end like this. No, she wasn't going to die this way, frozen to death like that sparrow she had found beside her bird feeder last winter, an object of pity, unknown and unmourned. She had gotten this far, and no seductively soft snowdrift was going to lull her into giving up. So what if her feet were numb? So what if the flashlight batteries were almost gone, and the temperature was dropping, and those trees she had glimpsed looked exactly the same as the ones she had passed twice before?

"No way." Her voice was nothing but a rasping croak against the screaming wind. She braced her arms and pushed herself up, then staggered backward out of the drift. "No way you're going to stay here, Jenna, old girl. You've got too much to do."

One step forward. And another. The dimming flashlight showed little more than a pale swath where the lane should have been. She knew there was a strong possibility that she was going in the wrong direction, but she forced herself to keep moving. It would be too easy to stop, to lay her weary body down in the next snowdrift and let the cold envelop her in its illusion of peace. It would be so simple to close her eyes and let the storm take away the choices and the problems and the pain.

Jenna refused to let doubt take hold. This wasn't hopeless. As long as she kept putting one foot in front of the other, she was making progress. How far could she be from the cabin? It was bound to be nearby. Surely she had walked the two miles by now. Maybe it was around the next bend. She raised her head and squinted against the driving snow. Was it her imagination, or had the blizzard eased?

"There," she mumbled. "It's getting better already. Another few yards and you'll be fine. Think positive."

Sure, positive. A steaming mug of hot chocolate. With marshmallows melting into a gooey foam. And a roaring fire to thaw the ice crystals from her joints, and warm, fluffy blankets to wrap around her shivering shoulders. And soft music, something light and airy to remind her of the promise of spring...

The soothing bubble of her fantasy popped. No, not spring. That was more than three months away, and she had already waited too long. She had to reach that cabin. She had to find Damien Reese and convince him to help her. The private detective had quit. The police were losing hope. Every day that passed was one day too many.

A surge of renewed determination tingled through her body. Jenna Lawrence would not give up. Not this time. The stakes were too high, and she wasn't about to let some measly weather system get in her way. Her feet might be numb, but her legs were still working. Her lungs might be raw, but at least she was still drawing breath. She fumbled with her scarf, feeling ice crunch where the moisture from her breath had frozen on the wool. Leaning into the wind, she plodded forward.

Twelve minutes later, the meager beam from her flashlight winked out, and no amount of shaking, pounding or pleading made it reappear. Jenna kept going, aiming for the center of what she had to believe was the lane to the cabin. The drifts grew deeper, each step forward became an agonizing test of endurance as the overworked muscles in her thighs burned. Not much farther, she told herself. Around the next bend, that was all. She couldn't stop yet.

The snow hit her face without warning, stinging her eyes, clogging her nostrils. It took a moment for Jenna to realize that she had fallen. Rolling to her back, she gasped for air. She had to get up. She braced her hands beside her and pushed. Her arms sank into the powdery snow to the elbows. She tried to bring her feet underneath her, but she couldn't get her legs to move.

With a groan, she shifted to her side, clenched her jaw and curled her knees to her chest. She lost count of the number of attempts it took, but eventually she managed to regain her balance and roll to her feet.

Two steps later she fell again.

Lifting her head, she blew the snow out of her mouth and turned her face to the storm. In the eerie glow that filtered through the clouds, trees were black shadows on shadows, waiting like mourners at a deathbed. And for the first time since she had left Minneapolis and started on this mad, desperate mission, Jenna was truly afraid. It couldn't end like this. Could it?

"No." She barely recognized the weak, wavering voice as her own. Dredging up the last reserves of her strength, she filled her lungs with the numbing air and shouted defiantly into the darkness. *"No!"*

The echo was faint, distorted so that it sounded deeper. And different. It might have been a trick of the gusting wind, but for a second there, it seemed as if she'd heard another voice.

Jenna blinked against the wind-whipped flakes and saw a light flicker beyond the trees.

"Hey!" she croaked. "Over here."

The light moved past her, a swirling beam of brightness tunneling its way through the storm. Within seconds it was lost.

Whether it was real or a hallucination brought on by exhaustion, she didn't care. Just the hope that there might be someone else out in this frozen hell gave her the ability to get to her knees and crawl out of the snowdrift that shrouded her. Help was out there. Maybe just around the next bend. "Hey! Hey, you!"

The light reappeared as a pinpoint shining from the way she had already come. It swung from side to side, strengthening with each passing second until she could see the flattened disk of white that traveled over the surface of the snow. Whoever it was seemed to be following her tracks.

"Hello!" The voice was strong and deep and male. And it was the most beautiful sound she had ever heard. "Can you hear me?"

For a moment Jenna pressed her lips tightly together, fighting the urge to give in to tears of weariness and relief. "Yes," she managed. "I'm here."

The light steadied and advanced directly toward her. A large figure took shape out of the darkness an instant before a powerful beam of light struck her full in the face.

Jenna shielded her eyes with her forearms. "Thank God," she said. "Thank-god-thank-god-thank-god—"

"Can you walk?" The gruff question sliced through her senseless mumbling.

Blinking at the brightness, she focused on the man in front of her. He was an imposing figure, tall and dark, like a phantom suddenly materialized from the storm. She blinked again. A hood shadowed his features, and a bulky parka ballooned over his body. Large boots were laced up to his knees. Snowshoes allowed him to stand easily on top of the drift that had nearly swallowed her. Phantom or man, it didn't matter. He was her only chance of getting out of this blizzard. She reached out for him, grasping his leg above the ankle as she tried to raise herself up. Could she walk? She couldn't feel her feet, and her knees seemed to have dissolved. "I don't know."

He set his flashlight down on the snow and leaned forward to catch her under her arms. Roughly he pulled her upright. "Try."

The moment he released his grip her legs collapsed. Swallowing a groan, she fell back into the snowdrift. "Give me a minute to rest," she said. "I'll try again."

"Are you hurt?"

"Can't tell. Can't feel anything."

"Any broken bones?"

"No. I don't think so." She set her jaw and shifted to her side. "I got this far."

With a muttered curse, he lowered himself to one knee and yanked her into a sitting position. Before she knew what he intended, he ducked his head, twisted his body and slid her across his shoulders.

"Hey, what—"

"Just keep still," he ordered, adjusting her position so that she was draped around his neck. He grasped her left leg and arm securely in front of his chest, reached for his flashlight with his free hand and rose smoothly to his feet.

Her head bumped against his shoulder and her chapped cheek rubbed painfully against the coarse fabric of his parka with every step he took. The position she was in was sending the blood to her brain in a nauseating rush, but Jenna wasn't about to protest. "Thanks," she gasped between steps.

He grunted and headed for the trees.

A low-hanging branch slapped against her thighs. Groggily she wondered where he was taking her. Not that she had a choice. Any place was better than that snow-drift. Her rescuer was moving quickly, his stride strong and steady despite the burden her limp weight must be. After a few minutes he reached a set of snowshoe tracks and turned to follow them. Evidently he was heading back wherever he had come from.

And there was only one place within ten square miles that could be.

The realization settled heavily over her exhaustion-fogged brain. She hadn't been able to see his face, but it had to be him. Damien Reese. She had come here to find him, to seek his help. But not like this. Oh, God. This wasn't what she had planned. It wasn't even close. She should have reached the cabin by noon, stated her case the way she'd rehearsed, convinced him to help her, then been back at the motel in Hemlock by dinner.

What she should have done, and what she had yet to do, whirled through her head like the snow that danced in the flashlight's beam. She closed her eyes to shut out the diz-zying upside-down view of moving snowshoes and tried to concentrate on the reason she was here, and what she would say to this phantom-man who was carrying her, and how she would salvage this situation.

But there were some things that even her usually in-domitable will couldn't overcome. Two dozen swaying, rocking steps later, the strain her body had endured fi-nally caught up with her. Silently, mercifully, Jenna slid from consciousness.

By the time Damien reached the shelter of the porch, the lull in the storm was over. Wind curled and moaned around the eaves, sending plumes of fresh snow over his tracks. He squatted down to unfasten his snowshoes, cursing under his breath when the woman started to shift sideways. Although she was lighter than she had appeared at first in that bulky jacket, after more than a mile of fighting for his balance in the wind and the drifts he was beginning to feel every pound of her slight weight. Twisting quickly, he shrugged her back onto his shoulders before he straightened up, stamped as much snow as he could off his boots, then maneuvered her through the doorway into the cabin. With a flick of his heel he kicked the door shut behind him.

The noise roused Smoke, who lifted his head and sniffed. Black fur rose stiffly at the back of his neck as a low growl came from the wolf's throat.

"Easy, boy," Damien said. He wiped his feet on the mat by the door and crossed the floor to the couch. Ignoring Smoke's increasingly ominous growls, he slid the woman onto the cushions, then stripped off his thick mittens and parka, unlaced his boots and tossed everything in the direction of the door. Puddles were already forming where he had walked. The extra logs he'd added to the fire before he'd gone outside had made the interior of the cabin hot enough to steam up the windows.

The woman shifted. Shivers racked her body, sending a trickle of powdery snow onto the floor.

"Hey, lady." He leaned over and lightly shook her shoulder. "Can you hear me?"

She moaned and curled onto her side, drawing her knees to her chest. Apart from the shivering, she didn't move again. She had passed out shortly after he had found her, which was little wonder. She had to be incredibly stubborn or incredibly courageous to have made it as far as she had in that storm. He'd seen her wavering tracks, the places where she'd fallen, the furrows she'd plowed when she'd only had enough strength left to crawl.

Damien tamped down the trace of admiration that stirred over this stranger's determination. He didn't know her, and he didn't want to know her. As soon as the snow stopped, he'd send her back where she came from. But in order to do that, he had to get her warmed up as quickly as possible.

Grasping her ankle firmly, he tugged at her boots. The soft leather was a tight fit, probably because of the thick socks she wore, and it took several seconds of wiggling before the boots finally came free. He dropped them to the floor and moved her arms aside in order to undo the zipper of her ski jacket. It was neon pink, and even the mellow firelight failed to subdue the outrageous color. He eased it off gently, then unwrapped her ice-encrusted scarf and slipped off her hat. Strands of fine blond hair spilled across the cushion and fell over her cheek, obscuring her face. One lock brushed his wrist, a whisper of silk. He hissed sharply and jerked his hand back as if he'd been burned.

He had to be sure not to touch her. After what had happened tonight, he didn't want to risk triggering anything else.

It's her fault.

She was the one who had called to him. She was the one who had resurrected the nightmare. And now it was all going to start again.

He straightened up and rubbed his eyes, then curled his hands into fists as he looked at her. If only he hadn't heard her, if only he hadn't gone out to check...

God, what was he thinking? Had living alone finally robbed him of his humanity? If he hadn't gone out to check, she might have died.

Tightening his jaw, he moved his gaze to her body. Her sweater appeared dry, but patches of dampness darkened the faded denim of her jeans. They would have to come off. Careful not to let his fingers come into contact with her skin, he unsnapped the waistband, lowered the zipper and peeled her jeans down her legs. He barely spared a glance at the peach-colored lace and the pale curves he uncovered before he retrieved the quilt from where he had dropped it earlier and spread it over the woman's form. He added the remaining blankets from his bed, tucking them securely behind her back and under her knees.

She still lay curled in a fetal position, shudders rippling spasmodically along her length. As long as she was shivering, it meant that her system was working to warm itself up. Since her breathing was steady, and she had been conscious when he had found her, she was probably suffering more from exhaustion than from hypothermia. When she woke up fully he'd try to get her to drink something hot to help raise her body temperature, but in the meantime, there wasn't much more he could do.

Smoke snarled, baring his teeth at the figure on the couch. Damien walked to the hearth and nudged the wolf aside with the edge of his foot. "That's enough, Smoke."

Yellow predator eyes turned toward him in a brief struggle of wills.

"I have to take care of her," he went on, talking to himself more than the animal. "I have no choice."

After another rumbling snarl to save face, the animal relaxed back onto his haunches and fell silent.

Damien briefly ruffled the fur behind Smoke's ears. He knew the wolf wasn't accustomed to visitors. It was only natural that the animal would react with hostility to a stranger.

The reasons for his own hostility were more complex.

Raking his hands through his hair, he moved to stand beside the couch and looked down at the woman. She was practically lost beneath the layers of blankets. She couldn't be more than an inch or two over five feet tall. He knew she didn't weigh much, and the bare skin he had glimpsed had looked as delicate as porcelain. Fragile, tiny and completely helpless, that's how she appeared.

She didn't look like someone who could shatter his life.

It must have been a fluke. It had happened in a moment of weakness. Hearing one hazy call for help didn't necessarily mean the gift was returning. Or it could have been a coincidence. . . .

He exhaled harshly, making a sound too rough to be called a laugh. Coincidence? That's what the skeptics had always claimed. Fluke? That was more likely. Sensing her need might have been no more than an echo of his former ability, like the way amputees claim to feel twinges from a limb that has been missing for years.

Whatever it was, coincidence, fluke or the resurrection of a nightmare, one thing was for sure. She was the cause. Whoever she was, this woman had barged uninvited into his life and into his mind.

And he wanted her out of both.

Warmth. It was one of those things Jenna had never thought much about, like air. She would never take it for granted again. Parting her lips, she inhaled greedily and drew the welcome heat into her lungs. There was no snow to choke her, no ice crystals to scrape her skin raw. She was lying on something soft. And she was surrounded by warmth, wonderful, blessed warmth. She could smell woodsmoke and hear the soft crackling whoosh of a nearby fire. Other sounds reached her—wood creaking in the wind, snow whispering against a windowpane, the ticking of a clock. The sounds of shelter, of safety.

Time held no meaning as she lay unmoving and simply relished the luxury of mindless physical comfort. Heat seeped slowly into her body. She floated on the edge of sleep as awareness drifted over her like cloud patterns on a hillside. Her strength, drained to the depths of her endurance by her struggle with the storm, began to return.

Minutes, or perhaps hours later she finally opened her eyes. Orange firelight danced over rough beams on the ceiling. She blinked, bringing the age-darkened wood into focus. The beams sloped down to a wall of squared logs. Logs. A cabin. Sleep beckoned, but she fought the urge to drift back into its soothing cocoon. She was in a cabin. She had been carried out of the storm. She shifted, and a groan vibrated from her throat. With the return of awareness came the aches of her awakening body.

"So, you're awake."

Jenna recognized that voice. It was the same deep, gruff tone that had sounded so beautiful in the storm. It belonged to her rescuer. To Damien. To the man she had traveled here to see. Full consciousness crashed over her. Damien. He had to help her. Brushing the hair from her face with the back of her hand, she turned her head.

Her lungs heaved as if she were a diver who had surfaced too quickly. Damn. She should have been prepared for this. She had seen his photograph. She had known what he looked like. But no film could have captured the reality of this man.

"You're in my cabin," he said tersely. "I brought you here so you could warm up."

Jenna tried to nod, but all she could do was stare. Handsome? The word didn't even come close. Handsome would have described what he had looked like in the five-year-old photograph she had studied. The glossy image had shown the chiseled jawline, the strong, hawklike nose, the piercing blue eyes, all the striking features that together formed a classic picture of masculine beauty. But that was five years ago. And Damien Reese had changed.

Rather than chiseled, his face looked honed. Deep lines bracketed his mouth, and wrinkles that weren't from smiling fanned out from the corners of his eyes. Several days' growth of stubble roughened his jaw, and the black hair that had once been neatly styled now hung in defiant disarray over his shoulders. His classic handsomeness had been carved down to its raw essence. He had an aura of... power around him. Power tightly leashed, passion held in check, something primitive and untamed that stirred her on a level she hadn't known existed. He looked lean, hard, hungry. Dangerous.

Fascinating.

"How are you feeling?" he asked. Firelight cast a bronze glow over his skin, deepening the hollows of his cheeks. His black sweater stretched tightly across his broad shoulders and clung to the muscular contours of his upper arms. He was leaning forward, his forearms crossed over the back of the wooden chair he straddled, his chin propped on his hand. He was watching her, no hint of his thoughts showing behind his ice-blue eyes, no trace of emotion on his rigid features.

Jenna parted her lips to answer but couldn't make more than a croak for a reply. She swallowed, grimacing at the rawness in her throat.

He rose smoothly from the chair and walked to the other side of the room. Jenna turned her head, watching him as he took a small pot from on top of a stove and poured something into a thick mug. His movements held the controlled grace of an athlete or a dancer, reinforcing the impression of power held in check. He returned carrying a steaming mug, the handle engulfed by his large hand. "Here, drink this."

Jenna braced her palms against the cushions and tried to push herself up. To her disgust, she could barely move. She let her head fall back against the arm of the couch. "Sorry," she whispered.

For a moment he remained motionless, standing by her side. Something flickered behind his icy blue gaze. Anger? *Hate?* It was gone before she could be sure she had seen anything. He knelt down and brought the rim of the mug to her lips. "Take a small sip at first. It's hot cider with honey. Should help get rid of the tightness in your throat."

She felt a crack in her lower lip sting as the liquid passed over it, but she forced herself to take a mouthful and swallow. The warm cider felt good, the honey tingled on the roof of her mouth. "Thanks."

He held the mug to her lips again and helped her take another drink. When she swallowed, he stood and moved back a step.

A cough rumbled up from her chest. She waited until the spasm had passed before she tried to speak. "I'm sor—" She breathed in another lungful of warm air and tried again. "I'm sorry to cause you all this trouble."

He didn't acknowledge her apology. Instead, he used the mug he still held to gesture toward her feet. "How are your toes?"

She shifted, feeling the weight of at least half a dozen blankets. "Okay, I guess. Feels like pins pricking into my skin."

"Then they're warming up. I didn't see any sign of frostbite. I removed everything but your sweater and your underwear. Your clothes should be dry by the morning, so I'll take you back down the hill when the storm clears. Where did you leave your car?"

"It went off the road. I skidded on a patch of..." The rest of what he had said filtered through her mind. "My clothes?"

"They were wet. You needed to get warm."

Experimentally she moved her leg and felt the slide of naked skin as her calves rubbed together. She lowered her hand beneath the blankets. Her palm skimmed over the soft angora that covered her breasts, then touched the folds where her sweater was twisted around her waist. More bare skin, a sensitive strip just below her navel, and then her fingers reached the textured lace fabric at the junction of her thighs. He had undressed her. Considering her situation, and everything else she had to worry about, it was stupid to think twice about this. Still, she couldn't prevent a rush of humiliation from coloring her cheeks.

His gaze never wavered from her face. "I didn't touch you."

Of course he hadn't touched her. It had been more than four years since any man had wanted to touch her. Stupid to think about this, too. Her humiliation deepened.

"I'll see what I can do about your car when it's light," he said. "Is it a four-wheel drive?"

She returned her hand to the edge of the blanket and cleared her throat. "No, it's a compact I rented in Hemlock. I flew in from Minneapolis. I wanted to get here as quickly—"

"We might have to leave the car until the county clears the roads. I'll take you into town with my Jeep. You should be up to the ride by tomorrow. Until then you should rest and recover your strength."

He wanted to take her to town? After what she had gone through to get here? "Uh, I really appreciate your help, but—"

"You can ask someone from the rental company to get the car later. It might be a few more days before the road's passable. You can probably find a room in the Hemlock motel while you're waiting."

"I already have a room there."

"Good." He glanced at the blankets that covered her. "Are you warm enough?"

"Yes. Very warm."

He put the mug of cider on a table beside the couch and turned away. "Fine. Bathroom's on your left, my bedroom's on your right. I'll see you at dawn."

In disbelief she watched him walk toward the dark archway on the right. This was happening too fast. She'd barely had a chance to regain her wits and the man was already planning how to get rid of her. She grasped the back of the couch with one hand and struggled to pull herself up. "Wait. Please."

He paused but didn't turn around. "What?"

"Don't you want to know why I'm here?"

Tension rippled across his shoulders. Beneath the black sweater his back stiffened. "No."

"My name's Jenna Lawrence, and I—"

"No."

A log popped in the fireplace. A gust of wind whipped around the eaves, making a noise like a growling animal. Jenna shivered. "But—"

"I don't care who you are. I don't care why you're here. It doesn't make a damn bit of difference."

There was an edge of anger to his words, a core of steel in the beautiful voice. She tried again. "I'm sorry about all the trouble I've been so far, but I really need to talk to you about—"

"Better get some rest. I'm taking you to town in the morning." He started moving toward the shadows.

With a sharp grunt, Jenna levered herself to a sitting position. Spots winked in front of her eyes until she took a deep breath to clear her vision. "Mr. Reese, please."

He stopped. "What did you call me?"

"You're Damien Reese, aren't you?"

His hands tightened into fists by his sides. Slowly he turned around. Even across the width of the room the coldness of his gaze sent a chill down her spine. "The fact that you know my name makes no difference, either. I'm taking you to town at dawn."

"Rachel sent me."

He crossed his arms over his chest and widened his stance. "So what?"

"Your grandmother. Rachel Beliveau."

"So what?" he repeated.

"She told me how to get here. She said that you would be able to help me."

A tremor whispered through his tense body. "I already helped you."

This was turning out all wrong. Jenna bit her lip and swung her feet to the floor. The room wavered briefly. She took several more deep breaths while she tried to remember the speech she had prepared. This wasn't how she had planned to state her case. Not like this—not weak, dizzy with fatigue and half-naked. "No. I mean, I'm grateful to you for bringing me to shelter, but I was coming to find you anyway before the storm hit. I've read about your abilities, and I've seen the newspaper accounts of how you used to work with the police, and Rachel told me—"

"My grandmother is old. She gets confused. And you shouldn't believe everything you read."

The window rattled. Icy pellets whipped against the glass. Sparks crackled up the chimney in a sudden draft. Jenna pulled the quilt around her shoulders and let the rest of the blankets fall to the cushions. She didn't believe everything she read. If she did, then she'd believe he was a fake, a fraud, a clever con man and a skillful hypnotist. But those were just labels that people used when they ran into something they didn't understand.

Labels. Like freak. Monster. Madman.

She had heard those words from her family when they had learned of her plans. But she hadn't believed those, either. "I believe in your gift, Mr. Reese. That's why I've come. Please. Just give me a chance to explain."

A muscle flexed in his cheek, the firelight rippling over the bronzed skin. "I have no gift. I have no abilities. If that's why you've come, you've wasted your trip."

"I've read about the people you've helped."

"I haven't helped anyone for a long time."

"There hasn't been any record of it for more than five years, but—"

"This discussion is over. You leave in the morning."

No! she thought. It wasn't going to end like this. She wasn't ready to give up, no matter how hopeless it seemed. Clutching the quilt around her with one hand, she grasped the arm of the couch with the other. She rocked forward and pushed herself to her feet, locking her knees when her legs threatened to buckle. "Do you want me to beg, Mr. Reese? I'll do that. I'll do anything."

He turned away.

"What do you want? I'll pay anything. You can name your price."

With long strides he covered the remaining distance to the shadowed archway.

Jenna lunged after him. She made it as far as the chair he had been sitting on before her strength gave out. Her bare knees hit the floor with a loud smack of skin against ceramic tile. She swallowed her cry of pain and grabbed the chair back to keep herself from collapsing completely. She hung on, pressing her face to her forearm, panting shallowly until she gained the strength to lift her head.

Damien was standing in front of her. With his wild black hair cascading to his shoulders and the flames from the fireplace painting his muscular, masculine contours in flickers of demonic orange, he dominated her senses. Hard, hungry, dangerous. Fascinating. He made no move to touch her, but his gaze was so intense she felt the impact like a physical blow.

This wasn't the way she had planned it. She knew all about negotiating deals, and she knew the importance of coming from a position of strength. Oh, God. She was on her knees. At his feet. But if she didn't ask now, he might not give her a chance in the morning. She moistened her lips with her tongue, tasting blood from the crack in the lower lip, and honey from the drink he had given her. *"Please!"*

He seemed to sway toward her. A flash of emotion sparked in his eyes. Anger? Hate? Beneath the shadow of bristling whiskers his jaw tensed. "No. I can't. Not anymore. All that is over."

"You have a gift—"

"No! No gift. It's gone. It's been gone for five years. If you really do know my grandmother, she should have told you that."

Jenna tightened her grip on the chair until her nails bent against the wood. "I don't believe it."

He leaned closer, looming above her but still making no move to touch. "My *abilities* don't exist. They're gone. Burned out. Used up. Whatever you want to call it. Is that clear enough? You came here for nothing. You walked through a blizzard and risked your life for nothing. Because I have nothing left to give. So it doesn't make any difference why you came—"

"It's my niece."

He hesitated. "It doesn't make any difference."

"My niece. My godchild." She felt the burn of tears behind her eyes but she held them back, just as she'd been holding them back for the past two months. Because if she let them come, she'd never be able to stop. "I want you to find her."

"No." His voice had dropped and roughened, as if his words were being dragged from somewhere deep inside. "No, I can't."

"She's only three." A lump formed in her throat but she talked past it. He was listening now, and she had to say it all before he walked away again. "She disappeared in broad daylight, on a trip to the zoo."

"Stop it. I can't help you."

"Her name is Emily. She's my widowed sister's only child. And I was the one who took her to the zoo that day. I was the one who lost her. I have to get her back."

His refusal was slower this time. "No."

"Since she disappeared, my family has tried everything. We went to the police. We hired a private detective. We put up posters and went on television and now my sister's near collapse. If there's even a chance that you could—"

"It's no use. I can't do anything."

Using the chair as a crutch, she pulled herself to her feet. Wind howled down the chimney and the fire flared. "I love my niece, couldn't love her more if she were my own child. I will not stop until I find her. And I believe you can help me."

A shudder rippled through his body. For an instant, for a span of time no longer than a heartbeat, the rigid control he had maintained over his expression faltered. Rage flashed across his face. He stared at her, clenching his jaw until the tendons stood out in stark, strong lines along his neck. His lips moved in silent denial.

She lifted her hand from the chair and reached out to him. "Please."

In the instant before her fingers could brush his wrist, the shutters slammed back down on his expression. He jerked his arm away from her touch and took a step back. And another. He kept backing away until he blended into the shadows beyond the firelight and was gone.

Chapter Two

Her name was Jenna.

Damien pressed his palm against the window to wipe away the circle of fog from his breath and concentrated on the storm. According to the clock beside his bed, dawn had broken half an hour earlier, but the only indication of sunrise was a slight graying of the whirling flakes. The snow showed no signs of stopping. Even if he put the chains on, the Jeep might not make it as far as town. The woman's car would be hopelessly buried. She would have to stay until the storm blew itself out.

She. Jenna. But he didn't want to know her name, he didn't want to think about her or lose the hostility that would keep her at a distance. He didn't want her in his life or in his head....

She had hair like silk. Fine silk, the color of sunshine behind a waterfall. She had brushed it over her shoulder, but pale strands had slid forward as she'd talked, shadowing her cheeks, teasing the edge of her mouth. A generous mouth, mobile, made for laughter. There was a crack in her lower lip. He should have offered her some ointment.

Hell, he'd saved her life, hadn't he? Wasn't that enough?

Her eyes were green. The color of new life, of leaves freshly unfurled, of gems sparkling with inner light. Her lashes were gold-tipped sweeps of softness, her eyebrows were delicately arched as if she saw a world that was filled with wonder.

He knew the world was filled with pain. He couldn't help her. He *couldn't*.

Her skin was as pale and translucent as the petal of a rose, her blush as warm as a new dawn. And yet there was strength beneath the surface, astonishing strength. She'd barely been capable of lifting her head, but she had dragged herself from the couch and tried to follow him. Although her knees had trembled and her hands had shaken, she had managed to rise to her feet and look him in the eye. Clothed in nothing but a wrinkled sweater and a scrap of lace, she had wrapped herself in her determination and refused to accept his denial.

And she had almost touched his wrist.

He grasped the windowsill, hanging on until the cold that seeped through the glass numbed his fingers, yet in his mind he imagined what it would have been like to feel the warmth of her skin against his.

How long had it been? Years. Long, careful, solitary years of keeping his distance, both physical and emotional. Years of self-imposed exile without experiencing something as simple and basic as the feel of someone's fingers on his skin. Someone. Her name was Jenna.

And she wanted him to find her niece.

He raised his cold hands to his face and rubbed his eyes. No. He had told her the truth. His gift was gone. It had burned out five years ago and he had no intention of risking its return. Hearing her in his dream last night had to have been a fluke. He couldn't help her. He wouldn't. He would be endangering everything he had built if he made the attempt to resurrect those powers.

She had offered to pay him, but she had no idea of the terrible cost of what she was asking.

Smoke padded across the floor and scratched at the bedroom door, then looked at it expectantly and whined.

Damien pushed away from the window. He'd had to keep the wolf in the bedroom with him while the woman had slept on the couch. He'd hoped that he would have been able to get rid of her this morning before there was a problem with the animal. From the looks of the weather so far, though, she'd be here for at least another day.

He pulled a heavy sweater over his black turtleneck, ran his fingers through his hair a few times, then took a firm grasp on the fur at the scruff of Smoke's neck and opened the door.

Light glowed from a pair of kerosene lamps. Logs blazed in the fireplace. The couch was empty except for a stack of neatly folded blankets. Damien glanced around the room. The mug that he'd left on the table for her was inverted on the drainboard beside the sink. Her clothes, the ones that he had draped over the spare chair to dry, were gone. His own coat, which he had left in a heap by the door, was hanging from a peg on the wall beside a flash of neon pink ski jacket. Two pairs of boots, his tall ones and her butter soft leather ones, stood side by side on the doormat.

Smoke tilted his ears forward, turned his head toward the bathroom and growled.

"Easy, boy," Damien murmured. Keeping a tight grip on the wolf, he guided him across the floor to the front door. Frowning in annoyance, he shoved the boots aside. He braced his foot against the frame and tugged until the door swung open. Several inches of snow instantly cascaded into the cabin. "Okay, Smoke. Out you go."

The moment the animal cleared the porch, Damien closed the door and turned back to face the room.

She had lit the lamps, stoked the fire and tidied their clothes. His frown deepened. She had left those boots in the way of the door. And she hadn't adjusted the lamp wicks properly. Already he could see black soot forming inside the glass chimneys. He realized she had been trying to be useful, but he didn't want to see these traces of her presence.

The bathroom door creaked open. Damien crossed his arms over his chest and braced himself to face her.

The woman stepped into the room tentatively, her hand skimming the wall for support. Freshly brushed hair crackled around her shoulders in a halo of gold. She paused to take a deep breath, and her soft angora sweater momentarily molded to her breasts.

Awareness jolted through him. Those small, femininely rounded breasts would fit perfectly into his palms. Faded denim hugged her slim hips, covering the curves that he hadn't let himself look at last night. When he had undressed her she had been limp and helpless with exhaustion. When she'd stood in front of him half-naked, he had been too intent on fighting the effect she was having on his mind to concern himself with the effect she could have on his body.

Hell, it had been a long time for that, too.

He ground his teeth together and thought of the smoking lamps.

She glanced up suddenly and from across the room she met his gaze. For a moment she stared without speaking, then she moistened her lips and cleared her throat. "Good morning."

"You should turn down those wicks," he said. "The chimneys are blacking up."

"Oh. Of course." She moved to the lamp on the counter and reached for the knob that controlled the wick. Light flared and the smoke thickened when she turned it the wrong way. "Sorry." It took her a few seconds to adjust the level properly. She managed the lamp beside the couch more easily. "Is that okay now?"

He nodded.

"I hope I didn't disturb you, Mr. Reese. I've been up for a while."

"So I see."

She motioned toward the stacked blankets. "Thanks again for helping me last night."

"You seem to have recovered."

"Yes, I feel much better. I, uh, I really do want to apologize for the way I imposed on you like this. We seem to have gotten off to a bad start."

"We're not starting anything. You're leaving as soon as the snow lets up."

Wind gusted around the eaves and she glanced at the window. "It doesn't look much better than it did last night."

"It'll stop. Eventually."

She tugged at her sweater before smoothing her hand over her hair. Her fingers shook. She hadn't fully recovered from the cold and exhaustion, that much was obvious. Only her astounding determination was keeping her upright. "I really didn't plan for this to happen, Mr. Reese, and I understand why you're annoyed with me. I have no right to make any demands of you. I hadn't meant to blurt everything out the way I did, but my anxiety over my niece can be overpowering at times."

Even if he hadn't heard her emotional plea last night, he would have been able to recognize those traces of suffering in her face. He didn't need any special power to feel her pain. He didn't want to add more, but it would be far crueler to give her false hope. "I gave you my answer," he said. "It hasn't changed. Go sit down before you collapse on me again."

If he had expected his gruff manner would make her back off, he was wrong. Beneath the softly feminine white angora sweater, her shoulders squared. "Well, I for one would like to start over." She took a step toward him and offered her hand. "How do you do? I'm Jenna Lawrence."

Damien looked at her hand, at the slender fingers and the small palm. For a moment he indulged himself and imagined what it would be like to enclose that hand with his, to touch her, to feel the friction of warm skin sliding together. A handshake. Was that so much to ask? Just a simple connection, man to woman, a fleeting pleasure. He could share her warmth, maybe step close enough to inhale her scent, hear the sigh of her breathing, see the pulse of life beating in the vulnerable skin at the base of her throat. Jenna, the woman of courage and determination and hair like sunshine.

Would it be worth the risk of what might follow the touch?

Tightening his jaw, he stepped around her and strode to the corner that formed the kitchen. "You already told me your name."

Jenna let her hand drop to her side. She had known it wouldn't be easy to confront him today, but she hadn't believed it would be *this* bad. Rachel had been wrong. She had described her grandson as a sensitive, deeply emotional man. And according to Jenna's research, he used to share his gift selflessly with any stranger who needed help. Obviously over the past five years more than his appearance had changed.

And this was the man she was counting on to find Emily?

Her gaze followed him as he stretched to take an enamel pot from a shelf. He tossed a few handfuls of coffee grounds into it and filled it with water before setting it on the stove. His movements were smooth and controlled. Once more she had the impression of power tightly leashed. She had seen it last night, and again when she had stepped into the room this morning and had looked into his face.

And God, what a face. Even with the rough, unshaved whiskers and the traces of a sleepless night in the shadows under his eyes, he still was enough to take any woman's breath away. He must have combed his hair with his fingers. It was pushed away from his forehead carelessly and left to curl toward his shoulders in unruly abandon, yet no amount of careful styling could have achieved such a dramatic effect. The thick locks gleamed with glints of midnight in the glow of the kerosene lamps, looking wild and wickedly inviting.

She sucked her lower lip between her teeth. It didn't matter what he looked like, or what he said, or how he acted. She had only one reason for being here. "May I help you with breakfast, Mr. Reese?"

He lifted a shoulder. "I don't eat breakfast. You want something?"

"I wouldn't want to impose on you further."

"Go ahead and eat if you feel like it." He jerked his chin toward the refrigerator. "But it's been awhile since my last trip to town so there's not much fresh stuff left."

Not the most promising or gracious of offers, she thought, but at least he wasn't throwing her back out into the storm. Yet. "Thank you." She walked to the refrigerator and opened the door. There was a cardboard carton with four eggs, a plastic bag with some bruised apples, a bottle of ketchup and a crumpled piece of foil with a smeared slab of butter. That was all.

"We won't starve," he said tersely as she hesitated. "I have enough canned goods to last another month."

Taking out the eggs and the butter, she closed the door with a bump of her hip and turned toward the counter.

Damien stepped back at the same instant. He saw the impending collision and dodged smoothly to avoid crushing the eggs, but as he moved to give her room, his elbow brushed the side of her breast. It was barely a breath of contact, yet he jerked away.

Jenna was suddenly conscious of how large he was. Even without the bulk of his parka, even with the added illumination of the lamps she had lit, he was as imposing as the first time she had seen him. He must be at least six feet tall, and she'd already felt the breadth of the shoulders that stretched out that fisherman-knit sweater. Beneath close-fitting black denim, his legs were long and solid with the kind of lean muscle that came from hard use. His body was as honed and rawly masculine as his features. In the best of physical condition, she would be no match for his strength.

So it was a good thing that he found touching her so repulsive. She inched backward to give him as much space as possible and placed the eggs beside the sink. "Would you like me to scramble some of these for you, Mr. Reese?"

He shook his head. "No."

"Do you mind if I call you Damien?"

"Suit yourself."

"You can call me Jenna."

"What's all this for? Do you think you can change my mind by being polite to me?"

Jenna sucked on her lip again. That's exactly what she had hoped. "As I said, we got off to a bad start, but since we're going to be spending time together until the weather clears, I thought we might as well try to get along."

He bent over to retrieve a cast-iron pan from under the sink and slammed it down beside the eggs. "You're only making this harder on yourself. Can't you accept no for an answer?''

"I'm not a person who gives up easily, Damien."

"So I noticed. But I can't help you."

"Because your abilities are burned out?"

"That's right."

"I don't think that's possible."

His knuckles whitened where he gripped the pan. "Why not?"

She had gone over this in her mind since he'd left her last night and again when she'd awakened this morning. She wasn't sure whether her reasoning was logical or a product of her own desperation, but she had to believe it. "A pianist can't lose his gift for music. Even if he doesn't practice or if he breaks his fingers, the inborn talent will still be there. He'll find some way to express it if he wants to."

"Talent?" He made a harsh noise in his throat. "I didn't perform in concert halls, I performed in sideshows. Telepathy isn't an ability that's generally acknowledged by society."

"Five hundred years ago society didn't generally acknowledge that the world was round. Some people did believe it, though. And I've always believed there are forces we don't yet understand. Telepathy is one of them."

"How can you put your hopes on something you don't understand?"

"No one needed to understand how you managed to find the survivors of that plane crash in Montana seven years ago, or how you directed the antiterrorist squad to that farmhouse where the vice president's wife was being held."

"The papers called it coincidence."

"Right. And some people see a spectacular sunset as merely the refraction of light rays through dust particles in the atmosphere. They know how to explain it now, but it's still a sunset.''

He rubbed his face, his palm rasping over his chin. ''This discussion is pointless.''

No, it wasn't pointless, not as long as she still harbored a breath of hope that Damien could help her. She stopped herself before she started making demands again. She had come on too strong last night. Whatever else he may be, Damien Reese wasn't a man who could be pushed.

She slipped her fingers into the pocket of her jeans and touched the vinyl folder that contained the snapshot of her niece. It was the same one that Brigit, Emily's mother, had supplied to the police.

For two months Jenna hadn't traveled anywhere without it. She kept it in her purse or in a pocket or beside her bed. It was the first thing that she'd checked when she managed to drag herself from the couch this morning. Zippered into an inner pocket of her jacket, the picture hadn't been hurt by the snow or the cold. Emily might be anywhere on the face of the earth, but at least Jenna knew where this photograph was. She could keep this safe. She wouldn't lose it, too....

Dear God, she had to find her.

A cloud of aromatic steam poured from the pot of coffee. The sharp scent made Jenna feel light-headed. She swayed, bracing her elbow on the counter.

Damien swore under his breath and stepped around her. Hooking a wooden chair away from the table with one hand, he thumped it down in front of the refrigerator and pointed. ''Sit before you fall.''

She didn't want this man to know how weak she felt, but it would be worse to collapse at his feet again. She pushed away from the counter and sank gratefully into the chair. ''Thank you.''

He picked up the mug she had left on the drainboard and strained a helping of thick, black coffee into it. He held it out to her so that she could grasp the handle without touching his fingers. "I'll fix the eggs."

She glanced in the mug. Clumps of coffee grounds floated on the surface of a substance that had the consistency of mud. Her head spun again but she set her jaw and looked at Damien. "Thank you."

He grunted and lit another burner on the stove before he broke all the eggs from the carton into the frying pan and scrambled them with a fork. Small pieces of eggshell gritted against the cast iron.

Swallowing hard, Jenna tried to focus on something else. "You don't have electricity in this cabin."

"No. It's too isolated to bring a line in."

"What kind of stove is that?"

"Propane. Same as the fridge." He poured himself a mug of coffee and emptied half in one gulp. "The water pump runs off a generator."

"It's very..." She struggled for a word. "Cozy."

"It's very private." He poked at the eggs for another minute. When they wobbled like rubber he emptied them onto a plate and shoved them toward her. "Here."

"Thank you." After only a brief hesitation, she took the fork he offered her and lifted a chunk of eggs to her mouth.

He watched her eat in silence for a few minutes. Shifting his weight, he crossed one ankle over the other and leaned his hip against the edge of the sink while he sipped his coffee. "How do you know my grandmother?"

It was the first real question he had asked her. Although it sounded more like a challenge than a polite conversational opening, Jenna felt that she might be making progress. "I'm a real estate agent. We met almost two years ago when some clients of mine bought her house."

"And she volunteered to tell you how to get here?"

Jenna grimaced inwardly. It had taken eight weeks of pleading to convince Rachel to "volunteer" her reclusive grandson's whereabouts. "Of course," she answered.

"Rachel hasn't been here since my grandfather died. That has to be at least thirty years."

"She drew me a map. The road seems to have changed since she used to come to this cabin, though. I would have beaten the storm if I hadn't taken wrong turns a few times."

"She knows I don't like visitors. She shouldn't have encouraged you to come."

"Don't blame her, Damien. She's my friend, and she knows how much Emily means to me."

"And you should have turned back as soon as you saw the snow starting. People can die in storms like this one."

"I know." She chewed and swallowed another mouthful of eggs, then raised her chin and met his gaze. "I thought it was worth the risk."

Her words seemed to have an odd effect on him. Emotion flashed briefly behind his piercing blue eyes. She saw a surge of anger, and something else that was almost like . . . respect.

Anger was understandable. He'd been angry last night. He hadn't asked her to come, and he'd made it perfectly clear that he didn't want anyone intruding on his privacy. She must have been mistaken about the respect, though. Jenna studied his face, but the glimpse of emotion was gone. Still, she was making progress. Despite the gruff way he went about it, he was continuing to take care of her, so things weren't yet hopeless. After all, a man who would rescue a stranger from a blizzard couldn't be completely merciless. . . .

Wait a minute. The blizzard.

Jenna's fingers tightened around the handle of the mug as the events of her rescue fell into place. Of course. Why hadn't she thought of it before?

Carefully setting her fork down on the edge of her plate, Jenna lifted her chin and narrowed her eyes. "If your telepathic abilities are gone," she said steadily, "how did you find me?"

Damien started, his gaze suddenly wary. "What?"

"Last night, in the storm."

"I followed your tracks."

"I know. I saw the way the beam of your flashlight wove back and forth over the snow. But what were you doing out there in the first place?"

Tension spread over his face, hardening his jaw, deepening the lines beside his mouth. "It doesn't matter. I saved your life, didn't I?"

"Yes, and I'm grateful for the care you've given me, but it *does* matter." She leaned forward, trying to see past the barrier he kept over his feelings. "Why were you out there, Damien? What made you decide to go walking through a blizzard in the middle of the night?"

He turned his back to her and dumped the remainder of his coffee into the sink. "I couldn't sleep."

"Do you expect me to believe that?"

"Believe what you want," he snapped, stepping past her. "I value reality too much to lie."

"You knew I was out there, didn't you," she insisted. She watched him stride across the room. She hurriedly placed her dishes in the sink and followed him, catching up when he reached the fireplace. "You weren't the least bit surprised when you found me, so you had to have known. You can't expect me to believe it was a coincidence."

Metal links rattled harshly as he pulled aside the spark guard. He added more wood to the flames, jabbed at the fire with a poker for a minute, then replaced the mesh curtain. He stared at the blaze without speaking.

Jenna felt her hope flare along with the fire. "You knew I was out there," she repeated. "You must have."

"I thought I heard someone call. That's all."

"You couldn't have heard me. I was too far from the cabin." She reached for his sleeve. "You *knew*, didn't you!"

He jerked his arm away and stepped back. "No!"

Taking a deep breath, Jenna carefully lowered her hand to her side. "Your abilities aren't burned out at all," she said, forcing a calmness she didn't feel into her voice. "They can't be, and I'm the proof."

"No. They're gone. They're not coming back."

"Why won't you admit the truth?"

"Just because I thought I heard you last night doesn't mean anything. I'm telling the truth. I haven't felt my gift for almost five years."

"Until now."

He raked his fingers through his hair, then grasped the mantel of the fireplace. A muscle twitched in his tightly flexed jaw.

"It did happen, didn't it? You *felt* my presence."

"It was a fluke. It won't happen again."

"Damien, please. You used your gift to save me from the storm. Couldn't you use it once more to find my niece?"

Sparks swirled up the chimney. He continued to stare at the fire as ripples of orange light chased across the rigid contours of his face. "No. You're only making it harder on yourself by holding on to this false hope."

"It isn't false hope. You still have your power. You have to, or I would be frozen in a snowbank somewhere." She knew she shouldn't be pushing him. That had been her mistake last night. But how the hell was she supposed to back off when so much was at stake? He *could* help her, but for some reason he didn't *want* to help her.

Another silence began to build. It wasn't the fragile truce of moments before. Challenge hummed in the air.

Tension crackled between them, blending with the hungry snapping of the strengthening fire.

Damien stood less than an arm's length away. Everything about him, from his height to his lean, muscular build to the unshaved stubble that cloaked his clenched jaw, radiated masculinity. Suppressed energy quivered through his body, making her acutely aware of the difference in their sizes. He looked rough-edged and dangerous. Yet the pounding of her heart still wasn't from fear. The same firelight that flickered over his harsh features gleamed sensuously on the soft waves of his hair. The strong, long-fingered hands that gripped the stone mantel had once held honey-laced cider to her lips.

If she reached out again, would he let her touch him?

Damien turned toward her, as if drawn by the same force that kept her from looking away. His eyes glistened, the icy blue burning with sudden heat. His eyelashes were long and as thick as sin and once more Jenna felt like a swimmer struggling for air. Power surrounded him, but there was nothing mysterious about it. Her body tingled with awareness, her blood throbbed with a response as old as time.

Good God! What was wrong with her? It was stupid, crazy, to respond this way, no matter what he looked like, or what capacity for compassion might lie beneath his gruff manner. This wasn't what she wanted from him. And judging by the way he had so scrupulously avoided touching her, he didn't want it, either.

A log fell over in the fireplace with a chinking rustle of shifting embers, startling Jenna into taking a step back.

The flash of heat in Damien's eyes winked out as if it had never been. "You're leaving tomorrow." His voice was low and hard, rumbling with the threat of distant thunder. "Even if I have to hook up a blade to the front of my Jeep and plow a track out, you're leaving."

She crossed her arms and locked her knees to keep them from trembling, trying to ignore the awareness that still pulsed through her body.

A sudden gust of wind howled outside the cabin, rattling the window like an animal trying to get in.

Damien scowled and looked at the door.

A whining noise, followed by a sharp scrabbling sound—nails? claws?—penetrated the thick varnished panels.

Jenna felt her mouth go dry. "What is it?"

"Stay here." He stepped around her and crossed the room, pausing when he reached the door. He raked his fingers through his hair and his scowl deepened.

"What is it?" she repeated. "What's out there?"

He glanced back at her. "Stay where you are and don't move, okay? Can you do that?"

The scrabbling sound intensified. Jenna's legs shook and she leaned against the wall for support.

He put his hand on the knob and pulled open the door.

Snow gusted into the cabin in a swirling cloud of white. Something moved over the threshold. Nails clicked against tile as a huge white dog bounded into the room. Damien slammed the door and the animal shook itself.

No, it wasn't white. A shower of snow arced over the floor and black fur emerged. "You have a dog!" she exclaimed.

The animal swung its massive head toward her. Golden eyes gleamed from the black fur. A growl puckered its muzzle.

"He isn't a dog," Damien said.

Chapter Three

Jenna stared, her breath catching. She saw the long banner of a tail, the narrow, powerful haunches, the deep chest and pointed ears. The animal stood with its forelegs locked and braced apart. Its body lowered slowly as if it were tensing to leap.

Damien grasped the back of the creature's neck where the black fur bristled. "Calm down," he ordered.

She wasn't sure whether he was talking to her or to the dog. No, not a dog. Her gaze flickered over the pointed ears and the glistening teeth that were bared in a snarl. "Oh, my God," she whispered, pressing her back against the hard logs of the cabin wall. "Oh, my God. That's a wolf."

"Yes."

"You've got a *wolf* for a pet?"

"Smoke isn't a pet."

The animal lunged forward but was stopped by Damien's firm grip. Its jaws snapped shut on empty air.

Jenna felt a scream building in her throat. "Do you mean he's wild? That's a wild wolf?"

"Essentially. He stays here when he's in the area—"

"He's staying here? That animal was here last night?"

"I shut him in the bedroom so he wouldn't bother you while you slept. Usually he sleeps in front of the fireplace, but you were in what he considers his territory."

"*Bother* me? What's that supposed to mean?"

"Smoke doesn't like strangers. He's doing a lot of posturing because he's nervous," he said, raising his voice over the continuing snarls. "I doubt if he'd attack, although while he's in the room I'd advise you not to make any sudden moves."

She tamped down the scream and tried to keep her body from shaking. "What should I do?"

"Just stay where you are. I'll introduce you to him once he's calmed down."

The wolf snapped at the air again, bunching its body in preparation for a spring.

With a quick movement of his leg, Damien nudged the animal off balance. "Cut it out, Smoke," he said firmly. He loosened his hold on the fur and came down on one knee, looking the wolf in the eye. The snarls subsided gradually. A minute later, Damien released his grip completely and ruffled the fur behind Smoke's ears.

Jenna blew out the breath she had been holding. "How did you do that?"

"Animal psychology. Smoke is a lone juvenile. He's accepted me as the dominant male of the pack we formed, so I have to assert my dominance." While he spoke, he continued to stroke the animal until it sank down and rolled over onto its back. Damien reached out to give a vigorous rub to the wooly fur on Smoke's belly. "Wolf behavior is very similar to that of domestic dogs. Most of their displays of hostility or aggression are just for show. You might say that his bark is worse than his bite."

"Having seen his bark, I wouldn't want to feel his bite."

Damien brought his other knee to the floor and used both hands to scratch the wolf's throat. His long fingers wove through the black fur with surprising gentleness. "Despite the legends, wolves don't attack humans unless they're provoked. He's far less dangerous than a dog like a pit bull that has been bred to be vicious. These are gregarious animals who have evolved to live cooperatively with each other. They've also evolved to be extremely intelligent."

"But that's a *wolf*," she said, still trying to accept what she was seeing.

"Smoke knows that while he's here I give him food and shelter, so he generally does what I ask him." A whine that sounded reassuringly canine emerged from between the wolf's glistening teeth. Damien paused, and the animal licked his hand. "I think he'll be all right now, if you come over here slowly."

Jenna watched, fascinated despite her fear, as Damien resumed his gentle stroking. His touch was filled with affection. His voice had changed, too. The gruff, rude tone he had been using before had mellowed as he'd spoken about the wolf. "Are you sure it's all right?" she asked.

He leaned back and Smoke rolled over to sit beside him. "I don't know. I've never had to accustom him to anyone before."

"Is it necessary now?"

"It is if you're going to share the cabin with us for another day. As far as I'm concerned, he has as much right to be here as you do."

Careful to keep her movements smooth, she pushed away from the wall and walked toward them. Her pulse hammered wildly. Sitting on the floor together like that, watching her warily, waiting for her to approach, neither the man nor the wolf looked tame. She stopped when she was about three feet away and rubbed her damp palms on her jeans. "Now what?"

Damien looped his arm loosely over the wolf's neck in a gesture that seemed almost protective. He had said the wolf wasn't a pet, but obviously he cared for the animal. "Show him you're not a threat."

Her? A threat? The wolf was the one with the inch-long teeth. "How?"

"Try kneeling down on the floor with us."

She lowered herself slowly until she was at eye level with them both.

"Okay," Damien said. "I'm not sure it would be wise to touch him just yet, but this will give him a chance to get used to you."

Smoke stretched his neck, his nose quivering. His upper lip curled back on a low growl.

Jenna forced herself not to flinch. This is for Emily, she told herself. She'd gotten this far, and she wasn't about to let the snarls from either Damien or his wolf drive her away. Not yet, anyway.

"Hello, boy," she said as steadily as she could. "I'm not going to hurt you, I'm just going to stay here—" Despite her resolve to remain calm, her words ended on a startled gasp when the animal nosed forward and she was able to see the side of his muzzle. "Oh, my God," she breathed. "What happened to him?"

Damien put his hand on the top of Smoke's head. "He was injured."

"I can see that." Pushing her fear of the wolf aside, she leaned closer in order to get a better look. Pink skin showed through the black fur in jagged slashes along the left side of the animal's jaw. Puckered red lines of recently healed wounds marred the skin. More scars snaked through the sparse fur on his neck and left foreleg. Jenna felt her stomach roil as she brought her gaze back to Smoke's face. No fur grew on the shiny red skin to one side of the moist black nose. A ragged chunk was missing from the right ear. "Oh, the poor thing," she said softly. "How did it happen? Was he caught in a trap?"

"No. His own kind did this to him."

"I thought you said that wolves weren't vicious."

"He was driven out of his pack, probably because he was different—black wolves aren't common around here." Using his fingertips, he lightly stroked the mangled ear. "Even intelligent species are prey to mob mentality. They attack what they fear or don't understand. When I found him he was too weak from his wounds to hunt for himself and was near starvation, so I took him in."

He said it simply, as if there were nothing out of the ordinary about taking in a wounded wolf, yet the statement spoke volumes, not only about what had happened, but about the man himself. "It couldn't have been easy."

"No, it wasn't. His left leg had been broken, and once he started to recover his strength, he kept chewing off the splint I'd fixed. He still has a limp."

"Did he ever bite you?"

His shoulder lifted in a negligent shrug. "Nothing serious. He was in pain, so his defensiveness was understandable."

Jenna sat back on her heels and watched Damien with Smoke. It wasn't only his voice that had mellowed. His face had lost some of the tension that had kept his features so rigid. He treated the wolf with tenderness and affection, and she realized that he was revealing a side of himself she hadn't yet seen. It must have taken sympathy and a great deal of patience to nurse this animal back to health. Were those the actions of the same person who was so steadfastly denying her request for help?

Sounds similar to those from the night before—the storm outside, the fire crackling, the clock ticking—slowly filled the silence that had fallen between them. The steady glow of the kerosene lamps combined with the firelight to cast an illusion of intimacy over the rough cabin. For a while they sat on the floor together, man, woman and wolf caught in a tentative truce. Something shifted inside her, and Jenna felt her initial impression of Damien begin to change.

What if Damien's snarling manners were as much for show as Smoke's? What if his antagonism was a result of wariness? Jenna glanced at Smoke's scars. Yes, the animal's defensiveness was understandable.

What had happened to Damien?

She studied his face, thinking about the old photograph Rachel had shown her. Had it been pain that had honed his features? Was it self-protection that had made him withdraw from the world? If only she knew why he insisted on living like this....

Giving herself a mental shake, she looked at the snow that still battered the window. It didn't make any difference, she thought, echoing Damien's brusque words of the night before. If Rachel was right and he had once been a different man, whatever had changed him couldn't concern her now. He was no injured animal, and she didn't have months to win his trust. She didn't care if he never let her touch him. All she wanted was to win his cooperation before the weather cleared and he sent her away. As long as the snow kept falling, the storm that could have killed her was now providing her with the perfect opportunity to convince Damien to help her.

The snow stopped falling at dusk. The clouds lingered until after sunset, then slowly fragmented and blew off to the east. In the fathomless black sky stars shone with harsh intensity, pinpricks of white stabbing through the subzero air. Crystals of snow glistened blue and silver, shifting restlessly across knife-edged drifts that stretched from the shadows of the pines to the porch steps.

Damien lifted his face to the night and inhaled deeply, welcoming the numbing sting in his nostrils and lungs. He moved away from the shelter of the shed, his snowshoes riding easily over the path he'd already packed from there to the cabin. Smoke trotted behind him, blowing panting huffs. This was the fourth time today he'd taken the wolf outside, and the animal was beginning to lose patience with these pointless outings. So was Damien. Yet even stumbling around in the snow in the dark was better than staying in the cabin with Jenna.

Jenna. With her leaf-green eyes and petal-soft skin... and her spine of pure stainless steel.

It was getting harder and harder to hang on to his hostility. He'd come outside to get away from her, but her image wouldn't leave him alone. *She* wouldn't leave him alone. No matter how disagreeable he was, he couldn't shake her out of her insistent good manners. He knew she was only acting friendly because she hoped she could use him, but that didn't make her any easier to ignore.

He shook his head and drew in another deep breath, letting the shot of frigid air clear his thoughts. Yet all he saw was Jenna's stubbornly lifted chin, and her generous mouth, and her wonderful arched eyebrows. And the womanly curves beneath the soft sweater and faded denim.

"Damn," he muttered, pausing at the foot of the steps. In less than a day, she had intruded into every aspect of his life. She had already left traces of herself all over the cabin. She'd cleaned the lamps she had blackened, but she hadn't stopped there. Each time he'd come in with Smoke, she had hung up his coat, set his boots by the door and taken a sponge and mopped up the puddles of melting snow they'd left. No wonder she got along with his grandmother. But she hadn't cleaned up everything. No, she had missed the long blond hairs that she'd left on his brush.

He remembered the jolt that had gone through him when he'd entered the bathroom and had first seen that blond hair shining from the bristles of his brush. The entire situation was too intimate. It made him think of how her hair would feel if he combed it with his fingers, of how it would smell if he pressed his head next to hers, of how it would look spread out on his pillow, tangled from a night in bed. With him.

"Damn," he said again. No matter what people had said about him or the labels they had given him, there was at least one way in which he was completely normal. Hell, it *had* been a long time. Living as a recluse hadn't done anything to dim the mindless, primitive response of his body to the proximity of a beautiful woman.

Yet it wasn't only her physical appearance that drew him. He admired her unswerving devotion to her niece and the very strength of will that had brought her here in the first place. But he couldn't let himself forget, even for an instant, what her presence meant. It was because of the effect she had on his mind that he couldn't even consider trying to satisfy the effect she had on his body.

Shifting the armful of firewood he carried, he started up the steps. Light spilled onto the porch in welcoming diamonds of yellow from the windows. He kicked off his snowshoes, stamped the snow from his boots and pushed open the door. Smoke rushed over the threshold in front of him, shook himself and loped to his spot on the hearth. Damien stepped inside and nudged the door shut with his heel.

Jenna was curled into a corner of the couch, her feet tucked beneath her. She glanced warily at Smoke before turning to face the door, a hesitant smile on her face.

He wanted to drop the wood to the floor, stride across the room and take her into his arms.

Instead, he toed off his boots and walked over to the woodbox. He felt like a first-class bastard, but he had to put a stop to this. For both their sakes. "It's cleared up outside. We should be able to get to Hemlock in the morning."

Her smile faded. She cleared her throat and lifted her chin in a gesture that was becoming too familiar.

Did she think he was made of stone? Did she think he couldn't recognize the pain and guilt and loss she was feeling? Each time she looked at him he could read the growing desperation on her face. Each time she told him another detail about her missing niece she stirred his sympathy and his conscience.

More than once today he'd found himself wishing that there really was something he could do to help her. He'd even caught himself toying with the idea of trying to see whether he could probe his long-dead abilities.

And that would be about as smart as walking up to a grizzly and kicking it in the side to see if it was truly dead or only sleeping.

The morning broke with sudden, merciless splendor. The sky was a sharp, clear, endless blue arching over the white-spangled landscape. Sunlight fingered delicately along the rippling drifts as if testing the strength of what it would melt when it grew stronger. A light breeze chimed through the trees, scattering snow from the laden branches in glittering veils.

If he'd been alone, Damien would have taken the time to appreciate the awakening hillside. He would have strapped on his snowshoes, packed his camera and his film bag and spent the day hiking through the bush in search of the perfect shot. But he wasn't alone. Tightening his grip on the steering wheel, he fought another sideways slide and turned the Jeep toward the center of the lane.

"Have we passed the spot where you found me?" Jenna asked, raising her voice over the noise of the engine.

"Yes, but you wouldn't have been able to see it from here. You were about half a mile away from the lane."

She braced a hand against the dashboard. "I was lucky you heard me."

He knew what she was doing. Even though they were on their way to town, she still wasn't giving up. He ground his teeth and steered around a bend. The Jeep hit a drift that would have stopped them in their tracks if they had been traveling any slower, but because of their momentum and the fact that they were going downhill, they bounced twice and burst through the other side in a spray of snow.

Smoke darted from one side of the back seat to the other, whining excitedly. Although Damien was always careful not to let the wolf loose near town, the animal enjoyed going for rides. And it was obvious that Jenna was uncomfortable around Smoke—another good reason for bringing him along.

Jenna twisted around to glance over her shoulder and was met with a sullen growl. She swiftly faced front. "Yes, I sure was lucky you heard me in that blizzard," she persisted. "Have I thanked you for saving my life?"

Only a few dozen times. "And have I told you that it was a fluke?"

"And have I mentioned that I don't believe you?"

Damien's fingers gripped harder. "Hell, what does it take to make you give up?"

She fell silent as they neared the end of the lane. Damien eased back on the gas pedal, letting the deep snow slow their descent. Twin tracks from no more than two vehicles were carved down the center of the unplowed road. He swung out without stopping, steering into the skid to keep the Jeep from fishtailing.

They found Jenna's car three miles from the end of the lane. It was nose-down in the ditch, buried by snow. After a brief inspection, Damien decided the car didn't have the size or the power to make it safely to town in these road conditions. Jenna agreed reluctantly and climbed back into the Jeep. Forty minutes later they reached the outskirts of Hemlock.

The town looked like a painting from a Christmas card. Curling streams of smoke rose from chimneys that poked through roofs pillowed with snow. A church steeple glistened against the sky. Stately trees spread their leafless branches over a frost-laced gazebo in the park. Bundled up in colorful scarves and bulky coats, a few hardy pedestrians hurried along the sidewalks.

Damien headed down the main street and pulled up in front of the town's only motel. He shifted the engine to neutral, put on the brake and turned to Jenna.

She was staring through the windshield, her bottom lip caught between her teeth, her hair falling like pale silk across her cheeks. Her hands twisted the ends of her scarf, wrapping and unwrapping the fringe around her fingers. She looked lost. For once, the vitality that usually glowed around her had dimmed.

From the time he had first seen her and known she wasn't a dream, he had been determined to get rid of her. Now that the moment was here, he found himself hesitating. From the seat behind him, Smoke whined inquisitively. The animal was anxious to get moving. And they *should* get moving. Instead, Damien reached back and ruffled the wolf's stiff black fur as he continued to watch Jenna. "Do you have your room key?"

She nodded and patted the side of her jacket.

"What about your purse?"

"I carried everything I needed in my pockets so I wouldn't lose—" She blinked hard and continued to stare out the window. "So I wouldn't lose anything."

He felt a tangled wave of guilt and love and sadness reach toward him. He cleared his throat. "Do you need any money?"

"Money wasn't what I wanted from you, Damien."

Make her leave. Now. He'd done all he could. But she looked so alone. The engine purred quietly, sending puffs of warm air through the heater in the dashboard. Damien still didn't make a move toward the door. "You'll find her without me, Jenna."

Her lips curved. Her expression held too much sadness to be mistaken for a smile. "That's the first time you've said my name."

It was, and he liked the way the syllables had felt on his tongue. He frowned. "You said that the police are involved, and you've hired a detective. They'll find something."

"Emily has been gone for two months. The private detective quit last week, and the police aren't very hopeful."

Damien struggled to hold on to his detachment. He didn't want to know more, didn't want to get drawn in deeper. After all these years, he'd managed to keep himself safe. He should make her leave. Now.

"There were hundreds of tips after we appealed to the public," she said. "The police were swamped with calls from people who thought they'd seen Emily. Every lead was checked out, but they were all dead ends." A shudder rippled over her as she said the last two words. "She's all right. I have to believe she's all right. We all do."

Once more Damien felt the urge to take her into his arms. But he couldn't help her. He hadn't been able to help anyone for five years. "What will you do now?"

"I ... don't know. We've already done everything else we could think of. When Rachel saw how desperate I was getting, when she finally told me how to find you, I took time off and arranged to get here the fastest way I could because you were my last hope—''

Jenna broke off and swallowed hard. In a way, Damien's sympathy was harder to take than his hostility. He hadn't changed his mind. No matter how many different ways she'd tried to approach him, he still maintained that he couldn't help.

She was starting to suspect he was telling the truth. Maybe the way he had sensed her presence in the storm really was a fluke. What did she know about telepathy? She could explain the fine print on a purchase agreement, or the reason sunsets were red. Had she been as recklessly foolish as her parents and Brigit had warned when she had chosen to put her hopes on something she didn't understand?

Letting go of her scarf, she undid her jacket and slid her hand inside to the zippered pocket. Yet instead of taking out the motel room key, she grasped the folder with the picture of Emily and drew it out. Running her fingers along the edge, she opened it up. "Brigit took this on her third birthday."

Damien lifted his hand from Smoke's neck and leaned closer, draping his arm along the back of her seat.

She tilted the photograph so he could see. "This is Emily."

He was silent for a moment. "She's a happy-looking kid."

"She'd just finished her birthday cake. See? There's a smear of chocolate icing on her chin. All the kids had crepe-paper hats. Emily's was a blue-and-gold crown. That's the crumpled bit of paper that she's holding in her hand. She hadn't left it on her head long enough for her mother to snap the picture." She sniffed, rubbing her nose with the back of her hand. "The week after, when I took her to the zoo, it was cold, but she kept...pulling off...her hat—''

The lump that had formed in her throat was too painful to speak past. She turned the picture toward her and touched her fingertips to Emily's image. Clear gray eyes sparkled with a glint of mischief. Cake crumbs clung to a cherub's smile. Baby-fine hair, more white than blond, stood up around her head.

Was it cold where Emily was now? Would whoever had her make sure she wore a hat?

Emotion crashed over her, as if opening the folder had opened a floodgate in her mind. All the love and worry and despair that she had struggled to control raged through her body and her mind until her eyes burned and her hands shook.

She closed her eyes and pressed the picture to her lips, holding on until the flood had receded. "Dear God, I have to find her, I have to get her back."

"I can't." Damien's voice was a low rasp. "I can't do what you want."

Startled, she turned to face him. She had been talking more to herself than to Damien.

"If this were five years ago, I would have gladly devoted my energy to helping you. But all that is over." He pulled back to his side of the Jeep, raking his fingers through his hair. "Hearing you in my head was a fluke. I can't help anyone."

There was genuine pain in his voice. No matter how abrupt and aloof he'd been with her, maybe he wasn't as hard as he seemed. Maybe the man he'd once been wasn't completely gone. Unthinking, responding automatically, Jenna reached across the small space that separated them and took his hand.

A tremor traveled through his fingers. His breath hissed between his teeth. "I can't do this. I can't."

"All right," she said, tightening her clasp. "I know I can't force you to help me."

His jaw flexed as his entire body tensed. His eyes held the angry desperation of a cornered animal. "No."

Beneath her palm, his skin seemed to burn with a strange, almost electric tingle. Jenna grew alarmed. "Damien?"

"Damn you, Jenna Lawrence," he whispered.

The tingling spread to her arm. She could feel his pulse beating and her own heart tripped to match its rhythm. His chest heaved... and her lungs gasped for air. "Damien?"

"I thought it was gone. I really thought it was over."

She tried to tug her hand away, but he twined his fingers with hers and brought her hand to his chest. He was staring past her, *through* her, as if his gaze was focused on something not visible. "What's wrong?" she asked.

"But it isn't gone at all. She has blond hair, like you."

Her other hand curled protectively over Emily's photo. "Yes, she has blond hair."

"And she's wearing a yellow jacket."

She tugged again but he still wouldn't release her. "No," she said, "she has a sailor suit with a navy blue collar—"

"Her boots are red, and she likes looking at her toes when she walks."

"Her rain boots are red, but it wasn't raining on her birthday." She shivered despite the warm air pouring from the heater.

"You let go of her hand to reach for something. Something she wanted. Her horse. She dropped her horse."

The image he was describing flashed through her mind. Oh, God. He wasn't describing Emily's birthday. He was describing the day...

"It was only a second. Less than a second. But when you turned around and looked for her, she was gone."

He was relating the details of that day at the zoo as if he had been there. "You know?" she whispered.

His jaw clenched, deepening the lines beside his mouth. Slowly, his eyes refocused on her face. He was breathing hard, as if he had traveled a great distance. The pain on his face was mixed with anger as he finally released her hand and slumped back against the door.

Jenna stared at him as the truth slowly dawned on her. "Damien? What just happened?"

His lips formed a silent curse.

"Damien!"

He raised his hands and splayed his fingers against his forehead, pressing until his knuckles whitened. His throat flexed as he swallowed, but still he didn't speak. From the back seat, Smoke whined. On the street behind them a snowplow rumbled past. In the distance the town-hall clock tolled the hour.

She grabbed his elbows, shaking him with a mixture of anxiety, impatience and crazy, irrepressible hope. *"Tell me, damn you!"*

Damien's chest lifted as he inhaled unsteadily. When he spoke, his voice was rough and distant, as if he hadn't fully returned from wherever he'd been. "I saw Emily."

Chapter Four

Jenna let go of Damien's arms and pressed her fingers against her cheeks. It was true. He could do it. He had already done it. But hearing about this from Rachel and reading about it in the newspapers she had found in the library couldn't possibly have prepared her for the impact of his muttered words. After two months of nothing, of worse than nothing, of doubts and discouragement, suddenly there was hope.

I saw Emily.

And he had. Exactly as Jenna had seen her that final time. Her eyes misted, but she stubbornly blinked back the tears. It had rained that morning, and Brigit had dressed Emily in her rain boots before they'd left so she could splash through the puddles on the pavement. The clouds had cleared away by noon and the sky had become the distant blue of autumn. Leaves fluttered in the air and fell to the ground in drifts of orange and gold. Emily had run through them like a laughing whirlwind, her throaty gurgle blending with the colors that spun in her wake. The breeze had been brisk with the threat of the season to come, and Emily had been wearing the bright yellow jacket from the two-piece snowsuit that her grandfather had bought her for her birthday.

Emily had run and laughed all morning, but by the time they had finished lunch her mood had switched with the suddenness of any tired three-year-old. They'd been heading for the zoo gates. Jenna had known that her niece would fall asleep as soon as they reached the car. But then Emily had dropped her horse. The blue plush animal, with a white mane and tail that had been worn thin with constant stroking from tiny fingers, had rolled under a bench.

It was only a second. Less than a second.

Her hands trembled as she clasped them together. Only a second. What she would give to have the chance to relive that moment. Emily had been right beside her. But Jenna had had to get down on her hands and knees to reach under the bench. She'd had to let go of her, but the little girl had been right beside her.

But when you turned around and looked for her, she was gone. Gone. Gone.

In one instant, in the blink of an eye, the world had shattered.

And Damien had seen it.

Jenna's body shook as she tried to bring the memory he had evoked under control.

Swearing under his breath, Damien slid from the Jeep. He stumbled briefly, catching the edge of the door for balance, before he pushed himself away. Smoke yipped and leapt over the seat, scrambling to follow.

Through the open door, Jenna watched Damien walk across the knee-deep snow that covered the motel parking lot. He held himself stiffly, his movements lacking his usual controlled grace. Wind whipped his black hair and sent puffs of snow spiraling from his boots. When Smoke loped to his side and nudged his hand, he ignored the wolf completely and continued to plunge through the drifts.

He had seen her niece. And he was walking away.

Jenna leaned over to shut off the ignition, then shoved the keys along with Emily's picture into her pocket. She flung open the door and jumped from the Jeep. "Damien, wait!"

Smoke glanced around, curling back his upper lip in warning, but Damien didn't show any signs of hearing her.

She rounded the hood and started after him. After what had just happened, he could no longer claim that his abilities were gone. He could help her after all. He *would* help her, whether he wanted to or not. Now that she'd seen it for herself, there was no way in hell that she was going to let him get rid of her.

He reached the edge of the street, stumbling over the ridge of tumbled chunks the plow had left. He swayed, then leaned forward and kept walking. He didn't see that the snowplow had turned around and was heading back on the other side of the road.

"Damien!" she cried, breaking into a run. "Watch out!"

He didn't stop, didn't change his pace, even when the blast of an air horn shrieked through the morning. He simply kept walking, the wolf by his side.

The plow swerved to avoid him. As it went by, the driver rolled down his window and shouted a string of obscenities over the noise of the engine.

Jenna waited until it passed, then scrambled over the snow ridge and ran after Damien. He seemed to be walking aimlessly, his wavering steps heading in the direction of the park. He passed a group of children pulling sleds, not appearing to notice when one of the girls screamed at the sight of Smoke.

"Oh, my God," Jenna muttered, increasing her pace. Luckily, the animal took no more notice of the children than Damien did. He kept going. He walked beneath a spreading oak, not even flinching when the wind knocked clumps of snow from the branches overhead. Jenna finally caught up to him as he reached the gazebo in the center of the park. "Damien, wait," she said, her chest burning from exertion and the cold air. She grasped his arm. "Stop for a minute."

At her touch, he paused.

And she got a good look at his face.

"Oh, my God," she whispered again.

He was as pale as the ice that coated the railing of the gazebo. Pain was etched into his features, deepening the lines beside his tightly compressed lips, shadowing the depths of his eyes. He looked at her blankly, as if he couldn't recognize her through the suffering in his gaze.

"What is it?" she asked. "What's wrong?"

He drew in a shuddering breath and leaned against the edge of the snow-covered steps as if he could no longer support his weight. Smoke circled around him, then sat at his feet and growled at Jenna.

She took a wary step back. "Damien, what's the matter?"

"Don't look so surprised," he muttered. "It's what you wanted, isn't it?"

"I don't know what you mean."

"You wanted me to use my gift. I did."

He was no longer denying it. Yet the triumph she should have felt was tinged with concern. "Are you sick?"

He closed his eyes briefly, his face tightening. "This is what always happens afterward. It's one of the costs. No gift comes without a price."

Concern changed to guilt. "Are you saying that the...vision, or whatever it was you had of Emily, caused this?"

"The vision was short. This reaction is mild."

Mild? He looked as if he had just run a marathon.

"Hey, lady!"

At the shout, she looked over her shoulder. The children had stopped near the oak tree. One boy, taller than the rest and bolder, stepped forward and cupped his hands around his mouth. "Better get away from that guy," he yelled. "He's crazy."

At the edge of the park, the snowplow was idling, clouds of exhaust streaming away on the wind. The driver who had narrowly missed Damien was standing on the road, gesturing toward them as he spoke with a man in a red plaid coat. A car slowed as it passed, its occupants drawn by the commotion.

"Craa-aazy," the boy shouted.

Jenna heard a grunt and turned back to Damien just as his legs crumpled and he slid down to sit on the ground. She fell to her knees in the snow. "What can I do? Do you need a doctor?"

He inhaled deeply, his nostrils flaring. "No. No doctor. It'll pass."

"You need help."

"I need to be left alone." He looked past her shoulder and swore roughly.

She followed his gaze. A black-and-white police car had pulled up behind the snowplow. When she looked back at Damien, she was alarmed to see that he had grasped the edge of the steps and was attempting to pull himself to his feet. "What are you doing?"

"I've got to get out of here."

"But they can help—"

"No." He took an unsteady step forward. "They'll make it worse. I have to go home."

She moved beside him and slipped his arm over her shoulders, bracing her weight against his side to keep him upright. His size shouldn't keep surprising her, but it did. She felt dwarfed by him, yet somehow she managed to keep them both from toppling over as they took another step.

"Leave me alone," Damien said. "I can make it."

Over his muttered protests, she wrapped her arm around his waist and hung on to his coat. Smoke snarled and snapped at the air beside her ankle. Jenna trembled, reminding herself that the wolf's aggression was probably for show. Probably. Biting her lip, she steered Damien back across the park.

A knot of people had formed near the police car. Jenna tried to guide Damien around them, but their path was blocked by a man in a sheepskin coat with a badge on the lapel. "What's the problem here?" he demanded. His hand rested on the holster that hung on his hip as his gaze flicked to Smoke.

Jenna tried to smile. "No problem, Officer."

"What's wrong with your friend? Is he drunk?"

Damien turned his head and stared until the policeman took a step back. "I don't drink, Deputy."

The man glanced at the crowd around him, then back at Damien, his expression turning belligerent. "We don't need you coming into town, causing trouble."

"We were simply taking a walk in the park, Officer," Jenna said, holding on to her smile as tightly as she held on to Damien's coat. She could feel the shaking in his body and knew it was only a matter of time before he collapsed again. "Now, if you'll excuse us, please?"

It was probably Smoke's snarl more than her polite request that caused the knot of people to part. Taking advantage of the opportunity, Jenna and Damien moved forward. She could hear muttering as they passed and caught glimpses of fear on several faces. She knew it wasn't only the wolf that inspired it. With his long hair blowing wildly in the wind and the fierce expression on his harshly drawn features, Damien was an intimidating sight.

They had reached the other side of the road before the deputy called out his parting challenge. "Don't bring that animal into town without a leash again, Reese, or I'll have to shoot him."

Jenna felt Damien's muscles tense and she bumped him hard with her hip before he could respond to the taunt. "We'll certainly see to it, Officer," she replied. She waved cheerfully with her free hand and turned toward the motel. She had a vague idea of getting Damien to her room so he could rest, but when they reached the parking lot, he headed straight for the Jeep. Over her protests, he pulled himself into the driver's seat, then sat there motionless, hanging on to the wheel as if he couldn't remember what it was for.

"You're in no condition to drive," she said. Smoke brushed past her and slipped into the back seat. Jenna moved to stand in the angle of the open door. "Come into my room and lie down until you feel better."

"No."

She looked around. No one had followed them from the park, but a pair of old women who had paused by the edge of the road were casting furtive glances toward the Jeep. Evidently, Damien was no more welcome in this town than Smoke had been in his own pack. Jenna made her decision quickly. "Okay, wait here and I'll drive you home."

He turned his head and glared at her. "No."

"I'll just grab my suitcase and call the rental company about my car first."

"No. Leave me alone."

She had no intention of leaving him alone. Not now. She was going to help him. And then he was going to help her.

No matter how much he snarled.

Reaching into her pocket, she pulled out the keys to the Jeep. "You have no choice. I've got your keys."

He hated her. Damien knew it wasn't fair, but emotions never followed the course of logic. He hated her for making him face the truth he hadn't wanted to admit. He hated her for showing him that he wasn't normal, never would be normal, and would have to spend the rest of his life fighting to hang on to reality. Yes, he hated her.

And he admired her. The courage he'd seen from the very start was stronger and deeper than he had suspected. She didn't back down. She didn't give up. She had stood up to him, and the wolf, and the good citizens of Hemlock, then had used every ounce of her physical strength to bring him safely back to the cabin and wrestle him into his bed.

And he wanted her. Oh, yes, he wanted her. His strength might be drained, but he wasn't dead. He'd never had a woman in this cabin, in this bed. Her presence was spreading through the solitary rooms like a spring breeze filled with sunshine. Her stubbornness, the astounding determination she exhibited, was all part of her appeal. And, of course, there was the way she looked.

Damien opened his eyes a crack and watched her through the open doorway. Sometime during the afternoon she had taken a shower and changed her clothes. A chenille sweater the color of jade draped softly to the middle of her thighs. Black leggings clung to her slim legs. She'd gathered her hair into a gold clip at the back of her head, but it was too fine to remain confined for long. Pale strands had already escaped to tease the soft skin of her cheeks and her nape. Each time she'd come near him, his fingers had tingled with the urge to feel that softness. After so many years of perfect control, all the needs that he'd managed to suppress were now straining to break free. His arms had never felt so empty or his bed so lonely.

The metal curtain in front of the fireplace rattled as Jenna drew it back to add more wood to the fire. From his usual spot in front of the hearth, Smoke yawned widely. Jenna froze, waiting until the display of gleaming teeth was over, before she cautiously closed the spark guard and stepped back. Moving carefully around the wolf, she picked up the tray she had left beside the couch and walked to the bedroom.

Mouth-watering aromas came from the tray. Damien inhaled slowly, savoring the rich smell of minestrone and fresh biscuits. After she had hijacked his Jeep, she had stopped at the Hemlock grocery store on the way out of town. He should have guessed that she would be able to cook. After all, she did get along with his grandmother. How long had it been since he'd had a home-cooked meal, since someone had cared enough to—

Fool. He knew she wasn't doing this because she cared. She hadn't brought him home and tended to him for the past hour out of charity. It was for the same reason as her good manners yesterday. She wanted to use him. She had already used him. It was her fault this had happened.

He waited until she had placed the tray beside the bed and had turned toward him before he spoke. "Did you feed Smoke?"

She leaned closer to look into his face. "Are you feeling better?"

"Obviously." He opened his eyes fully and pushed himself up on his elbows, startling her into taking a step back. "Did you feed him or not? If he's hungry he might snap at any fresh meat that appeals to him."

Her hand went to her throat as she glanced toward the main room. "I gave him a can of dog food. He already finished the whole thing. Should I give him more?"

He flung off the quilt she had covered him with and sat up, swinging his legs over the side of the mattress. "No. How much do I owe you for the groceries?"

"Forget it. I'm glad to see you're feeling better."

He caught her scent, then. It had teased him for two days. Fresh, feminine, with hints of something exotic, as if the pure water of a mountain stream had been infused with the essence of the life through which it flowed. Although she had stepped back, she was still standing near enough for him to reach. Would her body warm, would her scent change, if he caught her by the waist and pulled her toward him, if he spread his knees and brought her to stand between his legs and feel his hardness, if he touched her lips—

Fool! he raged silently. He shouldn't want her. He hated her.

Jenna curled her fingers into her palms and pressed until her nails dug painfully into her skin. It had been difficult enough to look at him while he had been lying there half-asleep. Stretched out on his back, on the massive hand-carved pine bed that was the perfect size for him, with the slanting afternoon sunlight casting a hushed glow over his rugged features, he had looked as fascinating as a fallen warrior. Even though his face had been drawn with pain, he still exuded that raw, dangerous masculinity. But now, with the power in those piercing blue eyes fully restored, he was more...himself than ever. A quiver went through her body, part fright, part fascination, but mostly pure feminine interest.

Oh, God, he was beautiful. Seeing him vulnerable had only strengthened his appeal. He was no longer remote or unapproachable. Feelings that she didn't want continued to surge over her. Sympathy. Desire. Protectiveness. Guilt.

Her fists tightened. Emily. She was what mattered. She was *all* that mattered.

Clearing her throat, she lifted her chin and focused on a point just beyond his left shoulder. "I've been thinking quite a lot about what happened when we got to town this morning. About the way you saw my niece."

"I figured you'd get to that sooner or later." He moved suddenly. She started and jumped out of the way, but he was only reaching for the soup bowl on the tray.

"I hadn't realized that your, er, abilities required such a terrible draining of your strength."

"You've repaid me for it," he said, gesturing toward the food.

"I think I'm beginning to understand why you're so unwilling to use your talent, if the aftereffects on your body and the reaction from the town are any example of what you've gone through."

He ate the soup in silence.

"But if we controlled the conditions, it might not be so bad next time."

Picking up a biscuit, he tore it apart with his fingers. "Next time?"

"Yes. Next time."

He looked at her, narrowing his eyes. "I figured you'd get to that sooner or later, too."

"What if we did it here? I can take care of you. And Smoke. We'll have privacy. I don't know how it works, but if you explain it to me, I'll do everything I can to help."

"Why?"

"*Why?* You saw Emily. You can find her just like you found all those other people."

He bit down on the biscuit so hard she could hear his teeth clack. He attacked the rest of the food, finishing it all before he spoke again. "And you're just like all the rest, too, aren't you? Coming to me with your demands and your pain, expecting me to accept them both. Offering to pay me for giving away pieces of my soul."

She forced down her rising guilt. "Please, Damien. She's only three. She's been gone so long."

He raked his fingers through his hair, then leaned his elbows on his knees and rubbed his eyes. "I thought it was over. But your feelings for your niece were too strong to resist. They reached me even in my sleep."

"What?"

"Your emotions." He dropped his hands and looked at her, his gaze burning with resentment. "That's how it works. There's a bond between you and your niece, the same way there are bonds between any people who are joined through emotion. No one has ever been able to see the bond, or touch it, but people have known about it since time began. Love is the strongest. Telepathy, or whatever you choose to call it, is the ability to tap into that current of emotion. I saw your niece because of you."

Currents of emotion. Bonds of love. She had never thought of it that way, but no one who had given birth to a child would doubt the truth of its existence. And he could tap into it? "I could show you her picture again," she said, unable to hold back her eagerness. "Would that help? I have the horse she lost—"

"I'm not a dog. You can't give me a scrap of clothing and tell me to follow a trail."

"Then how...?"

"With this," he said, holding his hand in front of him. "Touch. Joining my skin to yours. That's how it's triggered. Feeling your flesh, your pulse, your warmth—that's how the connection is made."

She remembered the strange, electric tingling that had spread from her fingers to her arm when she had taken his hand in the Jeep. "Touch? That's it? That's all you need?"

He spread his fingers, staring at the tips. "If the emotion is strong enough, yes. That's all I need."

"It's so simple. Why didn't it happen before..." Her words trailed to silence as his gaze met hers. Events flashed through her mind; incidents that she hadn't understood suddenly took on new significance. Damien flinching at an accidental contact, jerking away when she reached out to him, refusing to shake her hand.

I didn't touch you.

That's what he had said when she'd learned that he had stripped off her clothes. She hadn't taken it literally, but it was true, he hadn't touched her. Not until his eyes had held the panic of a cornered animal and he'd twined his fingers with hers. "You haven't touched me before."

"I haven't touched anyone for years. I wanted to believe it was gone."

"Years," she repeated, still trying to absorb what he was telling her. "You avoided contact for years, just so you wouldn't risk triggering your telepathy?"

"Didn't do any good, did it? You ended all that."

"Oh, Damien," she said softly, overcome with a wave of sympathy. "How lonely you must have been."

For a moment, just a heartbeat, the rigid barrier over his expression dropped. Loneliness didn't come close to describing what she saw in his eyes. Jenna couldn't imagine the isolation he lived with. She had grown up in a family where everyone hugged and kissed with uninhibited ease. She had always been a person who touched naturally. To willingly do without that...

"It was better than the alternative," he gritted.

She swayed toward him, her hand reaching out in an instinctive gesture of comfort. She caught herself before she could complete the motion. "I thought you didn't want—"

"Didn't *want?*" He clasped her arm before she could withdraw it, his fingers wrapping solidly over the sleeve of her sweater. "You thought I didn't want to touch you?" He gripped her other arm the same way, keeping the sweater between his skin and hers as he slowly drew her closer. "I'm a man, Jenna, with a man's needs and a man's desires. I haven't touched a woman in five years. What do you think I wanted when I saw your silky hair and your rose-petal skin and your curves pushing against that angora sweater? How do you think I felt when I knew I couldn't risk something as harmless as a handshake?"

Awareness of the strength in his grip shot through her, making her tremble. But not from fear. His thumbs moved over her sleeves, a gentle caress within a grip of steel. Power tightly leashed, passion held in check. Heat spread along the skin he still didn't touch and gathered in deep, hidden places.

"There were other reasons why I wanted you out of here, Jenna. Reasons that had nothing to do with what you were asking. Jenna." He said her name again, his voice flowing around the syllables like dark melted chocolate. "Your love for your niece glimmers around you like an aura, your face glows with wonder and hope and belief. Being close to you is like lifting my face to the sunshine and yes, I do want to touch you."

Her lips parted helplessly as she absorbed what he said. He spoke with the sensitivity of a poet. Those beautiful words, that deep, rich voice, captured her more firmly than his grip on her arms. It kept her from pulling away even when he drew her closer to stand between his knees.

"I haven't touched anyone," he said, sliding his hand up her arm slowly, as if savoring each inch of contact. "I haven't felt a woman's skin or shared her warmth." He lifted his fingers and caught a lock of hair that had slipped out of her barrette. "Silk," he murmured. "Smoother than I'd imagined."

She inhaled shakily, trying to control the reaction that had stolen her breath. He hadn't touched anyone. Until now. She hadn't been touched by a man for four years. Until now. "Damien." She was shocked by the roughness of her voice. "We shouldn't."

"Hell, I know that," he said, leaning forward, bringing his face level with hers. He lifted her hair to his cheek. The fine strands whispered against coarse black stubble in a contrast that was startlingly sensual.

She looked into his eyes, seeing the lush sweep of his lashes and the gleam of masculine interest. No, that word was too weak. Not interest, intent. Response skittered along her nerves. Her knees shook and she grasped his shoulder for support. Beneath the knobby texture of the knitted sweater, his muscles tensed, flexing like living steel. Her grip tightened as she imagined what his sweater covered, how his skin would glow in the lamplight, how her small hand would look against the hard contours of his chest. She looked at his mouth, noticing the perfect bow shape of his upper lip, and the moist smoothness of his lower one, and she wondered how he would taste.

Chocolate. Honey in hot, tart cider. Loneliness.

He turned his face, his nostrils flaring as he breathed in the scent of her hair.

She was so close. One move, and she would close the space between them. A deep breath, and her breasts would brush his chest. A twist of her hips, and she would learn the limits of his control.

Jenna clenched her jaw. No. *No.* It didn't make any difference. The way her body responded, the way his words tugged at her heart, none of that could be allowed to interfere with what she wanted from him.

The room suddenly felt colder, the lamplight looked harsher. She lifted her hand from his shoulder and let it drop to her side. "No."

He blinked. Gradually the tenderness seeped from his expression. He thrust her away from him and drew back his hands, splaying his fingers in the air beside him. "I'm a goddamn fool," he muttered. "You're just like all the rest."

"Damien, I'm sorry."

"No, you're not. You're going to get what you asked for. A command performance from the local crazy man."

The bitterness in his tone sliced through her conscience. Jenna felt torn between her love for Emily and her growing feelings for Damien. But there was only one choice. "Then you'll help me?"

"Of course I'll help you. I told you I would if I could. I don't lie. Now that you've taken care of my illusion of normalcy, there's no point in refusing anymore, is there?"

"Oh, thank you, thank—"

"Don't sound so surprised. I might be a freak, but I'm not a monster."

She wanted to apologize again, for how she wanted to use him, for the way the Hemlock residents treated him, for the labels, for the pain, for everything that had driven him to the isolation of this cabin. But the apology would be hollow. He was right, she wasn't sorry, not if he could find Emily.

"We'll do it now. Right now." He swept the tray from the bedside table with a swipe of his arm. Dishes crashed to the floor, shattering the last of the intimacy that had trembled around them. He rose to his feet and kicked aside a piece of the soup bowl. "Might as well get it over with. The sooner you get what you came for, the sooner you'll leave me in peace."

She crossed her arms, a reflexive defense against the frustration that was evident in his movements. "Here?"

"Why not? It's convenient. This time you won't need to strain yourself to get me into bed afterward." He strode to a door in the far wall, opened it and disappeared into what she had assumed was a closet. Minutes later he emerged with a handful of pencils and a pad of paper. He slammed them down on the table where the tray had been.

"When I used to do this for a living, I used a tape recorder. You'll have to improvise."

"Improvise?"

"Write down what I say." He reached out and fastened his fingers around the wrist of her sweater, tugging her arm away from her chest. "Are you right-handed?"

"Yes, I'm right-handed."

"Okay, I'll use your left." He pulled her toward the bed. "Let's get started."

"Just like that?"

"Did you want to wait?"

This was going so fast, it was difficult to take in. She shook her head quickly. "No, I don't want to wait another minute."

"All right." He pushed aside the quilt and sat cross-legged in the center of the mattress. "Come here."

She looked at the familiar scowl on his face. Was it only moments ago that he was so gently touching her hair while his words had touched her emotions? He had reerected the barriers, buried the poetry beneath the snarl. She had done this, she had destroyed that tentative connection between them. She had made him retreat, this sensitive man who had forced himself to live without basic human contact. She had put the wariness back in his gaze. She had ignored his need so that he could fill hers.

And for the sake of her niece, she would do it again.

Keeping a firm hold on her priorities, she climbed onto the bed, positioned herself so that she could reach the paper on the bedside table, and faced Damien. "All right," she said. "What do I do?"

He leaned toward her, determination in the set of his jaw, and a trace of vulnerability that he couldn't quite hide in the depths of his aching blue eyes. He held up his hand. "Now, Jenna, you touch me."

Chapter Five

Damien held his breath, watching her face, waiting for her to take his hand. This morning, in the Jeep, he hadn't been prepared. The strength of her emotions had taken him by surprise and he'd been drawn into the current before he'd had a chance to realize what was happening. But this was different. Deliberate. Just like old times.

He clamped down on his anger and tried to clear his mind. Just like old times. The pain, the ostracism, the demands...the satisfaction, the joy, the tearful gratitude...the joining, the giving, the sharing...There was a time when it used to balance out. It never would again, but still, he was willing to confront the darkness. For Jenna. For Emily, the child with the gray glint of mischief in her eyes. And, damn, for himself, too.

Slowly, carefully, Jenna lifted her left hand. She brought it to his right, holding it a whisper away, matching palm to palm, fingers to fingers. She hesitated for less than a second before she raised her chin, leaned forward and pressed her skin to his.

The breath he'd been holding hissed out between his teeth. He closed his eyes, savoring the sensation of her satin skin against his callused palm. Slowly he wove his fingers between hers, sliding each one against its mate until they meshed firmly into the valley at the base. Her hand was much smaller than his, yet she spread her fingers to accommodate him perfectly, her delicate strength enclosing him, accepting him. Flesh locked on flesh in an exchange of warmth and texture.

There were more erotic ways a man could join with a woman. But to a man who had lived without them, this was a glimpse of heaven. He curved his fingertips over her knuckles, finalizing his possession before he opened his eyes.

He didn't see her niece. He saw Jenna. As she was now. Sitting on his bed, with the lamp turning her hair to molten gold and her lips moistly parted. He didn't feel the tug of her bond with Emily. Instead, he sensed a confused mixture of regret and sympathy and longing.

"Concentrate," he said. "You need to help."

She curled her fingers, holding him as he held her. Her gaze lifted to his. "What should I do?"

He caught a glimpse of a face, but it wasn't a child's. It was a man's. A wild, unkempt, long-haired man with eyes full of pain. He jerked in surprised recognition. Was that him? Is that what he looked like to her? He raised his free hand to his jaw, rubbing his unshaved cheek. He was out of practice, to pick up on a casual thought like that. "Concentrate," he repeated. "On Emily."

She nodded once, quickly, and focused on their joined hands. The lock of hair that he'd touched swung softly beside her cheek. Her neck was bare and vulnerable. Her throat rippled twice as she swallowed. "Emily."

It began quietly. A trickle of awareness. Deep inside his head something stretched and tautened. He steeled himself against the accompanying ache. He shouldn't be trying this so soon after the last time. He should have allowed himself an opportunity to recover. A stabbing sensation, like a cramp from a muscle too soon exercised after being too long unused, formed behind his eyes. He shifted, pulling Jenna closer so that he could cradle her hand to his chest.

The bed creaked. Jenna leaned sideways to grab the paper and pencil, then put them on the pillow and inched nearer. Her knees nudged his ankle as she settled in front of him. "Are you all right?" she asked softly.

All right? He might have laughed at the absurdity of the question, but she was watching him closely, her green eyes troubled, ambivalent. He lifted a shoulder. "Keep concentrating. We'll get there."

"This is hurting you, isn't it?"

Her concern wasn't for him. It was for what he could do. He tightened his jaw. "It'll pass."

As naturally as if they had done this every day, she reached for his other hand and pulled it toward her, mating their fingers together. She curled her wrist, pressing the back of his knuckles against her sweater over her midriff, mirroring the way he held her. "I won't need to write down what you say. I'll remember."

I'll remember. Yes, after he gave her what she'd come for, after she politely thanked him and left him to pick up the pieces of his shattered solitude, he would remember the feel of her flesh meshed with his, the rhythm of her pulse, the gentle curve of her waist. He looked at where his hand rested beneath her breast. And he thought of the child she held in her heart.

The trickle of awareness became a stream, bubbling through his consciousness. The cramp eased. His lungs heaved, and he felt the warmth of Jenna's love for her niece flow over him. He was swept along, caught in her tangled anguish until old skills returned and he regained a hint of the control he used to have. Something flexed, and ached, and flexed again, and suddenly he was riding the current.

He went through the darkness. Nightmares yawned their gaping jaws around him, but he hung on to Jenna's hands and let the strength of her emotions guide him. How many times had he traveled these pathways? Each time was different and yet the same. He was a voyager, he didn't belong. A ghost, flickering in and out of others' reality, going where they led him, never knowing where the darkness ended, always hoping he'd find the way out.

There was a light. No, a window. The snow beyond it sparkled with sunshine so bright he had to squint. A shadow fell across his eyes. He strained to see what was there. A hand. A child's hand extended to the sunlight. Small fingers spread apart, and he could see the light glow orange-red through the translucent skin at the base of the fingers. The thumb wiggled. There was a blob of blue paint on the tip. It was fresh, dribbling over the nail, forming a fat drop that trembled on the curve of a tiny knuckle. The thumb wiggled again and the blue paint drop fell.

Damien clutched Jenna's hand, rocking forward. It was so vivid. So real. But he was still here. He heard the bed creak and felt her knees press hard against his leg.

He looked down as the paint spattered on a paper. His other hand, his left one, held a thick-handled brush. He dipped the stubby bristles into the pot of blue paint, lifted it and trailed a dripping line across the paper to the spatter mark. He pressed it down, smearing a circle of blue, pressing harder until the bristles flared out in a jagged skirt.

That was fun. He wiggled his thumb again, then shook his hand until another drop fell on the paper. That was fun, too. He sucked on his lower lip and glanced at the paint pots, then quickly stuck his thumb into the yellow one and put a sun in the other corner of the page. He grinned.

"Damien?"

It was Jenna's voice.

"Damien, what's happening? Why are you smiling?"

He lifted their joined hands to his mouth, running the back of his knuckle along his lips. "I'm painting."

"What?"

"It's more fun to use my fingers. I don't like that brush. I made a sun."

"What?"

His smile grew and he turned his hand over to rub her fingertips against his mouth. "I found Emily, Jenna. She's all right."

Her hand trembled. "Dear God."

"She's in a room somewhere. There's sunshine coming in the window. And fresh snow outside. Is she left-handed?"

"Yes! She's left-handed."

"Are you sure? She's holding the brush in her left hand but she's painting with her right thumb."

"She's all right?" she gasped. "You said she's all right? You did say that, didn't you?"

"Yes. She feels fine. Unhurt."

Her body shuddered violently. A sob burst from her lips and she doubled over, loosening her hold on his hand.

"Don't let go," he said quickly. "Hang on. I don't want to lose the connection."

Her grip immediately tightened until her nails bit into his skin. "Where is she?"

"All I can see is the room."

"Where?"

He felt himself being drawn back into the child. "I can only see what Emily sees," he said, his voice sounding farther away, even to his own ears. He let himself float, and the current swept him to the room with the window and the paint pots.

Silence descended and enveloped him once more. He looked down at his hands. There was paint on all his fingers now. He dabbed them on the paper, making bright spots across the bottom. The smell of the thick paint reminded him of the sand in his grandma's backyard when there were puddles.

Damien felt his consciousness twining with Emily's. Whose grandmother? Did he have a sandbox?

He gripped Jenna's hand like a lifeline. It had been so long since he'd tried this. It had seemed so familiar at first, but now he remembered the last time he'd traveled the darkness, the time it had caught him and he didn't come back, didn't want to come back. He'd had no lifeline, no anchor, and he'd been lost in the void for so long...

The paint smelled like wet sand, but it was smooth between his fingers when he rubbed his hands together. He dropped the brush. He didn't want to paint anymore.

Damien and Emily looked out the window again. It was a long, narrow window and it was covered with the stuff that made your hands wet if you drew pictures in it. There were icicles on the edge of the roof next door. He wanted to break one off, but he couldn't go out. He held his hand against the sunshine, squinting between his fingers, then brought his hand down fast on the painting. His palm stung. Vibrations traveled up his arm to his elbow. He hit it again and smushed the sun in the corner. He felt the heat of tears on his cheeks.

"Damien!"

Her voice called. It was all he heard. He felt the need to return, but he didn't want to leave Emily alone. The painting wasn't fun anymore.

"What's wrong? What's happening?"

Jenna. Damien fought the current and used the last reserves of his strength to keep his identity distinct. He couldn't go back yet. Where was he? Where was the room with the steamed-up window and the icicles next door? Why was he there? Straining to see more, Damien struggled to stay with the mind of the three-year-old. He needed more than this. He needed a clue, something that would lead them here. Emily was crying. Damien couldn't leave her like this. Alone. Alone.

Warm breath on his face. Her voice, urgent, loud. Nails digging into the backs of his hands.

Silence. The smell of the stupid paint. The sting on his palm where he smacked his stupid painting too hard. Dumb icicles he couldn't reach. Alone.

The grip on his hands relaxed. Arms encircled him, pulling him against a soft, warm, real body. Lips on his cheek, brushing away the moisture. Another current pulling him, more emotions, different ones.

One by one his senses withdrew. He could no longer smell the paint or feel the wet paper he was crumpling or hear the sobs that shook his chest, but he hadn't heard them, anyway. The sobs had been as soundless as the crash of his hand on the table. The light dimmed.

No! Emily! Where are you?

"Damien, come back," Jenna called. "Breathe. *Breathe!*" Silken hair slid over his face, arms tightened around him. "You're scaring me. Please."

He was traveling backward, recoiling like a snapped spring from the place he'd been. The light faded to a pinpoint and winked out. He was passing through the void, following a different current that guided him safely past the writhing nightmares. *She* pulled him back. The woman. His lips formed her name. "Jenna."

Hands stroking his brow, his chest. A mattress under his back. A scent as fresh and alive as a mountain stream. The bed creaking, the fire in the next room crackling.

Jenna's face above him, her hair swinging loose, concern clouding her beautiful eyes...

"I'm sorry. I didn't know. I'm sorry," she said, over and over, her fingers trembling as she smoothed his hair from his forehead.

"She's all right," Damien rasped.

Her hand stilled. She leaned closer, staring into his eyes. She glanced at his chest, then back at his face. Her eyes closed briefly as she pressed her lips tightly together. She nodded once.

He must have collapsed against her. He couldn't remember falling. "I hung on as long as I could, but I can't tell you where she is."

She nodded again, quickly, as if she didn't trust her voice.

"Couldn't see enough. Only weather. Angle of the sun. Type of building." He moistened his lips, the action thick and heavy, as if he were moving in slow motion. "Should have narrowed it down more."

Like a butterfly's kiss, her fingertips glided over his cheek. "You've already given me so much. You've told me she's alive. And unhurt. That's what really matters."

He could feel the pain waiting to take him, to claw at his mind and eat at his body, waiting to extract the cost of his voyage. He strained to hold it off. "Didn't want to leave her. So alone."

Her breath hitched. "You were there with her, really there."

"Yes. Shared senses. Saw, felt, smelled. No sound."

"There wouldn't be any sound."

No. That was wrong. There should have been sound. After sight, it was usually the strongest. Sometimes it was the sound he latched on to first. He frowned. Pain gathered behind his eyes. "Should have tried harder. Learned more. Listened."

Her lower lip trembled. She sucked it between her teeth in the same gesture he'd shared with her niece.

He could feel consciousness slipping away. He focused on her face, his frown deepening. "No sound. Why?"

She hesitated, her throat working as she struggled to bring her emotions under control. "You couldn't have heard anything, Damien, no matter how much harder you tried."

Something fell into place. He strained to understand. "Why?"

"Because Emily is deaf."

Jenna eased Damien's head from her lap, slipping a pillow beneath him before she reached for the quilt. Long, deep shudders shook his body. He was in pain and it was a hundred times worse than what she had seen in Hemlock this morning. He had said that was mild, but she hadn't believed him. She did now. She believed everything. "I'm sorry," she whispered, balancing on her knees to tuck the quilt around him. "I'm so sorry."

He shuddered again and the pencil she'd dropped on the mattress rolled to the floor. Impatiently, she pushed the pad of paper after it. She hadn't written down a thing. He'd said he used a tape recorder in the past when he'd done this for a living. Done *this?* He had stopped breathing. For a moment she hadn't been sure whether he was still with her, or whether he was coming back.

Yes, she believed everything. The bond of emotion, his ability to tap into it and follow it, everything. He'd been with Emily. Those details, the way he'd described her niece's method of painting—he must have been there. He'd mumbled things about smelling wet sand, wanting icicles, smushing the sun on the painting in a way that could only have come from the thoughts of a child. He'd described everything a child would have sensed.

Except sound.

Yes, she believed him. She hadn't told him that Emily was deaf; she hadn't thought of it. To her, it didn't make any difference, it wasn't relevant to her desire to find her niece. Yet Damien had noticed on his own. She'd seen understanding blossom on his face seconds before his eyelids had fallen shut. If she'd needed proof that he'd found her niece, he'd just given it to her.

"Oh, Damien." She brushed a lock of hair from his forehead and trailed her fingers over the lines that were etched into his skin. He'd called it giving away pieces of his soul. How could he do it? How could she have asked him to do it?

She snatched her hands away from him, sitting back quickly. She shouldn't be touching him. Not his skin. What if she triggered it again? In his weakened condition, what would another vision do to him?

Leave me alone, he'd said.

She hadn't.

This is the cost, he'd told her.

She'd tried to convince herself it didn't matter. She'd been wrong.

Unable to stop herself, she lifted her hand again, letting her fingers hover a breath away from his lips, tracing the shape of his mouth without touching him. He had smiled at first. She'd seen an echo of Emily's innocent grin, yet the smile had been Damien's. And it had been breathtaking. She had never seen him smile before. It transformed his face, shining through the harshness he had wrapped around himself, revealing the man who could speak like a poet and cry over a child's loneliness.

She lowered the quilt to his waist and leaned over to press her ear to his chest. Beneath the thick sweater he wore, his heart thudded slowly and steadily. "Damien?"

He didn't reply. He hadn't passed out the last time, but he must have known the aftereffects would be worse if he tried it again. That's why he'd insisted on staying on the bed. Taking care not to come into contact with the bare skin on his neck or his hands, she slipped her arms around him and held him tightly. She felt his warmth, and the inner strength that couldn't be diminished by his body's weakness. He'd asked her to leave him alone, but she didn't want to. And it wasn't merely because of what he could do to help find Emily.

Emily. She was in a room with a window, in a place where it had snowed. What had Damien said? Angle of the sun? Yes, they could get an idea of the latitude that way, and the time of day. The weather service should be able to help, too. They could get a list of places where it had snowed overnight. Already that ruled out at least half the country. Maybe when Damien awakened and had a chance to rest he could try again....

Try again? Do this again? How could she ask him?

How could she not?

At least her niece was alive. Jenna closed her eyes and listened to the reassuring beat of Damien's heart. Alive and unhurt. He had answered the one question she hadn't had the courage to consider. Oh, yes. He might not have pinpointed Emily's location, but he'd given her something worth even more.

No gift comes without a cost.

She tightened her cautious embrace. "Damien," she whispered. "What have I done to you?"

A low growl came from the doorway of the bedroom.

Jenna's eyes flew open. Damien still didn't stir. She lifted her head cautiously and looked over her shoulder.

The wolf was standing on the threshold, his legs braced apart, his body lowered. Firelight glinted from the black fur that bristled upright along the back of his neck. He growled again, his muzzle wrinkling to reveal gleaming teeth.

Jenna swallowed hard. Oh, God. How could she have forgotten the wolf? When they'd returned from Hemlock, Damien had been weak but at least he'd been awake enough to keep his pet under control with a few terse commands. Should she risk waking Damien? Should she make a lunge for the door and try to close it?

Smoke moved forward, his nails clacking against the tile floor. Yellow eyes reflected the glow from the lamps, shining eerily from the shadows.

"Nice boy," she said softly. "Nice Smoke." She slid her arms from Damien and turned to face the animal.

The wolf stretched his neck, his nose twitching. He padded forward, right to the side of the bed. Bared teeth glistened inches from her feet. He growled again, watching her steadily.

She rested her hand on Damien's sleeve. If the animal decided to attack, he couldn't help her. Trying to keep her fear from showing, she remained motionless and kept her gaze locked with the wolf's, waiting for his next move. "Uh, nice Smoke," she tried again. "Good pooch."

His nose twitched and he blew out a huffing breath. Slowly his head lowered. He sniffed at a piece of broken crockery. It was the soup bowl that Damien had swept onto the floor. He nudged it with the tip of his nose, then licked up a drop of minestrone that clung to the edge.

Moving as smoothly as she could, Jenna slid across Damien's legs to the other side of the bed. "Are you still hungry, pooch? Finished that can of dog food already? If you're looking for fresh meat, there's nothing in here for you. You like that soup? I'll get you some more." She was babbling. She knew the animal couldn't possibly understand, but she hoped her tone would keep him calm. "Sure, pooch. I'll just walk around you," she said, inching carefully toward the door.

The wolf turned to watch her, his ears cocked alertly. He ran his tongue around his muzzle.

She grasped the doorframe. "That's a good boy. Good doggy. Nice pooch. Soup, okay?"

Smoke took a step toward her, his tail swishing through the air twice. If he had been a dog, Jenna would have interpreted the tail-wagging as an overture of friendship. Wolf behavior was supposed to be similar to that of domestic dogs, wasn't it? Her gaze went from his teeth to the trail of a scar that zigzagged through his fur. As it had before, a wave of sympathy helped submerge her fear. Smoke might have been a very different animal if he hadn't suffered such horrible pain and rejection.

She glanced from the wolf to Damien. The comparison was too obvious to ignore. Pain and rejection. Defensiveness masked by hostility. The need for patience and understanding...

One cautious step at a time, Jenna made her way to the kitchen and ladled the leftover minestrone into a dish for Smoke.

Evening fell slowly, closing around the isolated cabin in cold-sharpened silence. Jenna moved restlessly around the interior, checking on Damien every few minutes while she struggled to contain her anxiety. It had been more than four hours since he'd fallen asleep. At least, she assumed he was asleep. Each time she approached his bed she had seen that he was still breathing, and whenever she put her ear to his chest she found that his heart continued its strong, steady beat. Yet he hadn't moved. Was that normal?

She shook her head sharply and stopped beside the fireplace to add another few logs. Normal? How was she supposed to know what normal was when it came to Damien's condition? What if he really did need a doctor this time? What did she know about nursing someone who was suffering from psychic exhaustion? On the other hand, what would a doctor know?

"If only you had a telephone," she muttered, not for the first time. If he had a telephone, she could call Rachel and ask her what to do. His grandmother would have to know about this, wouldn't she? And how long should Jenna wait before she did . . . something.

Each minute she stayed here was one minute more to wait before she could contact her sister and relay the information Damien had given her about Emily. Although the child's location was still unknown, at least Jenna could comfort Brigit with the knowledge that Emily was alive and unharmed.

She glanced at the reflection of the lamp that seemed to float in the void beyond the windowpane. By now it would be dark where Emily was, too. Was it cold there, as well? Was Emily asleep? Was there a night-light near her bed so she wouldn't be afraid of the dark if she woke? Had she cried for long this afternoon?

"Stop it," she said, lifting her chin and forcing herself to take a deep breath. She couldn't fall apart. For now, she'd take this one step at a time.

The clock on the mantel chimed softly. Jenna glanced at the time. Ten minutes since she had last checked on Damien. She pushed away from the fireplace, giving a wide berth to the sleeping Smoke, even though he hadn't growled at her since she'd let him finish the biscuits.

Just as she'd done for the past four hours, she checked Damien's condition the best she could without touching his skin. She knelt on the bed beside him, watching his face for signs of returning consciousness, but his features could have been carved from wax. Leaning forward, she pressed her ear to his chest and heard the steady beat of his heart. She wanted to hold him, but she couldn't be sure if it would make things worse. Frustrated, wanting to do something, she looked around for the extra blankets she'd used the night before. Picking up the lamp from the dresser, she walked to the closet in the far wall.

It wasn't a closet. As soon as the light reached past the shadowed doorway, Jenna realized this was a separate room. She lifted the lamp higher, surprised that she hadn't noticed this before.

It appeared to be an addition to the original structure, judging by the pale sheen of the log walls. There were deep shelves near the door, stacked with flat packages and cardboard boxes. She stepped over the threshold and saw a long table on the far side of the room with rectangular trays and plastic bottles aligned in precise rows. Ribbons of what appeared to be cellophane dangled from a cord that had been strung above one end of the table. There was no window in any of the walls. Instead, Damien had brought the outside in by decorating the room with photographs.

Jenna moved closer, her gaze caught by an enlargement that was tacked beside the deep shelf. It was a study in shades of white, a close-up of fresh snow balancing on the sun-whitened branch of a dead tree. The stark simplicity of the composition was deceptive. This photograph was a work of art.

Intrigued, she looked at another one. Unlike the first, it was a riot of color and movement. Birch trees swayed in the wind that twirled their golden brown leaves across a somber, brooding backdrop of pine. The next was different again. It was a picture of a pair of loons silhouetted against a sunrise, slicing through veils of mist on the surface of a glittering lake, evoking dignity and loneliness and a sense of isolated purpose.

The quality was exquisite, the images were haunting, like visions of someone's soul.

Jenna drew in her breath quickly, steadying the hand that held the lamp as the revelation struck her. She glanced around the room again. No window. A table with flat pans. Strips of cellophane. This wasn't a closet, it was a darkroom.

She saw the cameras then. There were three of them on a shelf in the far corner along with a bulky case. She moved forward, lifted the lid of the case and found extra lenses and filters. Small canisters of film were stacked beside the lense case with businesslike precision. A tripod leaned against the wall along with a multipocketed backpack that would be ideal for carrying a photographer's supplies.

Of course. These photographs would have to be his.

Filled with an urgency she didn't want to examine, Jenna explored the rest of the room. She found a cardboard box that contained neatly filed correspondence from several well-known magazines. In another box she uncovered copies of the articles that contained his work. The name that was given credit for the photographs was Duncan Rand, but there was no mistaking Damien's distinctive style. He'd worked from Arizona to Alaska, specializing in locations that were remote and unpopulated. And whether the scene was a desert or a mountainside, each picture captured its essence with the sensitivity of someone who saw...more.

"Oh, Damien," she whispered, turning back to the wall of photographs. This was what he did for a living. She already knew that he hadn't used his telepathy for years, but she hadn't considered what he'd been doing in the meantime. All she'd cared about was how she could use him. She had done her best to ignore everything else.

This explained so much. He might have withdrawn from human contact, but he hadn't withdrawn entirely. He channeled his energy into his work, sharing his vision in a way that would keep him safe—touching others without being touched in return.

Shaken, she walked back to the bedroom and went to stand by Damien's side. Some of the tension had eased from his face. The lines beside his mouth weren't as harsh as the last time she'd checked on him. The tears that he'd shed for Emily had dried hours ago, yet the hands that lay on top of the quilt were still clenched into fists.

And just as it had happened when she had sat on the floor with him and watched his strong fingers move gently through the fur of a scarred animal, Jenna felt her perception of Damien shift again.

He hadn't touched a woman in five years. Who had she been? What had she been like? Had he loved her? Had she loved him?

Jenna felt a lump form in her throat. He could ride the current of other people's emotions, he could see the beauty in a snow-covered branch, he could tame a wolf. He had so much to share and to give, yet he had condemned himself to live alone. He was strong, vulnerable, sensitive and fascinating. He was the kind of man who could inspire desire as well as admiration, who could make a woman question her priorities...

He was more dangerous than she had ever imagined.

Chapter Six

Emily couldn't hear. It was the first thought Damien had as he climbed his way out of the pain that clutched him. The child whom he had touched in his mind couldn't hear. She was different. Imperfect. Not normal. Had anyone called her a freak? Did the other children taunt her? Did her family reject her and tell her they wished she'd never been born?

No. Not if the rest of the family was like Jenna. She loved her niece and accepted her. Damien had felt the purity of her emotion and had no doubt about the genuineness of her feelings. She hadn't rejected her godchild because she wasn't perfect. She hadn't let her be driven away because she was different. She wasn't anything like his mother.

Darkness swirled around him, but it wasn't the darkness of the nightmares. It was memory. He'd been punished for saying things he wasn't supposed to know, shut into his room with no supper and no good-night kiss while his mother had smiled and laughed with the guests she entertained for the sake of his father's career. Miller Reese had become the mayor of Hemlock when Damien was Emily's age. The small town where he'd been born was supposed to be a springboard for Miller's political career.

But in a small town, word gets around about a child who goes into fits when he touches a crying playmate. Rumors spread about the boy who told his nursery-school teacher that her missing husband was in Duluth with the lady from next door, and soon the small-town springboard was in danger of becoming a dead end. So Damien's mother had tried to make him normal.

Normal. How that word had hurt. In a perfect world, no one would be judged on how close they came to that arbitrary standard. Children wouldn't be forced to feel less than human because of an accident in an obscure section of a DNA strand. They wouldn't be rejected the way his mother—

He wrenched his thoughts away from the useless loop of anger and resentment. How ironic that he'd come full circle, that during the struggle of the last five years he'd tried harder than his mother ever had to force himself into the mold of normalcy. He thought he had managed to carve a niche for himself in the imperfect world. Once Jenna left, would he be able to return to the safely separate life he'd established? Because of her, his illusion of normalcy was gone, and he'd have to live more cautiously than ever, yet he still had his work. Once Jenna left . . .

Only, she wasn't going to leave yet. She wanted to use him to find Emily. The imperfect child she was strong enough to love without reservation. The girl who sucked her lip and painted with her thumb and wanted to touch the icicles.

The agony that had weighed his eyelids shut had dulled to a rumbling ache. Damien ignored it, concentrating on completing his climb back to consciousness and opening his eyes.

Jenna was in the rocking chair on the other side of the room. Her shadow moved back and forth on the wall in time to the muted squeak of the runners. Beyond the reflection of the lamp in the window he could see nothing but blackness. How late was it? How long had he been out? He felt as if he had spent days trying to crawl away from the swirling void, but he knew from experience it could only have been a matter of hours. He shifted, easing muscles stiff from his body's inactivity. The bed creaked softly and Jenna looked up.

Their gazes meshed and locked as easily as their fingers had. Her open, trusting green eyes were shining with unshed tears. Sometime during the evening she had taken the clip from her hair. It spilled in sensuous waves across her shoulders, and Damien remembered the scent and the texture and the silky slide when he'd held it between his fingers. Soon another memory stirred. Emily had cried, and Damien had felt Jenna's fingers on his cheek, wiping away the tears. She had drawn him back from the edge and had held him in her arms. Her warmth had cushioned him, her sympathy had soothed him.

Ah, Jenna. It had felt so good.

She was the first to look away, breaking the tentative connection between them. She stopped the movement of the chair and cleared her throat. "You were asleep for a long time."

Her voice was distant. He'd seen this reaction before, when the vision was over. It was the awkward, morning-after embarrassment of someone who has awakened naked in a stranger's bed. He hadn't expected this from Jenna, though.

Fool. What *had* he expected? She had touched him only because of Emily. She'd made that clear from the start.

She glanced at him quickly, furtively, as if she didn't want to look too long. "Are you feeling better?"

He was already in too much pain to feel the stab of disappointment, wasn't he? Simply because her emotions for her niece were pure and unconditional didn't mean she had any left over for a man like him. He didn't want her to feel anything, anyway. It would be simpler if she didn't. His own feelings were still a turbulent mix of admiration and hate and wanting. He knew better than to expect anything more than gratitude from her. Once he found Emily, she would leave and he would do his damnedest to make sure his life settled back into the safe niche he had carved.

"Damien?"

He pushed himself up on his elbows. "What time is it?"

"Ten-thirty."

More than seven hours. He rubbed a hand over his face. The nerves in his skin twanged uncomfortably. He rubbed harder until the feeling passed.

"Is that . . . usual?" she asked.

"Pretty well."

"Would you like anything?" she asked, rising from the chair. "Soup? Coffee?"

"In a while. Not yet."

"I was worried. I didn't know whether to take you to a doctor, or even how I *could* take you to a doctor."

"Good."

"What?"

"I told you this morning that a doctor wouldn't help. If you had taken me to Hemlock and tried to explain what had happened, I would have ended up in a rubber room."

She took a step toward him, then changed direction and crossed the room, her back stiff beneath the jade sweater. When she reached the window, she turned to face him. "I don't know what to do to help you, Damien. Tell me what you need.''

"Why?"

She hesitated. "I feel responsible."

"You don't have to feel guilty, Jenna."

"But I do. It's because of me that you're . . . like this."

"I knew what I was doing."

"And I want to thank you, but anything I might say would be inadequate after what you've gone through. I had no idea how hard this was going to be on you. If I had known . . ." Her words trailed off and she flushed.

"If you had known, you would have asked anyway," he finished for her with brutal simplicity.

At least she had the integrity not to deny it. "Are you going to be all right now?"

"Yes. The physical effects are temporary. It's like a hangover." He gritted his teeth, waiting for a sudden wave of nausea to pass.

"How long will you need to rest before . . ." Her flush deepened. She lifted her hand in a wordless gesture.

He knew what she wanted to ask. He was surprised she'd managed to wait this long. "I won't be able to attempt making another connection with Emily for at least a week."

Her expression lost the guarded cautiousness that had shielded it. She looked directly at him, anxiety in every line of her face. "A week?"

He'd seen that look before, too. The morning-after awkwardness changing to the impatient demand for more. He rubbed his eyes wearily as another jolt of disappointment stabbed through him. "I doubt if what I saw will be enough to get close to her. We'll do some research and narrow the location down, but we can't learn more until I establish another connection."

"You can't try again for a whole week?" she asked, her voice breaking.

"No."

"But—"

"Even a trained circus animal gets to recuperate between performances, Jenna."

"Trained—" Something flashed behind her eyes. She strode to the foot of the bed and clasped the carved corner post. "That's not how I see you, Damien."

He looked at her over the tips of his fingers. "Really? How exactly do you see me?"

She parted her lips to reply, then slowly let out her breath. The guarded caution fell back into place. She glanced toward the door to his darkroom for a moment before she relaxed her grip on the bedpost and stepped back. "You're the man who's going to find my niece," she said, her tone flat. "That's how I see you."

If he'd had the strength in his limbs, he might have done something, then. He might have flung aside the quilt, leapt to his feet and shown her that he was more than simply a man she could use. Anger, yearning and resentment all combined with the throbbing ache in his head, and instead of easing his pain with her body, he lashed out at her with his words. "Fine. What are you willing to pay for my services?"

She started. "What do you mean?"

"The gift doesn't come without a cost, Jenna. You've barged into my life and resurrected a nightmare. Why should I continue to help you for nothing?"

Her chin angled upward as her jaw firmed with determination. "Name your price, Damien. To restore Emily to her mother, I'd be willing to pay whatever you want."

Whatever you want. He dropped his head back onto the pillow, closing his eyes to savor the image that sprang to his mind. What did he want? Soft blond hair sliding through his fingers, a smile sweeping the loneliness from his life like a spring breeze, Jenna curling over him, her thighs warm beneath his head, her hands gentle on his face. Ah, it had been so long, so long—

"Damien?"

It had been so long since he'd touched a woman or had any human contact, and his parched body had soaked up every precious moment Jenna had given him. Even the chaste joining of hands had been better than the years of loneliness. He hadn't been able to risk it before, because he hadn't wanted to trigger the nightmare.

But the nightmare had happened and he had survived. What did he have to lose if he touched her again? Touched more than her hand next time?

The mattress squeaked and dipped as Jenna put her knee on the edge and leaned over him. To Damien's surprise, she yanked back the quilt, braced her hands on his shoulders and laid her cheek against his chest. "Damien!"

He opened his eyes quickly, meeting her startled gaze. "What?"

Her gasp was immediate. "Oh!"

"What are you doing?" He felt her tense. She was close enough for him to see gold flecks in her green eyes and a sprinkling of freckles across her nose. Her lower lip was reddened and swollen, as if she had been biting it for hours, and he had a sudden urge to soothe it with his tongue. He raised his hand and caught her hair in his fist, trapping her where she was. "What the hell are you doing?"

She swallowed, staring into his face. "I thought you had passed out again. I thought—"

"So you crawled into bed with me? Because you thought I'd passed out?"

"No, I was checking your heartbeat." She moved her hands away from his shoulders and tried to lift her head, but he wouldn't release her hair. "I didn't know you were still awake. Damien, let me up."

He brought his other hand down on her back and pinned her to his chest. Her right breast pressed against his side, moving tantalizingly against him with each shallow breath she took. He shifted his leg and felt the warmth of her thigh beside his. Despite the fatigue that bound his body, a response stirred. Right now, he didn't care why she was here, he only wanted this moment to last. "Sure. In a minute."

She stopped trying to pull away and went completely still. Her eyes widened. "You said you shouldn't be using your gift to connect with Emily for a week. Is it safe to make another attempt now?"

Anger mixed with his budding desire. His gift. Everything came back to that, didn't it? His childhood had been warped by it, his life—his lack of a life—was defined by it. He couldn't simply enjoy a woman's closeness without it being the reason. Well, if she wanted a reason, he'd give her one. "We were discussing my fee."

"Your fee?"

"You offered to pay anything." Grasping her arms, he pulled her up until her face was above his, then hooked his leg over hers and rolled, reversing their positions, covering her small frame with his. "Or have you forgotten?"

Her hair spread across his pillow. Her heart thudded hard against his chest. "I haven't forgotten. I have money put aside. How much do you want?"

"Money isn't what I want from you, Jenna," he said, echoing the words she'd spoken in his Jeep this morning. Had it only been this morning? It seemed as if days had passed since then. He dipped his head, inhaling the delicate scent that rose from her throat. "No, I have enough money."

Her pulse fluttered in the vein at the side of her neck and her breathing quickened. "What do you want?"

"A trade. That would be fair, wouldn't it?"

"What kind of trade?"

This was insane. He knew it, even as the thought formed in his head. But everyone said he was crazy, didn't they? He adjusted his weight, partially supporting himself on his knees and elbows so he wouldn't crush her, yet still maintaining enough pressure to keep her from moving away. Even through the layers of clothing that separated them, the outline of her figure seared into his skin. His breath caught. Crazy. "We seem to have skipped the preliminaries, haven't we?"

"Preliminaries?"

"You came here demanding my help. When I agreed to cooperate, we were both in too much of a hurry to bother striking a deal. We'd better do that now before we go any further."

Jenna slid her hands between them and pushed at his chest. "I'm not negotiating any deal while I'm lying on your bed."

"But a bed is the perfect place to negotiate this particular deal, Jenna." He caught her wrists, careful to shield his palms with the cuffs of her sweater. He eased her hands down on either side of her head, holding her in place. "A trade," he repeated, watching her face. "You want the use of my mind. In return, I want the use of your body."

She didn't appear to understand him at first. Her forehead furrowed and the eyebrows that usually arched with wonder angled downward. "But I already know that we need to touch—" She broke off and pressed her head as far back into the pillow as it would go. "My body? You want to *use* my body?"

He nodded once, a sharp jerk of his chin. "Yes. And just to be sure you understand, I'm not talking about holding hands. After you leave, I won't be risking contact with anyone. Ever." The bleakness of his future unrolled in front of him like the cracked web of a dried-up riverbed. What had started as an angry impulse began to transform into something more, into need. *After you leave . . .*

He couldn't think about the emptiness to come. His grip on her wrists tightened. "Since you're here with me now, and you will be until I find Emily, I want to make the experience worth my while."

Shock clouded her eyes and slackened the muscles of her face. "That's insane," she whispered.

A corner of his mouth lifted in a bitter smile. "Exactly."

"You want to sleep with me in exchange—"

"Not sleep, Jenna," he murmured, moving above her so that his chest rubbed her breasts. "I wouldn't squander a minute of it in sleep."

At the friction of their bodies, she gasped. "But making love—"

"Not love, either. I don't want love. I can sense the emotion and ride its currents, but I want no part of it. No, what I want from you is sex."

"And that's your price? Sex?"

"To put it simply, yes."

"I can't believe you're asking this."

"Why not? It seems completely fair."

"Fair? It's obscene."

"You've destroyed my illusion and my hope. You've shown me that the nightmare is never going to end. Don't you think you owe me something for that?"

She hesitated, drawing her lower lip between her teeth. "I'm sorry for bringing you so much pain, but I can't—"

"You owe me," he stated.

"I'm not denying that. For what you've gone through today, you have a right to demand more than gratitude. I know I told you I'd pay anything, but what you're asking is impossible."

He pulled on her wrists, stretching her arms over her head until her back arched. "Impossible? Why? Do you find me repulsive?"

"No, of course not."

"I didn't notice a wedding ring. Are you married? Engaged? Promised to someone else?"

"I'm divorced. And I have no intention of starting a relationship with—"

"Relationship? Jenna, this is a business deal. That's all. I told you, I don't want love or any other insidious snares to complicate the purely physical."

"This is ridiculous. Impossible."

"Do you think I'm incapable of giving a woman pleasure?"

Color bloomed in her cheeks in a sudden flash. "I wouldn't know that, and I don't want to find out."

"Don't you?" Transferring her captured wrists to one hand, he trailed his other hand downward, stroking her hair, cupping her shoulder. He rested his fingers lightly on the upper slope of her breast, feeling the warm, resilient curve beneath the velvety sweater. Using the pad of his thumb, he traced an arcing path to her ribs. "I think your breast would fit perfectly into my palm. Do you want to find out, Jenna?"

"We don't even know each other. This is wrong."

"Wrong?" he asked, spreading his fingers over her midriff, absorbing the subtle quiver that traveled beneath his hand. "This is a woman's body responding to a man's. It's as natural as a bird singing to the rising sun. And you've thought about it, haven't you? I've seen it on your face."

Jenna felt the heat of his hand flow outward, a path of tingling awareness that gathered into a tight throb as her nipple hardened. As much as she wanted to deny what he said, the proof was mere inches from his fingertips. "Damien, don't do this."

"As for your other objection, it doesn't apply, either. We already know each other. Eight hours ago, on this very bed, we joined in a way that's more intimate than sex." He settled heavily on top of her, fitting his solid, muscular length firmly into place. "I opened my mind to you, Jenna. You touched me with your emotions. You can't pretend we're still strangers."

She was imprisoned by his strength and by his size and by his sheer male power. In the lamplight his face was all harsh planes and angles, giving a fierceness to his expression that struck a primitive cord deep inside. Her heart pounded, sending blood throbbing and surging into all the hidden places over which she had no control.

This shouldn't be happening. How could she feel this response when she was entrapped? She meant what she'd said. The pain of her divorce had cured her of the urge to risk her heart with another man.

But it wasn't her heart that he wanted. Or her love. Neither one of them was foolish enough to want love.

Twisting her arms, she broke his hold on her wrists. The ease with which she pulled away surprised her at first, but then she realized that at her first motion of resistance, his grip had become no more than a light caress. She could have broken it at any time. She lowered her hands slowly, cautiously, but he made no move to recapture her. When she brought her palms to his chest and pushed, he rolled to his side, removing his weight and his warmth.

She should jump from the bed, grab her coat and run from this cabin as fast as she could. She had managed to drive the Jeep up the lane this morning. It hadn't snowed since then, so even though she would be hampered by the darkness, she should be able to drive herself to town. She could stay at the motel, then find a way to arrange to get Damien's vehicle back to him somehow before she went home.

Yet she remained motionless, her entire body thrumming with reaction. Drawn by a power beyond thought, she turned her head and looked at his face.

He was lying a hand's breadth away, his elbow bent, his cheek propped against his palm. His eyes were half-closed, his jaw clenched. The lines beside his mouth were dark slashes of pain.

She should have been angry. The bargain he was proposing was too outrageous to consider, wasn't it? And he was obviously still suffering from the physical aftereffects of his connection with her niece, so she shouldn't be feeling this hard kernel of desire inside her, should she?

If he had dared to suggest this price two days ago, she would have turned around and taken her chances with the blizzard. Yet as he lay so close beside her, she remembered his helplessness when she had brought him back from town, and the sudden warmth of his smile when he'd found Emily, and the poignancy of his tears when he'd had to leave her.

"Well?" he asked.

His deep voice rumbled through the air between them, startling Jenna into motion. She twisted away, rolling to the edge of the mattress. Her feet hit the floor and she staggered, clutching the bedpost for balance.

"You don't have to run," he said. "I would never force you."

She eyed the long legs that had been pressed over hers, the strong fingers that had caressed her so tenderly, and a residual quiver whispered over her skin. She took a step back.

Lifting his hand, he rubbed his face hard for a moment before sitting up in the center of the bed. He rested one forearm across his upraised knee and turned toward her. "I wouldn't force you," he said again, more firmly this time. "I want you willing. And I won't expect payment in full until I've finished the job you want me to do," he continued. "As long as Emily is still missing, your emotions will be too strong for me to touch you without triggering my power, anyway."

She paused. "What?"

"Skin, Jenna. Your naked skin, remember? If I touch it while you're still preoccupied with the girl, I'll get caught in your bond with her. After she's found, when the intensity of your emotion drops, that's when we'll close the deal."

Close the deal? Expect payment? The everyday terms that she dealt with in her profession took on an entirely different tone. "I can't believe we're even discussing this."

"It would be a good deal for you. Guaranteed results. I don't get satisfaction until you do. What more could you ask?"

Shaking her head, she backed as far as the doorway.

He made no attempt to stop her from leaving. He watched her steadily, his eyes glittering with predatory determination. "I'll make it good for you, Jenna." His voice was low and coaxing, like a stroke of velvet in the dark. "Let me have some memories to take with me when I rebuild my solitude."

Solitude. Beautiful, moving, lonely photographs. A man who had so much to share, resigned to living alone. He said he would find Emily, but the price he was asking was too much.

Wasn't it?

"After the experience we shared, you can't maintain that we're still strangers. We've already joined," he said, his gaze never wavering. "I rode the current of your emotions. When we're together, you can—"

"No," she said shakily, trying to snuff out the reaction that still tremored through her body, but her imagination readily—and vividly—supplied the words she hadn't let him say. She felt the solidity of the doorframe behind her back and leaned into it, concentrating on keeping her knees from buckling. He was crazy to suggest such a trade.

And she must be going crazy herself, because she was actually considering it.

"I'm willing to help you, Jenna. I'll give you what you came for. I'll use all my abilities to find Emily, no matter how many times I need to travel the void. I'll do the research to put the clues together. All you need to do is tell me whether or not you agree to my price. Otherwise, I'll drive you back to Hemlock at dawn."

"You're giving me an impossible choice."

"I want your answer."

"Can't we discuss this in the morning, after you've had a chance to rest?"

"I won't change my mind."

"But I can't do what you want—"

"It seems to me we had this conversation before, only the roles were reversed. I wasn't willing to do what you wanted, but you didn't give up, you didn't leave me alone until you got it."

"You can't possibly equate my desire to find my niece to your desire for...that."

"I can. I do. I want your answer now. What's it going to be, Jenna? Do you agree to my terms?"

What he offered was everything she could hope for. What he wanted in return was...wrong. Wasn't it?

But did concepts of right and wrong matter when the welfare of her niece was at stake? Wouldn't it be worse to leave now, knowing that Damien had the power to help her? Didn't she love Emily enough to put the child's welfare above her own feelings?

She exhaled shakily. "You would find her first?" she asked. "You would wait until we actually could bring her home?"

He nodded slowly.

"And you wouldn't...force me?"

"I won't hurt you. How could I, when I would feel your pain?"

For Emily, she told herself. This was for Emily. She straightened her shoulders, curling her hands into fists by her sides. "All right."

"All right?"

What was she agreeing to? An affair? A fling? A one-night stand? How could she possibly consider bartering sex for... his services?

But what was the alternative?

"Yes," she said, forcing a strength into her voice that she didn't feel. "When Emily is reunited with her mother, I'll meet your price."

He didn't say anything more, didn't make a move toward her. Instead, he sat there in the center of his massive bed, with his wild hair brushing his shoulders and his icy blue eyes gleaming in the hushed light of the kerosene lamp.

And he smiled.

Jenna caught her breath. The air crackled with heat, as if she had stepped too close to the fire. Secrets, dark and sensual, pulsed in the hushed room. The smile was filled with pleasure, and potency. Challenge. And promise.

As carefully as she had backed away from the wolf earlier, Jenna kept her gaze on Damien and inched out of the bedroom.

Chapter Seven

The man who's going to find Emily. Jenna repeated it to herself over and over when she got her first glimpse of Damien the following morning. That's all he was to her. A means to an end. She couldn't allow this bargain between them to be anything more than a mutually beneficial deal. He was a recluse, a bitter, withdrawn recluse who wanted to use her because she happened to be convenient. There would be no possibility of a lasting relationship between them, no future, no commitment. What he had proposed was contrary to everything she had been raised to value.

She had to keep her distance, that was all. Emotional as well as physical. Until Emily was safely home.

But, oh God, the way he looked when he stepped into the living room.

He had shaved. The shadow of black stubble was gone. There was nothing left to disguise the dramatic angle of his jaw or cloak the smooth planes of his cheeks. His skin had the moist, taut gleam that was tempting, enticing and uniquely male. All male. Without the surrounding beard, his lips were chiseled curves, a contradiction of textures, firm lines promising sweet tastes. And his chin, oh Lord, his chin had a tiny cleft in the center, a subtle valley that added the perfect hint of softness to the hard contours of his face.

He'd combed his hair, and not merely with his fingers. The freshly shampooed strands still bore the neat, damp furrows from the teeth of a comb. Pulled starkly back from his face and caught in a ponytail at his nape, his midnight black hair conjured images of dashing pirates and soulful renegades and dangerous duels fought in the name of passion.

Yes, he was dangerous. His efforts to appear more civilized only emphasized his untamed appeal.

Jenna pressed her lips together and turned back to the couch where she had spent the night. Snatching the pillow from the corner, she shook it briskly a few times and tossed it to the cushions.

The stiffness that had restricted his movements yesterday had disappeared. He walked with the grace of a prowling animal as he crossed to the other side of the room and lifted the coffeepot from the stove. Such a simple motion, pouring coffee into a mug, but with his white cotton turtleneck molding his muscular arms, the motion turned into a study of restrained strength. He lifted the mug to his lips, took a sip and raised his eyebrows in surprise. "What did you do to the coffee?"

Jenna leaned over to smooth the blanket she had used, trying to keep her hands steady. "I scraped the layer of sludge out of the bottom of the pot and used a piece of cloth to hold the grounds," she explained.

Taking another sip, he closed his eyes, holding the liquid in his mouth as if savoring the taste. His face relaxed in pleasure. "Mmm."

It wasn't even a word, and it wasn't meant for her, but she couldn't help the tiny thud of her pulse at the masculine sound of satisfaction. She concentrated on folding the blanket into a neat rectangle.

He swallowed and tilted his head, glancing at the stove, then leaned over to pull open the oven door and look inside. "What's this?"

"Bread pudding."

His nostrils flared as he inhaled appreciatively. "What's in it besides bread?"

"Eggs, cinnamon and raisins. I remember that you don't usually have breakfast, but seeing as you haven't eaten anything since yesterday afternoon, I thought you might be hungry. There's some fresh orange juice, too."

He shut the oven and straightened up, doing a thorough survey of the kitchen area. He checked inside the cupboards, which she'd tidied, and the small refrigerator, which was still filled with the supplies she'd purchased the day before. "You've been busy," he said finally.

"I had a lot of time to fill last night while I waited for, uh..."

"While you waited for the next performance," he supplied. "I don't need a housekeeper, Jenna."

"It was the least I could do—"

"I want you in my bed, not in my kitchen."

Coming from any other man, the comment would have been too arrogant, too blatantly macho to be taken seriously. But from Damien, it wasn't a dare or a boast, it was a bald statement of fact.

Jenna finished folding the blanket and gathered up the stack of bedding, clutching it awkwardly to her chest like a shield. "Until you fulfill your half of our bargain, a housekeeper is all you're going to get. If that doesn't suit you, just say so. I'll pour the rest of that coffee down the sink and feed the bread pudding to your wolf."

Damien blinked. "You'd what?"

"You heard me."

His gaze darted to where Smoke sat on his haunches beside the refrigerator. The wolf ran his tongue around his muzzle as he watched the oven door. Damien looked back to Jenna, a wry smile lifting one corner of his mouth. "You and my grandmother must get along well."

"As a matter of fact, we do." She stored her bedding under the table beside the couch and went over to the fireplace. The blaze she'd built up when she'd awakened was burning well, but she added another two logs in an effort to keep her gaze away from that smile. It wasn't a real smile any more than his murmur of pleasure over the coffee had been a real word, but it seemed to have the same effect.

Straightening her spine, she lifted her chin and cleared her throat. "I need to go into town today. If you don't mind, I'd like to borrow your Jeep."

"Running away already, Jenna?"

"No. I'd like to get to a telephone as soon as possible so I can call my sister."

"Ah. And what would you tell her?"

"That you saw Emily, that she's all right. Brigit is sick with worry, and any shred of hope would—"

"And what will you say when your sister asks you how you know?"

"I'll tell her the truth, of course. That you saw Emily in your mind."

"She won't believe you," he stated flatly.

Jenna paused, taking a deep breath. "I'll find a way to make her listen."

He picked up his mug again and helped himself to more coffee, his silence serving as his reply.

"She might not have approved of my decision to seek your help," Jenna continued, "but once I tell her the details about what you saw, she'll have to believe me."

"Why?"

"You described the way Emily paints."

"So what? Most three-year-olds would prefer to paint with their fingers."

"And you realized that she couldn't hear. I hadn't told you that."

"That's not proof, either. I could have done some background research, found out some other way."

"You wouldn't have had the chance. I've been with you every minute for three days and I know you haven't had the opportunity to communicate with anyone else." She gestured impatiently. "I was there when you contacted her, Damien. I saw what you went through, so I don't have one shred of doubt over whether you did or not. Why are you saying these things?"

"Simply trying to prepare you for the reaction you're going to get. I've had plenty of experience with skeptics."

"If you ask me, you had a rotten deal."

"What's that supposed to mean?"

"I'm sure I'm not the only one in the world who is willing to admit that there are some things that science can't explain. Yet from what you've told me, you met up with a lot of narrow-mindedness and ingratitude during the time you exercised your gift."

"We trained circus animals don't expect anything different."

"Oh, stop it." Forgetting about her resolve to keep away from him, she walked toward the kitchen. "Maybe if you'd hired a good publicist, the media wouldn't have treated you so badly."

"Tabloids thrive on stories about freaks. It's understandable that—"

"You're no more a freak than Emily is," she said harshly. "Just because my niece is going to grow up to be different from the majority of people doesn't mean that she's inferior. She's just different. She can't hear. And I wouldn't let anyone get away with calling her a freak.''

''No, you wouldn't, would you?''

She halted beside the table and curled her fingers around the wooden slat on the back of the chair, leaning forward. ''Judging by what I saw in town yesterday morning, there are a lot of people in Hemlock who need a few lessons on tolerance and good manners. I'm sure if they got to know you, their attitudes would improve.''

''I quit worrying about what other people thought of me a long time ago, Jenna.''

''Did you? Is that why you act so rude all the time?''

''As I said, I don't care what they think.''

''Yes, you do. You act hostile deliberately because if you stopped growling, then people might approach you. And I think that you want to make sure you reject them before they get the chance to reject you.''

''I told you what I want from you, and it doesn't include amateur psychology. I have good reasons for keeping to myself, reasons you know nothing about.''

''That's why you don't publish your photographs under your real name, isn't it? You don't want anyone around here to get to know the real you.''

His breath hissed out between his teeth. ''What do you know about my photographs?''

''I found your darkroom last night.''

''You were busier than I thought.''

''I was looking for more blankets. I thought it was a closet. I've seen your work, Damien, and I know that it takes skill and tremendous sensitivity to take photographs like that.''

''Is there no part of my life that you plan to leave undisturbed?''

''I had no intention of intruding—''

"This is the life I have chosen," he said, pronouncing each word with the finality of a slap. "I'm fine on my own."

"Are you?"

He slammed his mug on the counter, splashing coffee over the rim. "I will be once you leave."

"I'll leave when I know where to find Emily."

"After you pay for my services."

"We're going in circles."

"No, *you're* going in circles. I know exactly what I want and I fully intend to get it." He moved toward her, his gaze holding the unswerving determination of a hunter who has lost patience with the chase. He stopped less than a foot away. He didn't touch her. He didn't need to. The power of his presence enveloped her as tangibly as the curling heat from the fire.

Jenna released her grip on the chair and stepped back. "Then we'd better get started."

"What?"

"Finding my niece. What do we do now?"

He looked toward the archway of the bedroom, a muscle twitching in his cheek.

"Damien?"

The silence stretched out, thick with tension. He swung his gaze back to her, pinning her in place as easily as he'd held her body motionless on the mattress the night before. "You held both my hands."

She crossed her arms, rubbing her palms over the sleeves of her sweater. "What do you mean?"

"Yesterday. I told you to take notes, but you didn't. I remember you pressed the back of my knuckles against your waist." His gaze lowered. "Your sweater was soft."

"I . . . wanted to help."

"You did. The connection was strong. But you didn't write anything down, and we need to remember the details."

"It's not too late to make a list. I haven't forgotten anything."

"All right. That's what we do first."

The timer on the stove chimed, an ordinary, homey sound. Jenna jumped nervously.

"I have some business I should take care of in Hemlock, later," he continued. "I'll drive you to town this afternoon and we'll use the library to research possible locations. You can call your sister afterward."

"Okay. Thank you."

He watched her steadily, his eyes gleaming. "Don't thank me. I'm not doing this for free."

The flag in front of the Hemlock post office snapped crisply in the breeze, a splash of vibrant color against the brittle blue sky. The building was long and squat, functional, unimaginative, a brown brick box that stood out starkly against the dignified stonework of the surrounding structures. It was considered an eyesore by some residents, and periodically there were suggestions to tear it down and rebuild, or to remodel it by constructing a facade that would better blend in with the architecture of the library that flanked it and the town hall across the street. Beautifying the post office had been among the campaign promises of the last four mayors, starting thirty years ago with Miller Reese. Yet budget constraints and bureaucratic inertia continued to allow the ugly little building a reprieve.

Its persistent endurance in the face of public disapproval was one of the few things Damien liked about this town.

A pickup truck backed out of one of the diagonal parking spots in front of the post office, puffs of exhaust trailing like banners from the rusted tail pipe. Damien waited until it moved down the street, then eased the Jeep into the vacant spot and pulled to a stop.

The heater blew gently as he sat unmoving, his hands still on the wheel. People moved quickly along the sidewalk, their chins tucked into their collars, their boots crunching on the snow. They all had their problems, their troubles, their stray emotions. Until today, each time he'd driven to town he'd dreaded the possibility of an accidental touch that might have triggered the power he'd hoped was gone. He'd preferred ignorance, avoiding any situation that might have revealed the truth. He'd made himself unpleasant and unapproachable in the hope that nothing would interfere with the safe illusion he clung to.

But then Jenna had touched him. What he had feared most had happened. And oddly enough, the sight of all these people no longer filled him with panic.

Muttering an oath, he shut off the engine and adjusted his gloves, making sure that the leather covered his wrists. No matter what Jenna said, or how stimulating her company was becoming, what he had told her this morning was true. He had good reasons for not changing his lifestyle or his attitude. He knew better than to risk random exposure to a stranger. The only reason his stomach wasn't knotting with anxiety this time was because it was too full of the lunch that Jenna had fixed.

He turned his head to look at her. She had jammed her hands into the pockets of her neon pink ski jacket and was chewing her lower lip again. Her glorious hair was stuffed under her hat, emphasizing the delicate beauty of her features . . . and revealing the shadows under her eyes. He tamped down the twinge of conscience he felt over what he had asked of her. He was offering her a fair deal. Besides, he'd seen the interest on her face when she looked at him, so he knew she wasn't as averse to his bargain as she claimed, no matter how much she protested.

Even in the sober light of day, he had no regrets about the price he had put on his services. If anything, he only wished that he didn't need to wait so long to collect.

Accompanied by Jenna, Damien went into the post office, where he mailed the package that contained his latest work and picked up the correspondence that had been accumulating in his box for the past month. Smoke had been left behind at the cabin, and without the nervous wolf by his side, Damien attracted less attention than the day before. No one went so far as to be friendly or cordial, but at least they weren't openly hostile.

From the post office they walked to the library. Damien occasionally did background research here before he left on one of his photographic assignments. Considering the library's limited resources, interpreting what he'd seen during his contact with Emily was going to be a challenge.

The list of details that Jenna had helped compile before they'd left the cabin was discouragingly short. The sunshine he'd seen through Emily's eyes was less of a help than he'd hoped. According to the national weather service, a massive ridge of high pressure had spread clear skies over most of the central area of the continent yesterday. As for the fresh snow, the storm front that had swept eastward through Hemlock earlier in the week had extended from northern Ontario to as far south as Kentucky.

The angle of the sun was even trickier to interpret. The farther east the location, the lower in the sky the sun would have appeared at that time of day. The same variation happened the farther north the location. Without knowing the direction the window was facing, all Damien could do was calculate an arc of possible locations. By the time he had assembled all the data into the form of a map, the afternoon was almost over.

They left the library just as the front doors were about to be locked. Jenna folded the photocopy of Damien's map and stored it carefully in one of her jacket pockets as they descended the steps. She paused when they reached the sidewalk. "At least I'll have something more definite to tell Brigit when I call her," she said.

Damien adjusted his gloves, stepping back to give plenty of space to a pair of boys who raced past, hockey skates banging against their shoulders. He waited until a third, smaller boy passed by before he started walking toward the Jeep. "I should have worked faster. You could have used the phone in the library."

She shook her head and hurried to keep up with him. "I'd rather go back to my motel room so I can have some privacy."

"I thought you had checked out yesterday."

"No. I wasn't sure how long I'd be at your cabin. I didn't want to let the room go."

"You can check out after you make your phone call. You won't be needing the room anymore since we'll be staying together until this is over."

Her steps faltered. "I'm not sure if that's such a good idea."

No, it probably wasn't. The more she stayed with him, the more opportunity she would have to poke and prod into all the other aspects of his life that he wanted left alone. And the more he saw her, the more difficult it would be to wait... "It will be more convenient," he said, walking past her to the Jeep and opening the passenger door.

She fingered the zipper over the pocket where she had stored the map. "Damien, what if this information is enough? What if you don't need to use your gift again?"

He paused, curling his gloved fingers around the edge of the door. A slow, thoroughly masculine smile deepened the lines beside his mouth. "Then I can collect my fee sooner."

She looked away, slipping past him and climbing into the Jeep. Her hand shook as she reached for the seat belt.

Damien eased the door shut and rounded the hood to get in the other side. He started up the engine and turned toward her, his smile mellowing. "Don't worry. Emily was fine when I saw her. Wherever she is, someone is taking good enough care of her to provide her with food and shelter."

"But she cried. She's lonely. She needs more than food and shelter."

"Yes, she does."

"She needs love, and security, and acceptance."

"All children do. We'll find her."

She nodded, shoving her hands deep into the pockets of her coat. She seemed as unwilling to accept his sympathy as she had been to accept his smile.

Damien's expression hardened. How many times did he have to be reminded? She didn't want sympathy or smiles, she wanted to use him. As he wanted to use her. That was their agreement, and neither of them was foolish enough to expect more. Someone honked from the street behind them. He jerked his gaze away from Jenna and put the Jeep into gear.

After the rustic coziness of the cabin, the sterile neatness of the motel room felt foreign to Jenna's eyes. She closed the door behind her, listening to the squeak of the Jeep's tires on the snow as Damien drove away. He had said that he needed to buy gas and that he would meet her here in half an hour, but she knew he was using the errand as an excuse to give her some privacy.

He was providing her glimpses of the understanding man he was capable of being, the sensitive, generous and compassionate man whom Rachel had told her about, the person he must have been before circumstances had changed him.

Sighing, Jenna pushed away from the door. She shouldn't be thinking about Damien, she should be thinking about Emily. That was her priority. She pulled off her hat, automatically smoothing the static from her hair as she moved to the bed and sat on the edge of the mattress. From her pocket she took out the map Damien had so painstakingly prepared and spread it out on her lap. She studied it in the light of the bedside lamp, tracing the shaded arc that indicated where Emily might be. The curving swath stretched across a thousand miles and eleven states.

Oh, they had narrowed down the search area, all right, but there were still dozens of cities, hundreds of small towns, millions of possible buildings where one small child might have looked at the icicles beyond a window.

Taking a deep breath, Jenna reached for the phone and dialed Brigit's number.

It took less than four minutes for her to admit to herself that Damien had been right. He had accurately predicted the precise reaction she would get from her sister. Leaning forward, she rested her forehead against her free hand. "I believe him, Brigit," she said firmly. "If you had seen what he went through— "

"For God's sake, Jenna, think what you're saying." Brigit's voice had risen, her usual musical tones approaching a grating shrillness. "Next you'll be consulting tea leaves. We're talking about my child, not some nightclub magic act."

"We've already narrowed down the possibilities," she persisted. She glanced at the map again. "Emily has to be somewhere between Fargo and Pittsburgh. There are less than a dozen possible states where she could be. You could relay the information to the police. Is Frank Novacek still working on the case?"

"As far as I know. He says he's pursuing every possible lead. But I'm not going to call him with this…this wild speculation."

"Has he made any progress since I've been gone?"

Through the phone line came the sound of a shuddering breath. "No."

"She's all right, Brigit," Jenna said. "She hasn't been harmed."

"I want to believe that. I *need* to believe that."

"So do I. That's why I had to call you as soon as I could to tell you—"

"Nothing. You have nothing, less than nothing. The word of some crazy hermit."

"He's not crazy."

"That man is taking advantage of you. He's preying on your emotions."

"He's not like that."

"How much are you paying him?"

She should have expected the question. It shouldn't have caught her by surprise, but she felt her pulse jump. "I can handle it."

"You've already done so much. I don't want you to throw your money away like this."

Money isn't what I want from you, Jenna. Her fingers tightened on the receiver. "He'll find her. I believe him."

There was a pause and a muffled noise as Brigit blew her nose. "When are you planning to leave...whatever the name of that town is."

"Hemlock. I don't know."

"Come home, Jenna. You've been my rock for the past two months. Please, come back to Minneapolis."

"But Damien can—"

"I can't handle worrying about you as well as Emily."

"Don't worry about me. I'm fine."

Another pause, a longer one this time. "I've never blamed you, Jenna."

She felt a tremor go through her as the words set off reverberations of guilt. No, Brigit hadn't said one word of recrimination. She hadn't needed to. Jenna had done it herself. "I should never have let go of her hand. If I had watched her more closely, it might not have happened."

"And if I had come with you instead of staying home and enjoying a day of peace and quiet, it might not have happened, either. How do you think I felt when I found out? I had been reading a book and drinking tea and feeling thankful to have some time alone. Time alone. It's as if I caused it."

"I'm sorry, Brigit. I'm so sorry. It was my fault."

"No. It was the fault of whoever took her."

"You'll get her back. I promise. Damien can—"

"God knows I love my daughter, but I love you, too." The tightly controlled desperation in Brigit's voice was obvious even through the long-distance line. "And I know full well how much Emily means to you. Please, be careful."

Jenna hung up the phone and braced her hands on her thighs, staring sightlessly at the patterned motel-room carpet between her feet.

It had been a mistake to call her sister. Until Damien could pinpoint Emily's location, all they had were vague assurances. To Brigit, who had no reason to believe in Damien's ability, those assurances would seem hollow, even cruel.

Setting her jaw, she reached for the phone once more and dialed the number of Detective Novacek. She caught him just as he was about to leave for the day, and he listened to her with barely concealed impatience. Jenna's own patience began to wear thin as she tried in vain to convince him to concentrate his efforts on the search area that was marked on Damien's map. Instead of questioning her about what Damien saw, though, he began to ask her about Damien, suspicion clear in his tone. Feeling frustrated and helpless, Jenna dropped the receiver back into its cradle and pushed to her feet.

What must it have been like for Damien, to always be doubted? He was too sensitive a man to have shrugged off the constant rejection. After the suffering he went through each time he used his power, how did he feel to be called a fraud and a liar?

Raking her hair off her forehead, she walked to the window. Across the road, beyond the building on the corner, Jenna could see streetlights come on at the edge of the park where Damien had staggered after that first time he'd seen Emily. He hadn't actually made contact with the child; he'd connected with Jenna's memory of that nightmare afternoon at the zoo. He'd said that he'd been caught in the strength of her tangled emotions. Love, despair, guilt, obligation.

Last night she had felt guilty over what she had done to Damien. What else did she feel? What would she let herself feel?

Damien. This was the first time they had been apart in days, but he still dominated her thoughts. And it wasn't merely because he was the man who would find Emily.

Chapter Eight

The highway rolled past between knife-edged drifts and patches of melting snow that spread a brilliant sheen across the pavement. Sunshine coming through the windshield had made the interior of the Jeep pleasantly warm. Jenna undid her jacket and moved her head against the back of the seat to look at Damien.

Almost a week had passed since she'd arrived at his cabin. He hadn't wanted to travel back to Minneapolis with her. She'd had to use all the arguments she'd prepared—her sister needed her, there wasn't anything they could do to find Emily for another few days, they might have more luck with Detective Novacek if they spoke with him in person—and even then it had taken most of the previous evening to convince him. In the end, she'd needed to resort to reminding him that he was essentially working for her.

So he'd agreed, but not before he'd pointedly reminded her that he'd still expect her to pay him, no matter what city they happened to be in.

She studied his profile. Etched against the glittering expanse of snow-covered fields beyond the window, the lines of his face were stark and uncompromising. Because of the glare from the sunshine, he wore aviator-style sunglasses. The reflective lenses concealed his eyes, making him look more distant and untouchable than ever.

He had abided by their bargain and hadn't touched her at all since the night he'd contacted Emily. He'd looked, though. Each time they were in the same room, she felt his glances stroke over her skin with an impact that was more than physical. The awareness between them had been steadily growing. Being this close to him in the comfortably warm confines of his Jeep was making her nerve endings tingle, as if she were sitting beside the crackling electric field of a high tension wire.

Shifting restlessly, hoping for a diversion, she twisted to look behind her. Apart from her suitcase and Damien's duffel bag, the back seat was empty. Although they hadn't taken the wolf with them the last time they went to Hemlock, she'd assumed that they wouldn't be able to leave him alone this time. "Is Smoke going to be all right?" she asked.

Damien lifted an eyebrow, as if surprised by her question. "Of course. He's a wild animal, he's accustomed to fending for himself."

She leaned against the door, propping her elbow on the back of the seat, putting as much distance as possible between them. "But you've been feeding him, and he's been staying in your cabin. Wouldn't he be expecting you to continue?"

"Providing him with a few meals doesn't change what he is. He's smart enough to take advantage of what I offer him, but he's perfectly capable of managing on his own. Hunting is bred into him."

"Wouldn't he lose his skill if he didn't practice?"

"What makes you think he doesn't practice? From the time his leg healed enough for him to run, he's been foraging whenever the mood strikes him. The day before the storm hit, he brought home a rabbit to share with me."

"And?"

"And what?"

"Did you share it?"

The reflective lenses that hid his eyes couldn't conceal the way the lines at the corners deepened with a hint of humor. "It was tempting, but I'd already eaten."

Another rare smile. Jenna hadn't seen more than seven in all the time since she'd met him, but each one hadn't failed to affect her. "What about the snow, though? Where will he sleep?"

"When I'm gone he sometimes sleeps in a corner of the woodshed, on an old blanket I put there for him. Sometimes he uses a shallow cave about half a mile from the cabin."

"You've left him before?"

He nodded. "Whenever I have to travel somewhere to work on an assignment. Except for one side of his muzzle, his fur has grown in over his scars. He'll be warm enough outside the cabin."

"That's good."

"I'm surprised you're worried. You didn't seem to care much for my wolf."

"We reached an understanding. He was starting to tolerate me. We would have found some way to manage—"

"I left him on his own for his sake, not yours, Jenna."

"Oh. I thought . . ."

"It would be cruel to expect him to survive outside his natural world. He can't wear a collar or a harness because it would rub too painfully on his old scars, and I'd never betray him by trying to restrain him."

"Yet he keeps coming back to you."

"That's because I don't force him to stay."

A silence fell between them as the Jeep's tires hummed along the road. Miles continued to roll past, the countryside sparkling. As they often had before, Jenna's thoughts turned from the wolf to the man. "You must enjoy the freedom your profession gives you. Being a photographer, I mean."

It was a while before he answered. When he did, he spoke with the guarded caution of someone not accustomed to casual conversation. "It has its good points. Living in that cabin, I have very few expenses, so I only take on the assignments that interest me."

"Your work is outstanding, Damien."

He hesitated. "Thank you."

She hid a smile. He'd sounded almost embarrassed over his polite response to her compliment. "How did you get started?" she asked. "When did you turn professional?"

"My grandmother gave me my first camera when I was thirteen. I made my first sale about five years later to a local paper. After that I sold the occasional shot to calendar companies or tourist boards for their brochures, but I didn't start pursuing it seriously until I retired from my other business."

His other business. Even though that's why she had sought him out and was with him now, somehow she didn't want to talk about it. "What was your most recent assignment?"

"I'm working on a few simultaneously. The major one is illustrating an article on Canada's national park system. It's been going on for several months, since I need to get shots that span the seasons. I'll be heading up to Wood Buffalo next month."

"Where's that?"

"Alberta."

So far away. That was her first thought. But it shouldn't make any difference. This association of theirs was only temporary.

He kept his attention on the road, guiding the Jeep around a long curve. "You don't need to pretend an interest in me, Jenna. I have no intention of backing out of our agreement."

Pretending? That wasn't what she had been doing. "I, uh, appreciate the way you agreed to accompany me home."

He glanced toward her, the lenses of his sunglasses flashing with harsh brilliance. "And you don't have to be so polite. I already told you that there's no need to thank me. I'm keeping a running total."

"What?"

"My fee. I'm adding it up as we go along."

She inhaled sharply. She had been lulled into relaxing by their pleasant conversation. She should have known he wouldn't be able to go for more than an hour without making some kind of reference that would ruin it. "Could we just not talk about this?"

"It's going to be another two days before I can touch your skin again, longer than that before I can touch you the way I want to."

"Tell me about that park in Alberta. Have you been there before?"

"I'd rather talk about what I'm planning to do before I go there. Each time I look at you, I remember how it felt to hold your hand."

Against her will, her gaze went to where his fingers gripped the wheel. "I'd rather hear about your photography."

He wasn't deterred. "I think about how your skin will glow in the light from a candle, about how your bare shoulders will look through the silky veil of your hair and about the sound of your naked limbs sliding across cotton sheets. I think about the way your skin will grow warm and damp. I wonder how many differences in texture I'll discover as I explore your body.''

The sunshine coming through the windshield had nothing to do with the sudden heat that flooded her. She clasped her hands in her lap. ''Damien, don't.''

''I'm not touching. I'm just talking.''

Technically, he wasn't touching, but his words stroked teasingly over her nerves. She flipped down the visor, blocking out as much glare as she could as she concentrated on watching the scenery. ''I'm not going to listen.''

''Your skin fascinates me.'' He lowered his voice to a pitch that recalled a massive hand-carved bed and the intimate shadows of late evening. ''But touch isn't the only sense I intend to indulge, Jenna. There's sight. I've seen your legs already. I saw them when I brought you to my cabin. I wonder how my hand will look against the pale, gentle curve of your thigh, and how the shadows will curl around the slope of your hip.''

She drew her lower lip between her teeth and studied the line in the center of the road.

''There are colors that I wonder about, places on your body that could be pink, or brown, or somewhere in between, places that respond to the pleasure you feel. And then there's the sense of smell.''

A maroon van went by, followed by an eighteen-wheeler with dried salt whitening its front grill. Jenna didn't see either one. ''Do you think this clear weather will last?''

''You have a natural scent that reminds me of springtime. It's fresh, clean and full of life. I wonder how you'll smell in that place at the base of your throat where your pulse beats like a fledgling bird.''

Unconsciously, her fingers went to the collar of her sweater. ''According to the information we got at the library, the high pressure zone is predicted to move off to the southeast.''

''Behind your ears, and your knees, at the bend of your elbows and the base of your wrists—anywhere the skin is thin, your scent is the sweetest.''

She reached forward and slid the temperature control knob as far to the left as it would go. Cold air drifted through the dashboard vents but failed to relieve the heat.

''And that brings us to taste,'' he whispered.

She slapped her hands over her ears. ''Damien!''

He fell silent.

Cautiously, she lowered her hands and glanced at him. A sheen of sweat had appeared on his upper lip. He gripped the wheel so hard his knuckles were white.

Jenna opened the window a crack and leaned toward the bracing rush of air. She checked her watch. It would be another two hours before they reached the city. Blood throbbed everywhere that Damien's words had touched. The man was unbelievable. He had been practically seducing her with nothing but his voice. If he kept this kind of thing up, by the time he collected his price, they would both be...

She closed her eyes, pressing her lips together. She was doing this for Emily.

Wasn't she?

Damien didn't shake Detective Novacek's hand. He didn't remove his gloves or his parka; instead he sat in one of the chairs that had been drawn up in front of the policeman's desk and acted as if he hadn't seen the gesture. Whether Novacek thought he was being deliberately rude or merely oblivious, Damien didn't care. He wasn't about to try explaining his behavior.

Jenna pulled off her hat and sat beside him, her gaze filled with sympathy. She looked at his gloves, and at her own bare hands. ''Are you okay?'' she asked quietly.

He nodded his head and glanced at the photocopied pictures that were tacked to the cork bulletin board beside the desk. Emily's was only one of them. There were two other girls and four boys, none of them much more than three years old. Their innocent smiles were frozen in grainy black-and-white, the facts of their disappearances printed in stark detail.

He hated police stations. They were places filled with so much misery, the echoes of suffering seemed to vibrate from the very walls. It didn't take any special ability to sense it, either. It was in the faces of the people who worked here, and those who had been brought here. And in the faces of those children whose lives had been reduced to photocopied notices on a stranger's bulletin board.

Emily Evans. Age three. Thirty-seven inches tall. Twenty-nine pounds. Blond hair, gray eyes. Mole on back of left shoulder. Deaf.

Jenna leaned forward and handed the map that Damien had drawn up in the Hemlock library to the slim, middle-aged man on the other side of the desk.

Frank Novacek had the tweedy, slightly fuzzy appearance of a college professor, right down to the pipe that was propped in the ashtray. Novacek's hairline had receded comfortably past the top of his head and the lines of his face suggested the mournful droopiness of a basset hound. Still, his dark brown eyes sparkled with intelligence as he peered through a pair of tortoiseshell glasses to study the map.

"This is nothing but guesswork," Frank said finally, pushing the paper back toward Jenna. "I'm sorry, but as I told you on the phone the other day, I can't act on vague speculation."

Vague speculation, Damien thought. Never mind the hours of painstaking research, the calculations of the sun's position, the correlating of sparse details. Never mind the cost of obtaining those sparse details.

Jenna held on to her polite smile as she put the paper back in her pocket. "I see. Would you tell me what you *are* working on, then?"

"Please, try to be realistic. It's been more than two months since your niece disappeared, and we've followed every lead we obtained at the time. We're coordinating our efforts with the national center in Atlanta, of course, but once the initial trail has gone cold, it will take considerable time before any progress can be made."

"You sound as if you're not expecting any."

He lifted his hand toward the stack of files that overflowed the wire-mesh basket on the corner of his desk. "We do our utmost for each case, Jenna." He turned his attention to Damien. "We pursue every legitimate avenue of investigation."

Damien met his stare evenly. "I know all about it, Detective Novacek. I've worked with officers like you before."

Frank rolled his chair backward and slid open the top drawer of his desk to withdraw a yellow folder. "Yes, I thought your name was familiar when Jenna mentioned it the other day." He flipped open the cover and leafed through a stack of papers. "I ran a background check on you, Mr. Reese."

Before Damien could respond, Jenna curled her fingers around the ends of the chair arms and leaned forward. "Mr. Reese is helping me to find Emily," she said firmly. "So should you, instead of wasting your time on that kind of thing," she added, nodding toward the folder.

"You haven't done any missing-persons work for several years," Frank continued. The amiable fuzziness of the professor dissolved as he tossed the folder onto the center of his desk. "Running low on funds? Is that why you've decided to come out of retirement?"

Damien crossed his arms and leaned back in the chair, steeling himself against the waves of animosity that rolled off the policeman.

"You had some phenomenal luck in the cases I read about," Frank said. "We've never been able to figure out how you did it. Was it inside information?"

"What does your file say?" Damien challenged.

"It says you've been too clever to be caught."

"This is absurd," Jenna exclaimed. "We didn't come here to—"

"The way I figure it," Frank persisted, "you only take a case if you already know where the missing individual is. Then you put on a show while you miraculously find them. Where is Emily Evans, Mr. Reese? What do you know about her disappearance?"

He'd been a fool to place himself in this situation once more, Damien thought. Clenching his jaw, he rose to his feet. "You know as much as I do, Detective."

Jenna jumped up to stand by his side. She placed her hand on Damien's sleeve and frowned at the policeman. "Frank, I really thought better of you."

He closed the folder and put it back in the drawer. "Just because I work Missing Persons doesn't mean that I intend to ignore a con artist. If he's trying to swindle money out of a vulnerable woman like—"

"There is no money involved, Frank," Jenna said, her voice steady even though her fingers tightened spasmodically. "You have no cause to make insinuations about Damien's honesty, either. I thought we were all on the same side here. Isn't the goal to find Emily?"

"Of course, that's our goal, but—"

"Then you should welcome any assistance, no matter where it comes from."

Although her hand was shielded by the thick sleeve of his coat, Damien felt the reassurance of her support flow into him. He glanced at the top of her head, once more struck by the surprising strength that was contained in her compact, fragile-looking form. His gaze moved to the scowling policeman. "We'll get back to you in a few days when we have more details," he said.

Frank pulled off his glasses, folded them with precise, steady movements and tucked them into the case that was clipped to his shirt pocket. He fixed Damien with a stare that prickled with distrust. "You do that."

Without another word, Damien turned to go.

Jenna's grip on his arm loosened. She jerked her hand away suddenly, as if only now realizing what she had done. Shoving her hands into her pockets, she was careful not to touch him again as they walked toward the stairs.

Her touch had been brief, and shielded. He shouldn't be feeling the withdrawal any more than he should have enjoyed her support. He hadn't needed her to defend him. That wasn't what he wanted from her, it wasn't part of their bargain.

Jenna had found this apartment shortly after her divorce, and decorating it had been a form of self-help therapy as each piece of furniture, each curtain and color of paint had been a way of reasserting her determination to get on with her life. The rich, earth-tone fabric that covered the couch and chairs was stubbornly durable; the splashes of vibrant red and gold velvet throw cushions added unexpected whimsy. Suspended in hanging planters in front of the window, sensible ferns and philodendrons thrived from steady nurturing, while the glass-top coffee table held a flamboyantly cheerful arrangement of fanciful silk flowers. The living room, with its sunny southern exposure and the delicate ivory patterned wallpaper had always seemed comfortably spacious.

It seemed anything but spacious now. Damien stood in front of the balcony doors, his tall, brooding form crowding the peaceful room. Beneath the black sweater and jeans, his lean body seemed to hum with tension. His feet were braced apart, his arms crossed tightly over his chest as he watched the scattered lights from neighboring buildings twinkle against the darkness.

He looked so alone, she thought, curling her legs underneath her as she snuggled further into the corner of the couch. Ever since they had reached the city, he had held himself with the defensive stiffness of someone bracing for a blow.

What was he thinking? Was he still angry over their pointless trip to the police station? Was he remembering those other times in the past when he had used his gift? Or was he remembering how it had felt to touch the skin of her hand?

She slammed the door on that particular direction of her thoughts. Since this afternoon in his Jeep, she had been doing her best to keep that door closed.

Taking a deep breath, deliberately pulling her gaze away from Damien, she turned to look at the photo on the side table. It was of Emily, of course, another snapshot from her third birthday party, one that had been taken before the cake. The white dress with the navy blue sailor collar hadn't yet been smeared with chocolate icing. The wide smile, the mischievously gleaming eyes brimming with laughter, had been frozen in time.

She dropped her head to her hand, feeling the continual strain of the past few days catch up with her. If she had thought she would feel better once she was back in her familiar surroundings, she'd been wrong. The emptiness was still here, waiting for her.

"How did Emily lose her hearing?"

The sudden question took her by surprise. She looked up. "What?"

Damien turned his back to the window, facing her across the width of the room. "Or was she born that way?"

Jenna rubbed her forehead and let her hand fall to her lap. "Emily was fine when she was born, but she contracted a virus in the hospital when she was two days old. She reacted badly to the medication that should have brought down her fever, and by the time it was under control, she was left with no usable hearing."

"Is it correctable?"

"No."

"How does her mother feel about Emily's handicap?"

"How does she feel? I'm not sure what you're trying to ask."

He shifted, uncrossing his arms to move his hand in a short, sharp gesture. "How does she handle her child's disability?"

"Brigit loves her," Jenna answered easily. "We all do."

"Any mother would claim to love her child. I want to know how she treats her," he said, moving forward restlessly. "Does she try to hide the fact that Emily isn't normal? Does she try to deny it?"

"Of course not. Brigit doesn't hide her daughter's lack of hearing, nor does she dismiss it. My sister doesn't have any illusions about the challenges ahead. Emily's deafness is a part of who she is, and it's going to shape the choices she has in life when she gets older, but right now, she's simply a child."

"And you love her without reservation."

She didn't need to reply. He'd made a statement, not a question. "My family has always been close. We're there for each other when someone's in need. There was never any question about accepting Emily the way she is."

"It won't be easy for her."

"No, it won't. I'm aware that no matter how much we try to support her, my niece is bound to run into narrow-mindedness and rejection over and over..." She fell silent, realizing that the words she was saying about Emily could fit Damien.

Something clicked in her mind, and she twisted on the couch to follow his restless pacing. He had talked about his grandmother, but he'd never mentioned his parents. Was his defensiveness due to more than the attitude of society? Was the rejection he had suffered deeper than she had guessed? "When did you first learn about your gift, Damien?"

He stopped beside the wall, reaching out to grip one corner of a bookshelf. "I don't remember. When did you first learn that you could see? Or taste?"

"So your ability was always with you?"

"Yes."

"How did..." She paused. "Was it inherited?"

"I don't know. If it is, it probably skipped a generation. Rachel claims that my grandfather had something similar."

"How did your parents deal with your difference?"

His back stiffened. "I told you before, you don't need to pretend an interest in me."

"I'm not pretending. We've known each other for almost a week now. It's only natural that I'd be...interested."

"Don't harbor any illusions about the kind of relationship we have, Jenna."

She should leave this alone, she thought. She was already getting herself far too involved with him. Neither of them wanted this temporary association to develop into anything more. That's what she told herself. But she asked the question, anyway. "What did they do to you, Damien?"

For a while he remained silent. When he finally did speak, his voice was low and strained. "They tried to make me normal."

"What do you mean?"

"They used excuses. And punishment. When that didn't work, they did what any ambitious, small-town political couple would do when confronting the potential of scandal. They denied it. They shipped me off to my grandmother's, hoping she could handle me. When that failed, they decided to cut their losses and my father took a diplomatic posting in Europe. They were in France, the last I heard."

"Don't you keep in touch?"

"No."

There was a wealth of old scars in that one word. Jenna's sympathy was tinged with anger. "Someone should have given them a good, swift kick thirty years ago. Made them thankful to have a child. Any child."

He let go of the bookshelf, rubbing a hand over his face as he turned around. "Somehow I knew you would react that way. You always seem to be defending me. I don't need defending, Jenna. I'm fine on my own. That's the way I want it."

"So you've said."

"I'm not a child anymore. I realize how difficult it must have been for my parents. There aren't any support groups for the families of telepaths."

"But—"

"And I was no angel, either. I probably courted the tabloids when I got older deliberately as a way to rebel against my upbringing."

"That doesn't excuse what they did. Every child is special in his or her own way and should be accepted. Children can't be custom ordered, and they don't come with guarantees."

"It takes strength to maintain an attitude like that, Jenna. That's something not everyone has." He walked toward her, pausing at the side of the coffee table until she looked up to meet his gaze. The tension slowly seeped from his features. "Not everyone can get up again after they've fallen in a blizzard. Or have the determination to crawl forward when their legs are too numb to hold them."

No, they shouldn't have gotten into this. She should have left it alone. But just like his rare and precious smiles, his compliment affected her far more than it should. She swallowed. "Thank you."

Still holding her gaze, he backed up to sit in the chair across from her. "You'll make a good mother."

He couldn't have known, she told herself as the tears sprang suddenly to her eyes. He couldn't possibly have known the old pain that comment would conjure up. She pressed her lips together, trying to keep them from trembling.

He leaned forward, his forehead creasing. "Jenna?"

She shook her head, swallowing hard to combat the lump that clogged her throat.

"What's wrong?"

This was foolish. It was ancient history. She had dealt with it. Why should these feelings still have the power to paralyze her without warning?

He stood up and moved around the coffee table, then sank down on his knees in front of her. He reached out hesitantly, but stopped before he could touch her, resting his hand on the arm of the couch. "Is it Emily? We'll find her. It's only a matter of time."

"I miss her," she managed. "So much."

"She's lucky to have you for an aunt."

No, he didn't know. He couldn't understand the depth of love she had for her niece. "Emily is special to me,

Damien. Not only because she's my sister's child, or because she's a wonderful, lovable individual.''

He didn't say anything further, didn't question her or press her to continue. He simply waited, his vibrant blue gaze filled with the compassion of someone who understood suffering and loss.

Jenna breathed in deeply, trying to control the emotion that had been there, waiting for her, prodding her forward in her desperate attempt to restore the missing child.

Oh, God. She had been so strong for everyone else.

He lifted his hand again, letting it hover in the air beside hers for a breathless moment before he pulled his arm back. ''Jenna?''

She raised her chin. ''I am a mother, Damien,'' she whispered.

''What?''

''I lost my child, but I'll always be a mother. That's something that never stops.''

''You had a child?''

''His name was Alex.'' Tears that she hadn't allowed herself to shed for Emily pooled in her eyes, making Damien's image waver in front of her. She blinked, feeling scalding drops fall on her cheeks. ''He was only two months old.''

''Oh, Jenna.'' His voice was deep, unsteady. ''What happened?''

''They called it SIDS. Sudden Infant Death Syndrome. They still don't know why it happens, or how to guarantee it won't. He was in his crib, and he had been sleeping too long, and I went in to check on him but I couldn't wake him up and I tried and I tried and he was so cold—''

Her words choked on a sob as she covered her face with her hands.

The couch creaked softly as Damien sat on the cushion beside her. "I'm sorry."

Coming from him, the standard response to someone's grief sounded neither meaningless nor trite. He *was* sorry, she realized, feeling his sympathy enfold her. "I thought I was over it. I really did. I don't dwell on it."

"Wounds may heal, but the scars will always be there," he said gently. The cushion dipped as he shifted closer. "I know how strong your emotions are about Emily. It's little wonder they stirred up your old pain over your son."

Something soft brushed the back of her wrist. She pulled her hands away from her face and saw that Damien was holding out a fistful of tissues. Her chin trembled as she took them from his hand. "He would have been four last December. I had so much love to give him, so much to tell him and teach him and show him. I never had the chance." She wiped her eyes and blew her nose, but the tears kept coming. "Two months. That's all we had. That's not enough."

He reached past her to pull more tissues from the box on the side table. Carefully, he dabbed the moisture from her cheeks.

"Damn," she said. "Damn! It wasn't fair."

"No. It wasn't fair."

The simple agreement was all she needed to hear. With a sob, she turned toward him and pressed her face to his shoulder.

His breath stirred her hair in a long, careful exhalation. Lightly at first, then more firmly, his hand settled on her back.

She felt the knobby pattern of his black sweater beneath her cheek, focused on the solid warmth of his gentle embrace, letting his strength soak up her anguish. "I would have died myself," she said, the words coming as easily as the tears. "I wanted to die. My marriage was falling apart, my husband had already found someone else. I had no desire to get up in the morning or eat or talk to anyone or even take care of myself. I wanted to follow Alex. I didn't want to leave him all alone.''

A shudder went through Damien's body. He wrapped his other arm around her shoulders and leaned back, pulling her securely against his chest. ''I know what you mean, Jenna. I understand.''

''I wanted to give up. I almost did.'' She pressed closer, nuzzling against him with a need that built with each breath she took. ''But then one morning Brigit marched into the house, opened all the curtains, yanked me out of bed and announced that I was going to be an aunt.''

''Emily.''

''Yes. Emily. All the love I couldn't give to my son, I gave to my niece.''

He stroked her back, his hand making soothing circles. The warmth of his palm absorbed her grief, drawing it away until her breathing steadied once more. He held her without speaking, letting her cry while her tears dampened the front of his sweater. For long, silent minutes he sheltered her in his arms, communicating his sympathy without using speech.

I understand, he'd said. She thought of the deep lines that framed his mouth, and the honed harshness of his features. Yes, he must know about loss. And pain. If it hadn't been for her family's unswerving support after Alex's death, she might have ended up withdrawing from the world permanently like Damien. God knew, she had wanted to.

And, of all people, he would know about love, about those invisible bonds that were stronger than anything that mankind had been able to create. He would understand how old pain leaves scars. Jenna listened to his heartbeat, taking comfort in the steady, rhythmic throb beneath her ear. She felt the heat from his body, and caught the clean, masculine scent of soap and after-shave.

And the emptiness that she had been fighting was gradually filled with Damien's solid, reassuring presence.

Had Roger held her after Alex had died? Her memory of that time had been mercifully blurred, but she didn't think that her husband had once held her like this. He'd never been comfortable with showing emotion. It was her family who had rallied around her after the funeral—her parents, her sister and brother-in-law had helped her get through what no mother can ever conceive of getting through. Their support had saved her life, but there was something very basic and primal about the desire to feel a man's embrace. Even after more than four years, the need was still there.

She slipped her arms around Damien's waist, curling against him, soaking up his comfort. It had been so long since she'd been held, since she'd felt the security of a man's masculine strength . . .

Since she'd been held?

Slowly, Jenna's thoughts steadied. The physical sensations that had been drowned out by her emotions finally began to register in her brain. The solid arm cradling her shoulders, the warm palm stroking her back, the hard thigh against her knee. The steadily accelerating throb of Damien's heartbeat.

Catching her breath on a gasp, Jenna raised her head.

Damien's lips were no more than a thought away.

Chapter Nine

Through vision still blurry from the remnants of her tears, Jenna stared at Damien's face. He was so close. They had been close before. He'd pinned her to his bed and had held her wrists against the pillow and had illustrated exactly what he wanted from her body. But this was different. Oh, how it was different. He wasn't only holding her—she was holding him.

She should have pulled away. Once she had realized what she had done, she should have apologized and straightened up, putting a safe distance between them once more. Touching him was dangerous, and it wasn't only because of the risk of triggering his gift. She didn't want this, she didn't need this. All she wanted from him was his cooperation in finding her niece. . . .

His gaze locked with hers, his icy blue eyes filled with a swirl of conflicting emotions. The moment spun out, as fragile as the sound of a cry on a moonless night. Then slowly, gently, his expression softened. Without saying a word, he slipped his hand beneath her knees and lifted her legs over his.

There were layers of cloth between them, but despite her cotton knit leggings and his thick denim jeans, Jenna could feel the hard, masculine contours of his thighs. She looked away, pressing her lips together. She should pull back. She should—

"Sometimes being strong is damn exhausting," he said quietly.

Her mouth trembled into a surprised smile. She blinked, and her gaze met his once more. "Yes, it is."

He shifted, pulling her with him as he relaxed more comfortably against the thick cushions of the couch. "I'm glad you told me about Alex. It explains why your feelings for Emily are so intense."

"I didn't mean to break down like this."

"We all have our lapses, Jenna. We're only human."

"I'm sorry I, uh, touched you."

"Are you?"

Under his steady scrutiny, she knew she couldn't lie. She wasn't really sorry. "We shouldn't be doing this."

"I know." He lifted his hand and caught a lock of her hair, rubbing it between his fingers.

"Damien, I—"

"I'll stop in a minute."

"We can't let this go... further."

"I know that, too. As much as I want to touch my lips to yours, and do everything I told you about this afternoon, I won't. Not yet, anyway." Still holding her hair, he moved his fist to his mouth, brushing a kiss over the pale gold strands that were wrapped around his fingers.

There were no nerve endings in her hair, she told herself. Yet she felt his leisurely caress all the way to her toes. She drew her arm away from his waist, laying her palm flat against his chest. "It's late."

"Don't run away yet, Jenna. Just because I have to wait before I can touch your skin doesn't mean that we need to deprive ourselves of all forms of contact."

She might have had the strength to crawl through a blizzard, but she was incapable of forcing herself to move now. A delicate tremor rippled through her body from all the places where she pressed against him.

He dipped his head, bringing his nose close to her neck. His chest rose as he inhaled deeply. "Mmm."

It was the same wordless, masculine sound of pleasure he'd made when he'd smelled the coffee. Instead of pushing him away, her fingers dug into the barrier of nubby knitted wool that was still damp with her tears.

He let the lock of hair he'd been holding fall to her shoulder, using the tip of his thumb to trace its outline against her sweater. His hand moved, and his thumb grazed the curve of her breast. "A few more minutes, that's all."

When had the mood changed? she wondered hazily. When had her need to feel this man's comfort transformed into a need to feel the man? Why couldn't he say something nasty or crude, use his well-practiced hostility to push her away? She parted her lips, prepared to remind him that until he fulfilled his half of their bargain she wasn't going to allow him...

At first it was no more than a kiss of contact. It could have been the weight of her sweater shifting over her silk blouse, or her bra pulling tighter as her chest expanded with her rapid breathing. And the warmth she felt could have been from the flush that was spreading over her skin as each charged minute melted into the next.

She glanced down, and her protest came out as a gasp. Mesmerized, she watched Damien's long, strong fingers splay. He rotated his wrist and cupped his hand. And with her next heartbeat, she learned that her breast really did fit perfectly into his palm.

"You see?" His voice was deep with pleasure, rough with restraint. "I'm not touching your skin. You're safe from me."

Safe? She was astounded by the arousal that followed his words. Knowing that what they were doing wouldn't lead to anything more somehow freed her to enjoy this moment. The same instinctive need that had made her seek the comfort of his embrace now sent her blood surging in a mindless affirmation of life. Instead of pulling away, she twisted her shoulders, fitting herself more fully into his hand.

"Ah, Jenna." Squeezing gently, he explored her shape and firmness through the friction of wool against silk. He lowered his head, laying his cheek above her heart.

Closing her eyes, she slid her palm to his shoulder, her fingers tingling as she measured the breadth of hard muscle and bone. She moved her hand higher and brushed the resilient silk of his hair, tracing it to where the elastic bound it tightly at his nape. Above the collar of his sweater his neck was bare. She could feel the heat of his skin in the air beneath her fingertips. The temptation to touch him was almost overwhelming.

"Not yet," he murmured. He lowered his hand, lingering over her midriff, her waist, her stomach, slowly skimming downward until his palm rested on her left thigh. "Soon."

Soon. Did he mean when they would stop, or when they wouldn't need to stop?

Raising her other hand, she unfastened the elastic from his hair, catching the thick midnight locks as they tumbled free. Recklessly, she indulged herself in exploring the texture, discovering a surprising combination of softness and strength. It was sleek, sensuous. Like him, like the sounds of pleasure that vibrated from his throat, like the tender, compelling movements of his hands and his body.

He tightened his grip on her thigh, his thumb slipping toward the sensitive flesh between her legs. "Soon there won't be this barrier between us, Jenna." He stroked her boldly, insistently. "Right here. That's where you'll feel me."

She quivered, arching against the arm he still held tightly around her back, engulfed by a sudden wave of desire.

"I'll make it good for you," he said. "I know I will. See how readily your body responds." Moving his head, he rubbed his nose against one hard, pebbled nipple. "They're pink, aren't they? Deep, ripe, budding pink."

In some distant, still-functioning part of her brain, she realized what he was doing. He was seducing her. Shamelessly, blatantly, skillfully seducing her. His words, his virile body, his sensual enjoyment of what was happening, all of it was wringing a response that was more powerful than anything she had felt in her life.

But it was more than his words and his actions. She was responding to *him*, to the man she was growing to know, to the man who...

To the man who would find Emily, collect his payment and then leave.

Her pulse thudded painfully. Nothing had really changed, yet the pleasure he was giving her gradually dimmed. Sex. That was all he wanted, that was all this was to him. And for her own sake, for the sake of her heart, which had already been battered by too many losses, that's all it could be to her.

Without warning, he shifted her legs from his lap, clasped her against his chest and stretched out on the couch. He held his head so that his face didn't touch hers, but from the neck down their bodies fused together. Her curves fit his angles, her softness reshaping against his lean strength. His hands lost their gentleness as he staked his claim to what he had been promised.

Denim slid over cotton, wool glided on silk and he pressed his knee between her thighs, holding her with an urgency that shimmered through his frame.

On a sob that was half frustration, half panic, Jenna brought her hands to his chest and pushed. She rolled off the couch, landing on her back on the carpet. Her body still vibrating in mindless protest, she sat up, curling her shoulders to her knees and wrapping her arms around her legs in a defensive ball.

Silence, tense and brittle, broken only by their labored breathing, settled rigidly around them. Seconds stretched into minutes before Damien shifted to his back, flung an arm over his forehead and directed a long string of curses to the ceiling. "You could have said no," he muttered.

"I just did."

He rubbed his face. "Right."

"Damien, I should explain."

"Don't bother. You made yourself crystal clear. Hell, I said it myself. I don't get satisfaction until you do."

There was a bank of clouds on the horizon, looming behind the silhouettes of the buildings, smothering the first tentative rays of sunrise. The maples at the edge of the street stretched listless, skeletal limbs in the gray morning. Damien braced his hands against the sides of the window frame, letting his body sway forward. Until he'd turned sixteen, he'd lived in Minneapolis on and off whenever his parents had banished him to his grandmother's, so he was no stranger to this area. Still, as he watched the traffic on the street below and saw the increasing activity of the awakening city, he was seized by a gnawing wish to be back in the safe familiarity of his cabin.

How was Smoke managing? Despite what he had told Jenna yesterday, and what he knew about the wolf's staunch independence, he couldn't help wondering how the animal was faring. Wolves were gregarious. The first time Smoke had disappeared for a few days after his wounds had healed, Damien hadn't expected to see him again. He'd thought that the wolf would try to find another pack, seek the company of his own kind. But Smoke had returned. Evidently the life of an outcast suited him. The wolf wasn't fool enough to risk more injury.

Too bad Damien wasn't as smart as the wolf.

Abruptly he stepped back from the window and shoved his hands into his pockets, turning around to face the room. It would be one more day before he could try to establish another link with Emily. One more day of seeing Jenna, and hearing her and smelling her... Damn, he shouldn't have touched her last night. Touching her without really touching hadn't eased the need inside him. It had made it worse.

A door opened from the hall that led to Jenna's bedroom. There were muffled footsteps, the click of another door closing, then the sound of water running. She was taking a shower. That meant she was naked.

He clenched his teeth, listening to the changes in pitch as the water struck the shower curtain, the tile walls and firm, soap-slicked flesh. He fought against the image that slipped all too easily into his mind, but his imagination readily supplied what his memory couldn't. Pale satin skin, curves that were made for his hand, slender, supple limbs...

And devotion to another woman's child, and grief for her own, and strength enough to wrest another chance from life. His admiration and his respect for her were deepening almost as fast as his desire. So was the danger she presented to the life he had so painstakingly built. It was bad enough that she had stirred up his latent power. It would be a thousand times worse if he allowed her to stir his love.

He hadn't touched her skin last night, but he had touched her tears and felt her emotions. If he were any other man, he would seize the opportunity he'd been given to get to know this exceptional woman. She had so much to give and to share. Any other man would consider himself blessed to be part of her life, to plan a future, to give her the promises she needed and deserved.

But he wasn't any other man, was he?

Swearing under his breath, he strode across the room, snatched up Jenna's apartment keys from the shelf beside the closet, threw on his coat and slammed out of the apartment. After locking the door securely behind him, he pulled on his gloves, bypassed the elevator and headed for the stairs. He had to get out, he had to get away from her. When he reached the street he turned left without thinking, needing physical exertion to burn off his excess energy.

For more than two hours Damien walked, his stride swift and his posture rigid. He went past the parks where he had played as a child, and the schools he had irregularly attended. Eventually his steps took him to the old, rambling brick two-story where his grandmother had once lived. Pausing on the sidewalk, his hands in his pockets and his shoulders raised stiffly against the wind, he studied the house. The new owners had planted a hedge and had hung a tire swing from the oak tree. Two crooked snowmen with stone eyes and carrot noses stood in the center of a yard crisscrossed by small footprints.

Children. Jenna was a mother who had lost her child. He'd felt her pain last night, and he'd understood more than she knew. He'd felt the same sense of rage and denial and helpless despair over the death of someone he loved.

It had been more than five years since he'd been here, but his memory of that day was as vividly indelible as the white center of an old scar. He'd said goodbye to his wife in Santa Fe, when he'd scattered her ashes the way she'd asked him to. He'd left everything they'd owned behind and had driven straight through in a desperate attempt to make it to the isolation of his cabin before he lost his crumbling grip on his sanity. Yet he'd taken the time to stop in Minneapolis in order to say goodbye to Rachel.

With the last of his strength he'd told her why he needed to cut himself off from his gift and from the risk of loving again. His grandmother hadn't tried to stop him. She had listened patiently, then had nodded her head, given him a careful hug and a picnic lunch and told him to visit when he was ready.

The low-rise seniors' building where Rachel now lived was three blocks east of here. He'd recognized the address when she'd written to him about her new apartment. In a matter of minutes he could bring an end to his self-imposed exile. . . .

A curtain moved in the front window of the house and a stranger's face peered out curiously. Damien turned away. He no longer belonged here; he'd never really belonged here. He was a voyager, traveling on the fringes of other people's lives the same way he could travel other people's emotions. The consequences of getting ensnared in either were unthinkable. He would never allow it to happen again.

Despite what his grandmother had hoped, he would never be ready.

Jenna slid the pan of brownies into the oven, closed the door and set the timer on the stove clock. The knot that had begun forming in her stomach three hours ago tightened as she focused on the time. Where was Damien? Why had he left? And was he coming back?

She had felt his absence the moment she had stepped out of the shower. He'd left his duffel bag and the keys to his Jeep, so she reasoned that he intended to return, but it had been more than three hours. It didn't matter how many times she told herself that they needed some time apart, especially after what had happened on the couch yesterday. And it made no difference how sternly she reminded herself to control her feelings. She missed him. It was as simple as that. She was getting accustomed to his tall, dark, brooding presence, no matter how temporary it was going to be.

"Do you need any help in there, Jenna?"

At her mother's voice, Jenna pushed away from the stove, wiping her fingers on her terry-cloth apron. She had been in the middle of sliding chocolate chip cookies off a baking sheet when her mother and Brigit had arrived at her apartment a few minutes ago. They had made themselves at home in the living room while she'd finished mixing the brownie batter. "No, thanks. I'll clean up later," she called. She transferred a dozen warm cookies to a plate and carried them to the living room.

"Those smell delicious, but I really shouldn't."

Jenna paused in front of her mother and waved the plate under her nose.

Sighing, Nora Lawrence picked up a cookie and leaned back in the chair. At fifty, she wore the gray in her hair and the lines beside her sparkling green eyes with pride. Badges of a life well lived, she always said. "I'm going straight to the gym from here. Give the rest of those to your sister."

Jenna turned to where Brigit sat in the corner of the couch and offered her the plate. Brigit refused with a delicate shake of her head, her gaze straying to the picture of Emily that was on the side table.

"Go on," Nora coaxed. "The chocolate will do you good. You look as if you've dropped another five pounds."

"These cookies weren't really meant for us," Brigit said. "You know Jenna always bakes when she's upset."

"And I eat, but you don't," Nora replied. "Honey, you can't let yourself get run-down."

Jenna shared her mother's concern. Brigit didn't look well. Her once-vibrant auburn hair hung dully to her collar. The bruised shadows beneath her gray eyes grew darker each time she saw her. Although Brigit took after her father and was several inches taller than either her mother or her sister, she now weighed considerably less than Jenna.

"Can I get you something else?" Jenna asked. "The brownies should be done in half an hour."

Brigit's lips lifted in a sad smile. "Brownies, too? You're worse off than I thought."

Placing the plate on the coffee table within easy reach of her sister's hand, Jenna sat beside her on the couch. Drawing her lower lip between her teeth, she glanced at her mother.

Nora took a large bite of her cookie and chewed slowly before she swallowed. "This recipe never tasted so good when I made it."

"That's not true, but thank you, anyway."

The conversation continued with talk of everyday topics, the kind of trivia of daily living that continues no matter how horrible the circumstances. They discussed the basketball league the girls' father, Ian, had joined, the cost of replacing the furnace in Brigit's house and the possibility of another storm before the end of the week, but underneath it all was their concern for Emily.

Finally, though, Nora reached for a second cookie and broached another subject entirely. "Where's your visitor this morning?" she asked Jenna.

"Visitor?"

"The hermit you brought home with you."

"What?"

"This time Mom's eating because of you, Jenna," Brigit said quietly, "not just me."

She should have known, Jenna thought. The minute these two showed up unannounced at her door she should have guessed the reason for the visit. She reached behind her back to untie her apron, then concentrated on folding it into a square and laying it on her lap. "I told you what I planned to do when I took time off from work to go to Hemlock, Mom."

"We're all worried about Emily. God knows, we're doing everything within reason," Nora said. "But consulting a psychic?"

Jenna's grip on the apron tightened before she tossed it to the cushion beside her. "There's no need for you to use that tone. His name is Damien Reese, and he's the grandson of my friend Rachel Beliveau. And before you can start into it, he's not a crackpot and he's not a con man. He's a very talented professional photographer. He's also very intelligent and sensitive, and he doesn't deserve all the narrow-minded suspicion that—"

"Whoa, there! I never said anything."

"I could hear you thinking, Mom."

"All right, to be honest, I'm concerned about the situation you're getting yourself into. When Brigit told me that you actually brought the man back with you, it was only natural that I'd worry." She hesitated. "The way you spoke of him now makes me worry more. You're in a vulnerable state, Jenna. It would be easy for an unscrupulous man to take advantage of you."

She knew she was vulnerable. Her sudden loss of control last night had proven it. But Damien had dried her tears and held her and ... And wanted nothing but sex.

"Jennifer?"

The name she'd left behind with her childhood startled her. "I know what I'm doing, Mom. There's no need to worry about me."

"Be careful of this Damien character."

The advice was exactly what Jenna had been telling herself since that moment a week ago when she'd opened her eyes and had first seen Damien's face. It bore repeating. "I will."

"You know that I'm no prude, and I don't make a habit of intruding on my daughters' personal lives, but a divorced woman on her own might seem like easy pickings for—"

"Mom, please. I get the point."

"It's natural that you'd feel lonely."

"Damien is going to find Emily," Jenna stated, as much for her mother's and sister's benefit as for her own. "That's why he's staying with me, the only reason he's staying with me. When it's over, he's going to leave."

She hadn't realized her voice had risen until she heard the silence that followed her words. Nora exchanged a look with Brigit. Seconds later, the silence was broken by the sound of a key scraping in the lock. All three women turned to look at the door.

Jenna rose slowly to her feet. All morning she had wanted him to return, but why now? She loved her sister and her mother as much as they loved her, yet at that moment she wished they were somewhere else. She had been hoping to avoid or at least postpone this meeting, not to save herself more well-meaning advice, but to shelter Damien from the reaction she feared he would get.

A burst of cold air accompanied him as he stepped into the apartment. Closing the door behind him, he slipped off his coat and turned to face the room.

The silence deepened. He hadn't shaved yet today. Or tied back his hair. His pale blue eyes gleamed fiercely above lean cheeks that were reddened by the burn of the wind. With his height and that firm, rangy body and his midnight black hair flowing to his shoulders, he looked as dangerous and untamed as the wolf they'd left behind at his cabin.

"Oh, my," Nora breathed.

"*That's* the man?" Brigit whispered.

Jenna lifted her chin and forced a smile. "Hello, Damien. You're just in time to meet my family."

He stayed where he was, crossing his arms over his chest.

"Mom, Brigit, this is Damien Reese," Jenna said, as if good manners could smooth over the tension she felt growing around her. "Damien, this is my mother, Nora Lawrence, and my sister, Brigit Evans, Emily's mother."

He looked at each of the women in turn, his face warily watchful.

Nora cleared her throat, brushed some cookie crumbs from her lap and stood up. She glanced sideways at Jenna, then took a step toward Damien and held out her hand. "How do you do, Mr. Reese."

Damien tightened his crossed arms, not making a move to come forward and take the hand she offered, or to give an explanation.

"I should have warned you, Mom," Jenna said. "Damien doesn't shake hands. If he makes contact with someone's skin, he risks triggering his telepathy." She looked steadily at Damien. "He's not being deliberately rude."

"Oh." Nora dropped her hand and tilted her head. "How...odd."

Clenching his jaw, he walked to the window and stood with his feet braced apart and his back to the light. It was difficult to see his expression.

Brigit shifted on the couch so that she faced him. "I spoke with Frank Novacek yesterday, Mr. Reese, after your visit to the police station. He seems to think that you may know more than you're telling about my daughter's location."

"I've shared everything I know," he said.

"Frank thinks you might be connected to whoever took her."

"Brigit, please," Jenna said. "That's just not true."

"If you know where she is," Brigit persisted, "for God's sake, quit playing games. Tell me. I won't press charges. I won't tell the police." She leaned forward, her fingers twining together in her lap. "I don't care about punishing whoever took her, I just want her back."

"That's what we all want," Jenna said. "I know how upsetting this must be for you, Brigit. You don't want to put your hopes on something, only to be disappointed again. But trust my judgment in this, all right? It's no game, no trick. I sought Damien out, not the other way around. I've seen the agony he goes through each time he uses his abilities. I admire his strength and I believe in him completely. He's a deeply emotional, caring—"

"Jenna."

At the sound of his voice she stopped. Biting her lip, she walked toward him and stood close enough to feel his presence but far enough not to touch him. "I'm sorry, Damien," she murmured. "They don't know you like I do."

"I told you before, I don't need you defending me."

"Why not? You weren't doing it yourself."

"It doesn't matter what anyone thinks about—"

"Yes, it does! If you gave them a chance—"

"But I don't want to. Once I find Emily and this is all over, I'm gone."

"I know that."

"Do you?"

"You keep reminding me. But for the time that you're here, I'm going to keep defending you. It's long overdue." She turned around to face Brigit and her mother, unconsciously aligning herself with Damien. "Now, why don't we all sit down. The brownies should be ready any minute."

Nora was studying them both, her eyes narrowed shrewdly, her expression guarded. Obviously she wasn't yet prepared to accept Jenna's opinion of Damien. "I'm due at my aerobics class in half an hour, so I can't stay."

"I'll drop you off, Mom," Brigit said, rising from the couch. Her hand trembled as she pushed a limp lock of hair behind her ear. She took a deep breath and faced Damien. "My daughter is my life, Mr. Reese. She's all I have left, and I love her with all my heart."

Jenna sensed rather than saw the defensive stiffening of Damien's frame. Even without any special power, she could feel the impact of her sister's raw emotion.

"I'll be honest with you," Brigit went on. "I don't believe in telepathy, but I've tried everything else. I've put up posters, I've gone on television. I've sorted through hundreds of dead-end tips and false trails."

Nora walked to Brigit's side and slid her arm around her waist, her eyes moist.

Brigit's chin trembled. "Whether you're a criminal or merely a fraud doesn't matter to me. All I want is to see my daughter again, to hold her in my arms—" She broke off, swallowing hard.

"I understand," Damien said.

Drawing herself up as if preparing for battle, Nora fixed Damien with a hard stare, a stare made all the more intense by the unshed tears in her eyes. "Something else you should understand, Mr. Reese. Just as Brigit loves her daughter and is willing to do anything to make sure she's all right, I feel the same way about my own girls. Jenna might believe in you, and Brigit might be desperate enough to overlook what you're doing—"

"Mom," Jenna interrupted. "Please don't start—"

"But I'm not that forgiving," she continued. "If you can really restore Emily to us, then I don't care if you're the devil himself. But if you end up hurting either one of my daughters, I'm going to make your life a living hell.''

There was nothing more to say after that. Jenna watched her mother and sister leave, then turned to face Damien, prepared to apologize again.

He was looking at the door, his expression so bleak that Jenna's heart clenched. His lips were pinched as if he were bracing himself against a wave of pain. The dark stubble on his cheeks deepened the grim lines around his mouth. And his eyes, oh, God, his eyes gleamed with a reflection of the tears she had seen in Nora's and Brigit's.

"Damien?" she whispered, lifting her hand. She stopped before she could touch him, letting her palm hover in the air above his shoulder. "I'm sorry."

His nostrils flared as he took in a long, calming breath. "This isn't going to work."

"What?"

"The waiting. I can't afford this."

"What do you mean? Waiting for what?"

"To finish." His eyes focused suddenly on her face. "I never should have left the cabin. I should have known the risks I was taking."

She let her hand fall to her side. "I'm sorry about what they said, and the way Frank treated you yesterday."

A muscle twitched in his jaw. "I have to go back."

"What about Emily? And our deal? You said—"

"I'll find her. Now."

Her pulse thudded. "Now? You can't mean you're going to try to contact her again so soon. You need another day to recover."

"I'll manage."

"But—"

"This is what you want. It's all you want. Why are you arguing?"

She hesitated. "Please, don't let what my mother said push you into hurting yourself."

"Every minute I stay here, I'm exposing myself to more and more emotions. I can't risk being caught by them. Let's get this over with today."

"You know I want to find Emily as soon as possible, but—"

He reached out to her, focusing on his fingers as they settled lightly on her sleeve. "The longer I stay, the closer I feel to you. But that wasn't our bargain. I don't want to hold you when you cry. I don't want to wake up with this need to hear your voice."

At his words, something tightened inside her. What he was describing was too similar to what she had been struggling against herself. "What are you saying?"

"I don't want to feel good when you defend me, or to get accustomed to the sight of your chin lifted in determination or enjoy the smell of your damn cookies." Although his grip on her arm was light, suppressed power seemed to vibrate from his hand. His voice roughened. "You know what I want."

"Yes. I know."

"Sex. Physical satisfaction. No emotional snares."

"I'm not trying to snare you."

Breathing in deeply, he shook his head in a slow, sad negative. "With your springtime eyes and your pure faith in love, you're more dangerous than a steel trap. I've been on my own most of my life. For the past five years I haven't spoken with more than a dozen people. I need isolation the same way I need air. It's how I survive."

"But—"

"It's time to stop confusing the issue here. Time to fulfill this bargain between us. That's what we both want, isn't it?"

The answer should have been simple. But nothing about this entire situation could be described as simple. She said nothing, because she couldn't be sure that any response she might have made would have been completely truthful.

Chapter Ten

There had never been a man on this bed. The thought of sharing a bed with a man again had been the furthest thing from her mind when Jenna had furnished her bedroom. The brass scrolls of the dainty headboard were delicate and feminine. So were the rose-patterned bedspread that draped softly over the mattress and the swaths of ivory curtain that filtered the light from the window. The extra pillows were for propping herself up when she read, not for accommodating a guest. No lover had held her between those sheets, or whispered sweet, meaningless phrases in her ear, or left his clothing on the carpet or greeted the morning with a kiss....

Damien sat on the edge of the mattress, his shoulders rigid as he braced the heels of his hands on his thighs. His black sweater and black jeans made a jarring contrast to the muted pastels surrounding him. She had never seen him wear anything but black and white, Jenna realized. For a man who used film to capture every nuance of color from the subtle to the extreme, he was determinedly restrained in his choice of clothing.

"Whatever happens," he said suddenly, "don't call a doctor, all right?"

Jenna moved the lamp aside so that she could position the portable cassette recorder on the small table beside the bed. Her hand shook as she leaned over to fit the plug into the electric socket. "Last time you were barely breathing. If it's worse this time—"

"No doctor. Promise me, or I'm not doing this."

Although she didn't want to agree, she knew she'd probably already pushed him as far as he would allow. She'd convinced him to eat a nourishing lunch in the hopes that the food would help sustain his body during the aftermath of what he was about to do. They had already delayed for more than two hours. Why was she continuing to stall? She straightened up, tugging the hem of her sweater over her hips. "All right."

"And I'll probably sleep for seven or eight hours afterward. Because it hasn't been a full week since the last time, don't start panicking if it's nine or ten."

That endless evening in his cabin, when she had been waiting for him to wake up, loomed in her memory. "Is there anything I can do to help your recovery?"

"No. My mind will need the sleep even more than my body will." He looked around the room, concentrating as if he were memorizing everything. "It won't make any difference to me where I spend that time. Do you want to change your mind about doing this in here?"

"It's the most sensible choice."

Bedsprings creaked as he shifted to the center of the mattress. Resting his forearm on his updrawn knee, he twisted to look at her. "Are you ready?"

Fumbling behind her, she activated the recorder, then pushed up her sleeves and walked to the bed. She sat in front of him, curling her legs beneath her. "Yes, I'm ready."

Holding her gaze, he lifted his hand, palm outward. "We'll start like before. The link will probably be established more quickly this time, since I've ridden it before and I know her now."

Heart pounding, Jenna lifted her hand to mirror his. The air between them seemed charged, as if a power were building up. Her skin tingled. When she glanced down, she saw that the fine hairs on her arm were standing on end. "I can already feel it," she said.

"Your emotions are strong. They draw me even without the benefit of touch."

Jenna raised her gaze to his face. He was watching her, his eyes gleaming with purpose. Something simmered below the surface, as if awaiting the chance to break free from his control. Anticipation stretched and grew as the gap between their hands shrank. She felt his warmth, she caught his uniquely male scent, and then, finally, there was a whisper of skin.

A quiver traveled between them at the first contact. The air whooshed from her lungs as she felt his long, strong fingers curl possessively over her knuckles. He had touched her in more personal, more sensitive places through the barrier of her clothes, but there was nothing to compare with the sensation of naked flesh sliding together.

"Concentrate," he said.

She trembled, telling herself to think of Emily, to focus on her love for her niece. Yet there were other feelings mixed in with that love, strong feelings. And so many of them concerned the man who was touching her.

He leaned forward to clasp her other hand. "Close your eyes. You're seeing me, so your thoughts are muddled with my image."

It was only their hands that touched, only a tiny fraction of the surface of their skin, yet the impact shook her. And it was stronger than the last time, because her feelings for him had grown and deepened. She knew there was no possibility of a future between them, and that she had to keep her heart safe from the impossible yearnings that were budding inside her. She knew that their bargain was for sex, not love. But she had no control over—

"Jenna, no. I'm still seeing myself. Close your eyes," he repeated.

Her eyelids lowered. "Emily," she said softly.

"Yes," he whispered. "Yes. That's it."

Clutching him more tightly, she turned her thoughts to the laughing blond child who meant so much to her, the girl who loved splashing through puddles and painting with her fingers. The niece whose very existence had drawn Jenna out of her grief and back into life.

"There."

She felt so close to her, now. The long months since that day at the zoo disappeared. She knew she was sitting in the center of her bed, linked with Damien, but it seemed as if a breeze stirred past her face, bringing the presence of the child.

"Not fun," Damien murmured. "He took the fire truck."

She swayed. "You found her?"

"He won't share. He keeps crying."

"Who?"

"New boy. He sucks his thumb."

Cautiously, Jenna opened her eyes. A frown puckered Damien's forehead as he gazed at a scene that only he could see. His lower lip trembled.

"What is it?" she asked quietly. "What's wrong?"

His voice was raw. "Such loneliness. So much loneliness. Emily wants to come home."

She blinked back sudden tears. Even though she'd known what to expect, the reality of the contact with her niece still hit her with the force of a miracle. "Where is she, Damien?"

"The same room. No sunshine this time, no paint. She's watching another child who's sitting in the corner. He's holding a toy truck to his chest and is sucking his thumb. He's so lonely and scared." He paused. "Damn, what *is* that place?"

"What else do you see?"

There was another pause, a longer one. "Hungry. I'm tired of that orange macaroni. I want ice cream."

"Damien," she said more firmly. "Hang on. Tell me what you see."

He shuddered, tucking her hands against his chest. "There's something sticking up on the other side of the building next door. Thin. Like an antenna. No, a cross."

"Could it be a church? With a cross on top of the steeple?"

"Yes. That's it. A church."

"What about the weather?"

"Snow. Light, fat flakes. No wind."

She glanced at the sky outside the window. It was a flat gray overcast, but there was no snow falling. "Okay. Now the room. Describe it."

"Pale yellow walls. Low shelves beside an old accordion-type radiator. Braided rug in the center of the floor. Clock on top of a portable TV set."

"A clock? What time is it?"

There was a pause. "Don't know. The big hand—"

"Damien, stay with me," she urged. "The time."

"Two o'clock. No, two-ten."

"That's what it is here. It's the same time zone."

His breathing was becoming strained. He curled forward, drawing air into his lungs in long, deep gulps. "That boy in the corner is still crying. My vision's blurred because Emily's starting to cry, too. Oh, God! They're so alone.''

The sharp pain in his voice made her throat close. She shifted, tugging at his hands until his head rested against her shoulder. "Lean on me. Let me help."

"Emily still wants the truck. She's going over to the corner and reaching out for it," he said, his words muffled. His grip tightened. "No, she's touching him. Touching. Oh, God, *no!*"

Shudders shook his frame. Jenna felt the tremors transmit themselves to her spine. How long could he keep this up? Already he had maintained the connection longer than the last time. She pressed her face to the side of Damien's head, trying to give him support.

"I feel his suffering," he whispered. "It's both of them, now. He wants to go home. He wants his mother. He's looking up at us..." He shuddered again. "I know that face. I know it. I saw it before. Where? Where?"

She rocked with him, her lips brushing his hair. She wanted to call him back. She wanted to ease his pain and tell him to end this. But she wanted Emily. The lump in her throat grew heavier.

"Black-and-white. I saw it in black-and-white. His picture. On a wall. No, a bulletin board."

"What?"

"At the police station."

A tear fell on their joined hands. Jenna knew it wasn't hers. What was he seeing? What on earth had they found?

His muscles quivered. "She's coming back. She's mad that he's still crying," he said, his voice altering. "I don't like her. I hate her. Go away. I want Mommy."

"Damien, stay with me. Who do you see?"

"Lady with the mean face. She's big. I feel her walking. Smells like onions. Go away. Go away."

He was shaking uncontrollably. Jenna felt the heat drain from his body. His hands grew cold, his teeth chattered and he breathed in short, desperate pants. She moved her lips to his ear. "That's enough, Damien. Come back. Come back now."

"*No!* The woman shakes Emily when she can't hear. She gets angry. She ridicules her. I can't leave a child to endure that."

"Damien, please. You're letting this go on too long."

"They'll take him away. He'll go away like all the others. I don't want the truck. I want Mommy."

"Damien!"

"I can't leave her." His voice was no more than a broken whisper of sound, fading into a distance not measured in miles. "So alone."

It took less than a second for Jenna to make her decision. As much as she wanted Emily's safe return, she wasn't prepared to sacrifice Damien to whatever nightmare he was caught in. Releasing his hands, she wrapped her arms around his shoulders and held his head to her breasts. "You've done enough," she said. "It's time to come back, Damien."

He trembled. "No. No-ooo-ooo..."

"Let go of Emily. We'll find her. You saw so much more this time." Jenna stroked his hair, his back, rubbed his shoulders, anything to make him reconnect with reality. "Come back, Damien. Come back to me."

Although the curtains at the closed window didn't move, a breeze seemed to swirl coldly around them. Jenna braced herself, holding Damien with all her strength, fighting against the current that pulled him away.

Suddenly he collapsed, folding inward like a discarded puppet. Still holding him, she fell sideways on the bed. Tremors rippled through him and she pressed her body full length against his, sharing her warmth, absorbing his pain. "All right," she whispered. "It's all right. I've got you."

He moved slowly, heavily, lifting his arm until he could drape it over her back. His lungs heaved and he breathed her name. "Jenna."

She blinked hard, realizing that her cheeks were wet. "Yes, I'm here."

"Saw more. Maybe enough. Don't know."

"Rest, Damien. We'll figure it out later."

"Have to find her, get her back. And the other child. The boy. So frightened." He shuddered, raising his head to look into her face.

His expression was so ravaged, so full of agony that a cry was torn from her throat. She pressed her lips together, her fingers clutching his shoulder.

"That woman...doesn't understand. Angry at Emily's deafness."

"Does she hurt her?"

"Shakes her, but Emily's still unharmed. Physically."

"Oh, God."

"Have to get Emily home. Her mother...loves her. All...of you love her."

The tenderness that mixed with the pain in his expression almost broke her. She stroked a damp lock of hair from his cheek, wishing she could risk touching him once more.

"A ring, Jenna. Has to be organized. Explains...the others...Emily saw." He was weakening, slipping away. The fierce gleam in his eyes dulled.

"Damien?"

"Find them." With those words, the remainder of his strength ran out. He slumped unconscious against the pillow.

Jenna didn't move away. She listened to his breathing, feeling the shallow but steady rise and fall of his chest against her breasts while his tortured words echoed in her head.

She'd always assumed that Emily had been the victim of a random, opportunistic child snatching. But an organized ring? Somehow it seemed all the more cold-blooded and brutal. But who? Where? They still couldn't be sure. If only Damien could have—

No. He'd done enough. She wasn't going to lose him, too. Turning her head, she rubbed her cheeks against her pillow to dry her tears.

There was a brief whine and a click when the tape finally ran out and the recorder shut off, but Jenna didn't get up. Instead, she closed her eyes and nestled closer to Damien, feeling the need to maintain some kind of connection with him even though their skin no longer touched.

Once I find Emily and this is over, I'm gone.

A sob shook her shoulders. Not yet. She didn't have to let him go yet.

Frank Novacek leaned back in his chair, sucking on the stem of his unlit pipe as he listened to the tape Jenna had brought. His expression was running the gamut from impatient to incredulous as he looked from Damien to Jenna. "You're either very good actors or you're suffering from the same delusion," he muttered.

Jenna hit the pause button and frowned. "You said you would hear this through, Frank."

Pressing his lips together, he motioned for her to continue.

Damien rubbed his hand over his face, blocking out the sound of his own words. His entire body ached with residual stiffness, but it wasn't as bad as it might have been. He'd awakened briefly, around midnight, when Jenna had tucked an extra blanket around him, but then he'd fallen into a normal sleep until the morning.

The hellish reaction that should have followed his too-early contact with Emily had never materialized. While he'd battled the darkness in his head, he'd felt Jenna's presence supporting and guiding him back to reality. Her familiar scent, her warm breath, her womanly softness had been his beacon. Whether it was Jenna's voice or her butterfly touch, he didn't know, but whatever she had done, she had caused the aftereffects to be almost mild.

He didn't want to think about why there had been a change in the pattern any more than he wanted to examine his reasons for his growing urgency to find Emily. There was the bargain, of course, but he suspected that he was getting too involved with the child. When he'd done this in the past, he'd managed to maintain a protective aloofness from the emotions he traced, but with Jenna and her niece—hell, with her entire family—that aloofness was faltering. He had to complete this before it failed altogether.

The sound of the tape rewinding brought his attention back to Frank. The policeman put his pipe in the ashtray, then ran his fingers through his thinning hair. "I don't believe in this stuff. I really don't."

"Then handle it the same way you'd handle any other tip," Jenna said, pulling a paper from her purse. "There are several solid leads to pursue. I've listed them here."

Frank took the list and studied it carefully before glancing up at Damien. "You claim you saw a second child. Which one?"

Curling his gloved fingers around the arm of his chair, Damien nodded his chin toward the bulletin board. "The boy on the bottom row. Third from the left."

"That's Tim Sorensen. Disappeared from a shopping mall in Des Moines only four days ago."

Damien studied the face on the black-and-white image while he saw a crying, frightened child. "The details printed under the picture don't mention the fact that he sucks his thumb, or that his eyes are the color of caramel. There's a small scrape on the back of his left hand, almost healed. The skin on his forehead turns blotchy red when he cries. The hair on the top of his head sticks up like fine wire. It must have been slicked down for that photo."

Frank pulled a file out of the stack on his desk and flipped it open. "His parents gave enough information to fill a book." Pushing his glasses up on his nose, he read through the papers in silence. A few minutes later, he looked up, his forehead wrinkled. "Everything you've said matches." His eyes narrowed. "How did you do it?"

"You heard how I did it."

"What's your angle? How much are you making off this?"

"Frank," Jenna began.

"You said you want me to treat this like any other tip. Standard police procedure is to check out the reliability of the informant."

Damien saw Jenna shift in her chair and he knew that she was preparing to come to his defense yet again. Before she could open her mouth, he decided to answer for himself. "If you need references, contact Joe Sandoval. He's one of the magazine editors I've recently worked for. And if you have doubts about my solvency, feel free to phone my bank," he said, slipping off his right glove so that he could pull his wallet out of the pocket of his jeans. He took out one of his business cards, scribbled the names and numbers on the back and tossed it on the desk.

Frank picked up the card. When he read what Damien had written, he sat straighter in his chair. "*That* magazine? I've had a subscription to that for the past twenty years. The back issues are filling my basement." He looked up. "I don't remember seeing your name."

"I don't use it. Check the front of that card."

He did. His lips pursed.

Damien put his glove back on. "And if you still aren't satisfied, call the American Embassy in Paris and ask to speak to Miller Reese. My father and I haven't seen each other in almost fifteen years, but I guarantee that he'll be quick to vouch for my honesty."

"The embassy?"

There was a fitting irony about making use of the respectability and position that his parents had valued more than their son. He smiled grimly. "My parents are with the diplomatic corps. They still have political connections here."

Jenna crossed her arms and leaned back, a look of quiet satisfaction on her face. "Shall we continue, Frank?"

There was a long silence while Frank tapped the card Damien had given him against the desk. Finally, though, he tucked it in his shirt pocket and cleared his throat. "Okay, I'll check out what you've said, but you still can't expect me to believe in this...hocus-pocus," he muttered. "The theory about a child-snatching ring is feasible, though. I'll give you that much."

"The very idea is abhorrent. Inhuman," Jenna said.

"And very profitable. Sad to say, there are illegal adoption networks everywhere. Abducting a toddler is easier than snatching an infant. Kids between two and three are difficult to keep track of at the best of times, but in a crowded area, they're easy prey for a ruthless adult."

"In a crowd. Like at a shopping mall or a...zoo," Jenna said.

Damien heard the distress in her voice and put his hand on her sleeve. He knew how strong her emotions were about the afternoon she lost her niece. "You were up against professionals," he said. "The ring would probably scout out an area, choose a vulnerable child and then move in."

Frank nodded. "The whole operation would be coordinated ahead of time. One follows, looking for an opportunity, then makes the snatch while accomplices aid in the escape. If what you saw was true—" he glanced at

Damien "—*if* it was true, then the ring would want to get the child out of the area as quickly as possible and finalize the adoption."

"What kind of monster would adopt a kidnapped child?"

"They might not even realize where the child came from," Frank said. "Kids that age have no choice but to believe what an adult tells them. As long as the transition to their new home was made smoothly, they would eventually suppress the memory of their real parents."

"That fits with what I learned," Damien said. "The toys in that playroom would entertain a child for a short time. And Emily knew there had been others who hadn't stayed long. She thought the boy, Tim, would be taken away when that woman came into the room."

"But if they want to get rid of the children quickly, why is Emily still there?" Jenna asked. "It's been more than two months."

"Those children are worth a lot of money," Frank explained. "They're chosen not only for the ease with which they can be taken but for the way they look. Emily and Tim are good-looking kids." He hesitated. "I don't think the ring knew Emily was deaf when they took her. When they discovered she was flawed merchandise, they couldn't find a buyer."

"I think I'm going to be sick," Jenna muttered.

"I got a good look at the woman," Damien said, rubbing Jenna's arm gently. "She appeared to be in her mid-forties, about five feet seven, a hundred and sixty pounds. Emily thinks she has a mean face because of her small eyes and narrow lips. Hair was blond but it looked dyed. I'd recognize her if I saw her again."

Frank swore under his breath. "This is all still speculation."

"Then speculate about the weather and the church I saw while I look through your mug books."

Still muttering, Frank pushed to his feet and walked away. He returned a short time later with several thick books and dropped them on the desk in front of Damien.

It took over an hour for Damien to find the face. Although the woman's hair was black, and she weighed at least fifteen pounds less, the eyes were unmistakable. He gritted his teeth, remembering Emily's reaction when the woman had appeared. Flawed merchandise, Frank had said. Damien knew firsthand the invisible wounds that could be inflicted by someone with that attitude. And how much longer would the ring be willing to keep Emily? What if they couldn't find a buyer?

And what would happen to Jenna if she lost this child, too?

No matter what it took, he had to find Emily. He had to bring her home.

"Is that the woman?" Frank asked.

Damien stabbed his index finger against the small, plastic-coated photograph. "Yes. There's no doubt in my mind. That's her."

"Bernice Moss." Frank swiveled toward his computer, tapping rapidly with two fingers. "String of arrests dates back to 1979. Started out with bad checks, progressed to bootlegging videotapes. Served time for involvement with a ring that smuggled exotic birds into the country." He tapped the keys again. "Released on parole almost a year ago."

"If she's on parole, her parole officer would have her current address," Jenna said. "If she's living within the area we've narrowed down—"

"Let me make some calls," Frank said, reaching for the phone on his desk.

Jenna clasped her hands together to keep them from trembling. Finally, finally, it looked as if they were making progress. She gazed at the picture of the woman Damien had seen. If that was the "lady with the mean face," then they had the key that could lead them to Emily.

Frank dropped the phone back into its cradle and scowled. "Moss skipped parole seven weeks ago. They don't have a current address."

These highs and lows were getting to be too much, Jenna thought, wiping her palms on her skirt. "What was her last address?"

"Chicago." He dialed another number. "I'll contact a buddy of mine who works Missing Persons there. See if they've heard any rumors."

"It's in the same time zone," she said. "It's in the area we narrowed down. All you need to do is search the buildings near churches..."

"We'll do this my way," Frank said, his scowl deepening. "Through police channels. There's a warrant out on Moss for parole violation, so it won't hurt to question her about her recent activities when she's picked up. It's a long shot, but it's not impossible. As for checking out the buildings next to churches, forget it. There's no way we can justify search warrants on the basis of—" he gestured toward the tape "—that."

Jenna knew he was right. Logic told her that they should leave this to the police. They would get farther, faster, with Frank's cooperation and resources. But how could she sit here and do nothing when they were closer to finding Emily than they'd ever been?

Frank spoke into the phone while he shuffled papers in Tim Sorenson's file. Then he flipped open the cover of Emily's and relayed the cold facts of her disappearance.

Although she tried to close out the sound of his words, she once more felt the stomach-wrenching panic of that day at the zoo. A child-snatching ring. They must have been watching her, realizing that she was alone with the child, waiting for their opportunity to swoop down like a pack of jackals and—

"We've done all we can here," Damien said gently. "It's time to leave."

As had happened so often before, he had accurately gauged her mood. After one last, long look at Tim's and Emily's pictures, Damien rose from his chair and walked toward the stairs. Jenna said goodbye to Frank, making him promise to call her and Brigit the second he heard anything positive, then followed Damien out to the parking lot.

It had started to snow while they'd been inside the police station. Breathing deeply to cleanse her lungs with the crisp, cold air, Jenna watched Damien clean off the shallow layer of snow that had accumulated on his Jeep. "I'm too restless to go home and wait," she said. "I know there's nothing more we can do, but . . . it's hard."

He brushed off his gloves and squinted against the flurry that whitened the sky. "Then I won't take you home."

"I don't know where else to go. We can't do any more good with Frank. He has all the information we have, even more."

"How about Chicago?"

She pressed her hands to her sides to hold down her skirt against the strengthening wind. "What?"

"They're predicting a storm, but we should be able to get a flight out before it hits. I'll rent a car there, and we'll start our own search."

He said it so easily, but she knew what the prospect of traveling to a city that size must be doing to him. He hadn't wanted to leave his cabin, he hadn't wanted to go farther than Hemlock. Yet now he was volunteering to take her to Chicago. "You'd fly there with me? And check out the buildings near churches? But Frank said—"

"I know what he said." Damien came around the hood and opened the passenger door for her. "I also know how you feel."

Yes, he must know. He *would* know. "It seems impossible, like checking for a needle in a haystack."

"You were willing to tackle the wildest odds in order to find your niece. You wouldn't let mere logic or police procedure stand in your way."

Her heart raced. "No, I wouldn't, would I?"

"There's always the other option. The aftereffects from last night weren't as severe as I'd expected. If I rest another day, I could try making contact—"

"No!" Alarm shot through her at the prospect of Damien exercising his gift again so soon. "No. I'd never ask that of you. After what I saw..." She swallowed hard. "Please, don't risk yourself. We'll find her."

"Yes, we'll find her." Looking into her eyes, he lifted his hand to her cheek. The leather of his gloves, butter soft and warmed by the heat of his fingers, glided lightly over her skin. "There might be hundreds of churches in that city. Even if the police aren't going to check them out, I'm willing to take a look at each of them, one at a time, until we find the one that I saw."

She pressed her face to his palm. "Oh, Damien, thank you."

"Don't thank me, Jenna," he said, pulling his hand back quickly to hang on to the open door. "No, don't thank me. I'm not doing it for free."

He'd said the same thing to her before, many times. Somehow, it was different now. There was no longer any anger or defiance in his tone. Instead, she heard regret, as if he didn't want to remind her as much as he wanted to remind himself.

Chapter Eleven

The light changed to green, but the intersection was blocked by a stalled truck. A car inched ahead, squeezing past the truck and turning onto the cross street, skidding sideways when its tires hit a patch of ice. Pedestrians leaned into the wind, shielding their faces with collars or scarves as they wove between the snarled traffic. Black smoke puffed from the truck's exhaust pipe and it lurched forward, clearing the intersection just as the light turned red.

Damien struck the steering wheel of the rented sedan with his hand and leaned back in the seat. "We have to find another route."

The windshield wipers swished and thunked rhythmically. The whirring heater puffed warm air onto her face as Jenna held the map up to the window, struggling to read it in the fading daylight. "Turn right at the next street past this one, go down four blocks and make a left. That would bring us to the north side of the next church."

"How many have we checked so far?"

She peered more closely at the detailed street map. They'd purchased it at the airport as soon as they'd reached Chicago. In order to search as efficiently as possible, they'd divided it into sections, making note of each small, cross-topped square that indicated a church. Neither of them was familiar with the city, but Damien had been able to navigate with a steady competence, despite the deteriorating weather. Every time they found a church with any kind of cross or steeple, he drove carefully around the entire area, looking at the scene from all angles, but so far he'd recognized nothing.

There were so many. How could they possibly find the right one? And what if that Moss woman wasn't even in Chicago any longer? No, Damien was convinced that she would be keeping the children here, where she had criminal connections and where she would be in familiar territory. Territory, like the domain of any scavenging animal...

"Jenna?"

She shook herself out of her useless anger and counted up the small penciled-in X's she'd made on the map. "Seventeen."

"How many more are left in the square we're working on?"

"Eight."

He eased the car into gear as the line of vehicles crept forward. Flicking on his turn signal, he took the street that Jenna had indicated. "All right, it's not as congested here."

"The city is so huge," she said, her eyes blurring as she tried to focus on the map. "How are we ever going to find the right place. And what about the suburbs? The newer subdivisions? We haven't extended the grid that far."

"We can rule out a lot of them. I think the place we want has to be in an older neighborhood. The window had a wood frame and small, separate panes of glass, and the radiator was one of those fat accordion styles. They stopped putting in windows and radiators like those decades ago.'' He slowed down and turned again, then let the car coast to a stop.

Jenna looked through the windshield, trying to suppress a moan of frustration when she saw the eighteenth church. It was a single-story white building, with a long, curving glass front. No steeple, no cross.

''I'll check around it, anyway,'' Damien said, even though she hadn't spoken.

He drove around the block, stopping frequently to concentrate on a particular angle, but then he shook his head and pulled away.

Biting her lip, she marked another X on the map.

She penciled in three more before darkness fell completely. As the storm intensified, the traffic gradually dwindled. Jenna blinked back her weariness and concentrated on giving Damien directions. Although the rental car didn't have the power or the traction of his Jeep, he was no stranger to blizzards and was able to maintain control as he steered through the deepening drifts.

Gradually, the thickening snow reduced their visibility to the extent that Damien couldn't be sure whether or not he might miss the scene he sought. Neither of them wanted to give up, but they both knew it was futile to continue under these conditions. Deciding to resume the search the minute the weather cleared, they turned their efforts toward finding a place to spend the night.

The wind shrieked around the building, vibrating the glass in the window, sending icy drafts past the edge of the frame. Jenna grasped the curtain and peered outside, but all she could see was a swirling veil of white, pierced only by the streetlights at the edge of the motel parking lot.

Had the blizzard been this bad the night she had found Damien? Or to put it more accurately, the night he had found her? Surrounded by hulking buildings instead of pine trees, she felt the same eerie sense of isolation and borderline despair as that other time. Had it been only ten days ago?

She focused on the reflection of the room where it appeared to float in midair outside the window. According to the motel manager, business was heavier than usual tonight as many people decided to spend the night in the city rather than risk the long and treacherous drive home. It had been fortunate that she and Damien had been able to obtain this room. It was beige and comfortable, with its standard bland furniture and a forgettable painting over the pair of double beds. Most customers would probably find the decor soothing and inoffensive. But to Jenna it just seemed . . . empty.

The tears that she'd fought all day threatened to well in her eyes. She blinked, tightening her grip on the curtain. Empty, like her life had been after Alex had died, and after Emily had been lost. Like her life would be after Damien left.

Her gaze moved a fraction of an inch, and she could see his long, black-clad body stretched out on top of the far bed. And suddenly, the room didn't feel so empty.

A shiver whispered down her spine, and it wasn't from the cold draft. Her awareness of Damien had been curling at the edge of every conscious thought, like an itch . . . or an ache, filling her with a steadily escalating restlessness.

As if his thoughts were mirroring hers, he jackknifed to a sitting position and turned toward her, one forearm propped over his upraised knee. The position brought back an image of another bed, another time, when he had sat like that and watched her with a predatory light in his ice-blue eyes . . . and she had agreed to his bargain.

It seemed so long ago in one way, and like no time at all in another. Her anxiety over her niece clung to each passing minute, dragging it almost to a standstill. But the time had been filled with Damien, and the confused tangle of feelings he inspired.

Oh, he was much more than the cynical, disillusioned recluse she had first met. And he was more than the sensitive, generous grandson Rachel had told her about. He was deep, complex and utterly fascinating. A lifetime wouldn't be long enough to learn everything she wanted to know about him. All she had was a matter of days.

She wanted to find Emily. She did. But she wanted more time with Damien. If she could, she would postpone his departure. Yet she didn't want to postpone their search. But by finding one, she would eventually lose the other.

Oh, God. How could her heart survive being ripped apart like this?

He rolled smoothly to his feet and walked to stand behind her. "She'll be asleep by now," he said.

Her tears threatened again. She had never known anyone so attuned to her moods. "I hope it's warm enough where she is," she said, wincing as a gust of wind drove a sheet of snow against the window. "That building she's in is old, and the heating system might be inadequate in a storm like this."

"She's all right."

"We have to find her."

"We will." He raised his hands. In the reflection in the window she could see him hesitate, his palms inches away from her shoulders. But then he curled his hands into fists and dropped them to his sides.

She let the curtain fall back into place and sighed. "She could be on the other side of the city. Or she could be on the next block. The not knowing is frustrating."

"We'll start looking again as soon as the snow lets up enough to see the roofs across the street. Until then, there's nothing more we can do." He paused. "Unless—"

"No." She spun around, worry over Emily switching to concern for Damien. "I already told you, I won't let you risk contacting her again."

Compassion softened the lines beside his lips as he tipped his head to look into her face. "You're a special woman, Jenna."

She rubbed her eyes, then crossed her arms over her chest. "I don't feel special. I feel as if my nerves have been stretched to the point where they're ready to snap."

"It's been a long day. You should get some rest."

"How can I rest when I'm this close to Emily?"

"Worrying yourself sick isn't going to help. She's going to need you when we find her. Save your strength for that."

Why was it that sympathy and kind words could threaten her control so easily? She felt a tear slip over her cheek.

He shifted closer. "Jenna?"

"Would you hold me, Damien? Just for a little while?"

His fingers were already resting on her sleeve. "You know that probably wouldn't be safe."

"I don't want to come apart. Just hold me like you did before. You can do that if you don't touch my skin, can't you?"

"Yes." He slid his hand upward until he cupped her shoulder. Gently, cautiously, he pulled her toward him. "Yes, I can do that."

She uncrossed her arms, flattening her palms against his thick sweater, feeling his warmth reach out to her, wanting more.

With a muffled curse, he wrapped his arms around her back and drew her closer. "Yes, I can do that," he repeated, his words tinged with determination. He braced his legs apart, anchoring her more securely. "Whatever you need."

Beneath her ear, his heart thudded loudly. She felt surrounded by his presence, his power. Closing her eyes, she inhaled deeply, filling her senses. She needed this, she needed him. It was frightening to realize just how intensely she needed him. It was more than the circumstances, or their damn bargain.

There was a low rumble from outside, an odd, bass counterpoint to the wail of the wind. Thunder. It was rare in winter, but if the conditions of the storm were right, it happened even in a blizzard. Jenna knew there was a reasonable, scientific explanation for it, but that couldn't prevent the tremor of foreboding that shook her body.

"You need to go to bed," he murmured.

She snuggled against him. She didn't want to move away. He seemed like the only stability in her world right now. "Not yet. Not by myself."

"Jenna." There was a warning in his tone, a low rumble as ominous as the thunder.

"I held you last night," she said. "While you slept. You didn't know I was there, but I couldn't leave you alone."

"What?"

"You seemed so cold. I stayed beside you until you stopped shaking."

He paused. "The reaction wasn't as bad this morning."

"It wasn't?"

"No. It was milder than I'd thought it would be. It must have been because of you." His palm moved in a gentle circle on her back. "That's what was different."

"I was careful. I didn't want to hurt you, so I made sure not to touch your skin."

Another peal of thunder sounded in the distance. He pressed his cheek to the top of her head. "You're always giving. And sharing. How do you do it? How can you give away so much when you've endured so much misery?''

"Please," she whispered. "Just hold me."

For long, stolen minutes, he did just that. Outside the window, the storm built to a swirling frenzy, but in the circle of Damien's arms, Jenna knew she was safe. She felt his warm breath stir her hair, felt his hands move gently over her back. And as she absorbed his comfort, she felt it replaced by tension. Familiar tension.

She didn't pull away. When his caress changed from comforting to seeking, she melted closer. She molded herself to his hard planes and angles, reveling in the muscular, masculine strength that made him so different from her.

His hands cupped her bottom, lifting her against him, showing her how their embrace was affecting his body. That time on her couch came back to her. Vividly. The sensation of wool sliding on silk, gentle fingers stroking through cotton. She had made him stop then, because she knew he would never stay with her. Their situation hadn't changed. Yet now the thought of his leaving had the opposite effect. She didn't want him to stop. Clasping her hands behind his neck, she raised her head.

His eyes, those piercing, ice-blue eyes framed by the sinfully lush black lashes, were filled with passion that he didn't try to hide. And promise. So much promise. "Jenna, there are things we can do," he said, his voice rough, his breathing rapid. "Even without joining our skin. There are ways."

Her response was swift and primitive. Right now, in this strange room in an indifferent city, with the fury of the blizzard isolating them from the rest of the world, all the reasons she'd gone over in her mind so many times no longer seemed relevant. Caution crumbled. Restraint dissolved. She quivered, moistening lips that throbbed for a touch she knew he couldn't give her. "Show me," she said.

He smiled. It was a rare, beautiful smile. It held no triumph or smugness. Instead, it held...happiness. The lonely child, the rejected, isolated man, the defensive recluse faded away, leaving the open, loving soul he might have been if his life had been different.

And Jenna knew she was lost.

With a rippling of muscle that made the movement seem effortless, he bent down and scooped her into his arms. She trembled, burying her face against his shoulder as he carried her to the bed.

Bracing his knee against the edge of the mattress, he lowered her slowly, letting her slide down his body, making no attempt to hide his low groan of pleasure as her hip rubbed past the front of his jeans. "Feel what you do to me, Jenna."

Because it was the one sense she knew they had to restrain, suddenly her sense of touch seemed unbearably heightened. Through the barriers of her corduroy skirt and his denim jeans, she felt every inch of him. Her fingers ached to test his length and firmness, to feel his texture and heat. She clutched his sleeve. "Oh, Damien."

He steadied her so that she sat in the center of the bed, then came to his knees in front of her, his fingers busy with the buttons at the neck of her sweater. "What's underneath this?"

"My blouse, my bra."

"Is your blouse like the one you wore two days ago? Silk? Long sleeves?"

She nodded, her mouth going dry.

"Good. It'll be enough." He tugged her sweater over her head and tossed it behind him. Slowly, watching her face, he placed his hands on her breasts.

Pleasure flooded her, along with an overwhelming feeling of...rightness. The fine lace of her bra and the thin silk under his palm couldn't stop the flow of heat and sensation. Her nipples hardened, pushing against his fingers. She needed this. She needed more.

He bent forward and blew on the fabric. The moist warmth of his breath molded her blouse to her breast, outlining the pattern of lace, revealing the swollen nub of the center, sending tingles radiating outward, making her shake. She braced her arms behind her in an effort to stay upright. With a wordless murmur of encouragement, he slid one arm behind her back to support her and touched his lips to the puckered silk.

The shock stole her breath. Gasping, she arched against him. Through the fabric, she felt his cheeks round in another smile seconds before she felt the rich, slick texture of his tongue.

"Undo your bra." His voice vibrated against her flesh. "Let it fall open under your blouse."

The madness of what they were doing didn't enter into her mind. Her vision and her thoughts were filled with nothing but Damien, and how he was making her feel. She let his arm support her, leaning into his embrace as she slipped her hand beneath her blouse and unfastened the front clasp of her bra.

He did the rest. The silk was nothing but a token barrier to his touch as he eased her breasts out of the lace cups and into his waiting hands. He moved his thumb, rotating the place where he'd wetted the fabric, rubbing the cool silk over flesh that burned.

Blood surged and rushed in an exuberance of life. Jenna shifted to reach the elastic that held back his hair, then shivered with delight as she felt the thick locks curl between her fingers. Sensation built on sensation as she slid her hands down the knobby, ticklish knit of the wool that stretched over his chest.

"Go ahead," he urged. "I have a shirt underneath."

Eagerly, she grasped the hem of his thick sweater and pulled it upward, then dropped it to the floor with hers. Clutching his shoulders through the thin knit of his cotton turtleneck, she fell back on the bed, pulling him down beside her. With her fingertips, her palms, her wrists, she explored the contours of his chest, the firmness of his abdomen, the tapering slope of his ribs.

Denim rasped over corduroy. He slid his knee between her legs, molding her skirt to her thighs, easing her onto her back, matching their bodies together. "Ah, Jenna," he murmured, running his hand over her hip. "It's been so long. So long."

She knew that the length of time she'd been celibate had little to do with her reaction to him. Even before her marriage had started to fail, it had never been like…this. She felt the pressure building inside her, a need for completion that bordered on pain. "How?"

He understood her need, and her whispered question. He slid his knee higher, pressing gently at the junction of her thighs. "I have protection. In my wallet."

She hadn't given a thought to birth control. She should have. She'd known what their bargain entailed. But the price they had agreed to was to be paid *after* Emily was found. What was happening between them now had nothing to do with their deal. They both knew it. "But what about our skin?"

He parted her legs wider, kneeling between them. "Jenna. My sweet, pure, Jenna. We don't need to take off all of our clothes. We can use them, and the sheet, and the package in my wallet. We still don't have to touch."

Anticipation shook her body as she realized what he meant. Of course. They could manage. The barrier he would slip on to protect her from pregnancy would shield him from contact. They could touch in the ultimate intimacy, but not actually touch.

And suddenly, Jenna realized that wasn't what she wanted. No, she wanted completion, not simply physical relief. Not simply sex. Her body was on fire, thrumming its demands with every throb of her pulse. But her heart wanted . . . more.

He stretched out on top of her, balancing on his knees and his elbows as he leaned down to inhale deeply at the base of her throat. "Springtime," he murmured. "Generous. Healing. Hopeful." He caught the edge of her collar between his teeth and tugged it aside, then tilted his head and let the ends of his hair stroke teasingly over her skin.

"Damien," she said shakily. "Damien, wait."

The sound he made was dangerously close to a growl. The muscles in his thighs bunched and he fitted himself against her, twisting his hips in a promise of pleasure.

She grasped his arm, struggling for breath. "Damien!"

He raised his head, his nostrils flaring. "Not like this. That's what you're thinking, isn't it? You don't want it like this."

Her heartbeat was as rapid as the pulse she saw hammering in his throat. "I want you," she said. "You know I want you."

He pressed against her, pushing her into the mattress. "I can give you more. After. When we're free to touch."

It wasn't only his touch she wanted. And it wasn't only his body. She wanted the impossible. She wanted love.

But love was something that neither one of them could afford to give.

"Let yourself go, Jenna," he coaxed. He moved his hips again, then caught her hair in his fingers, shielding his palms as he cradled her face. "I won't hurt you."

He was wrong, she thought hazily. The pain wouldn't be physical, but he would hurt her just the same. When he left... No. She wouldn't think about that. She would think about now. This minute. This man.

Let yourself go. It wasn't difficult. She was already too close to the edge. She emptied her mind of everything else, all her fears and her cautions and her conflicting emotions. What he offered would have to be enough. Holding his gaze, not trying to hide the desire in her own, she nodded her head. "Yes."

He smiled again. This time the expression held more than happiness. Much more. It held passion, determination and raw, burning need.

Deep inside her, something leapt in reply. She put her hands on his shoulders and pushed until he rolled to his side, then reached beneath her skirt and pulled off her panty hose and underwear. Tossing it to the floor on top of their discarded sweaters, she felt her lips curve in a smile that ended the need for words.

"Ah, Jenna." He lowered his head, blowing gently on the delicate curve of her ear, laughing softly when she shivered in reaction. "This is just the start."

She had asked him to show her. And he did.

Time lost its meaning. As the storm raged outside the window, their world contracted, leaving room for only each other. Fabric slid, sheets crumpled, springs groaned and creaked as they explored sensations that were all the more vivid because of their limitations. They learned angles without learning textures, scents without learning tastes, building pleasure on pleasure until need became necessity.

Lost in a sensual haze, Jenna heard the snap of a stud and the rasp of a zipper as Damien opened his jeans. She trembled, waiting, yearning, reaching...

He caught her wrists, keeping the damp silk of her sleeves against her skin, and stretched her arms over her head. "Can't... touch," he said. "Not yet."

Groaning with impatience, she pressed her palms to the headboard and arched her back. "Damien!"

He pushed up her skirt and settled his weight on top of her. She felt denim rub her bare thighs, smooth cotton float over swollen moistness. Blocking out her frustration over their inability to really touch, she drew him closer, tighter...

Until they glided together.

Delight exploded through her body in a dazzling wave of color and light, glowing across every inch of untouched skin. She gasped, feeling the supple shift of corduroy against her hips as Damien slipped his hands beneath her and lifted her even higher. He called her name, his body shuddering, and the wave crashed over them both.

Echoes pulsed through the air, felt more than heard, as the room slowly came back into focus. Snow swished against the window, a door at the other end of the motel corridor opened and closed. Damien made a sound in his throat, one of his masculine murmurs of pure pleasure that sent an answering vibration singing through Jenna's nerves. He rolled away, dropping a hot, wet kiss on the silk between her breasts when she whispered a protest. Pausing only long enough to readjust the clothing they still wore, he pulled her back into his arms.

Closing her eyes, she pressed her face to his chest, listening to the steady beat of his heart, trying to ignore the voice of reason that was struggling to be heard in her head. Her body was too weary and too sated for her to summon the energy to move.

"Go to sleep, Jenna," he said. "I'll be right here."

She slid her arm around his waist, splaying her hand over his shirt. "Damien, what we did was—"

"Good. It was good, Jenna. It was what we both needed."

"It was just...so...I don't know. Carnal."

"It was what we both needed," he said again.

"But our deal—"

"Isn't over. We're going to finish what we started here. That much I can promise you." He pressed his cheek to the top of her head. "But for now, let me hold you, all right? The way you did for me last night. Keep the nightmares and the emptiness away."

How had her request become his? Feeling the warmth of his embrace surround her, she snuggled more firmly against him. As sleep finally claimed her, she thought she heard his voice whisper her name.

But somehow she knew he hadn't spoken.

. . . .

. . . .

. . . .

. . . .

. . . .

. . . .

. . . .

. . . .

. . . .

. . . .

. . . .

. . . .

Chapter Twelve

The overcast gradually cleared as the day wore on, but the driving conditions grew worse. Not all the roads were plowed. The snow that remained formed lumpy, uneven ruts in the center of the side streets and compacted into hard, slippery sheets of ice at the intersections. The morning crawled past with frustration following disappointment. By noon Damien had found, and eliminated, thirteen more churches.

Jenna marked another X on her map and let her head thump against the back of the seat. Everything was worse than yesterday, not only the driving. She let her gaze drift to her silent companion. If he'd been a wolf, he would have been growling and bristling. Despite the incredible experience of the night before, the barriers, those damn, invisible ramparts he'd perfected over the years to keep the world at bay, were slipping back into place.

She should have known this would happen. She should have known better than to invite his touch. But he hadn't touched her. Technically, they were still sticking to the letter of their agreement. Last night had been . . .

A mistake. A reckless, mindless, primitive mistake. In the clear, sober light of day, she was able to see how wrong it had been. Obviously, so had Damien. She'd been overcome by loneliness and need. What they'd done had been . . .

Fantastic. Sensual. Satisfying. And the way they had made love, the exquisite care he'd taken to bring her so much pleasure without actually undressing her was enough to bring a blush to her cheeks even now. Yet she had been the one to initiate it, and it was too late for regrets.

There would be time enough for those when he left. Whenever that would be.

Whenever they found Emily.

"Something wrong?" he asked.

Her laugh held no humor. "You mean besides the fact that we're looking for a needle in a snowy haystack? And that you slept with me and now you're treating me like a complete stranger?"

He stopped at a red light and took the map out of her hands. As he spread it open over the steering wheel, his fingers weren't quite steady. "We have three more to check before we move to another grid."

The tremor in his fingers startled her. She turned her head in order to look at him more closely. "Those ramparts aren't as sturdy as you want me to believe, are they?"

"I don't know what you're talking about."

"The walls around your feelings."

He placed the map on the seat between them and put the car back into gear as the light turned green. "Leave me alone, Jenna."

That would be the smartest course of action. She'd managed to avoid this humiliating confrontation all

morning, hadn't she? Why not let him barricade himself
for good? He was continuing to search for her niece, so
what should it matter to her if . . .

But it mattered. God, it mattered.

Lifting her chin, she twisted on the seat so that she was
facing him. "Don't you think we've come past all this,
Damien?"

"All what?"

"This rudeness. You're trying to pretend that last night
didn't happen. But it won't work."

"I'm not pretending anything," he said brusquely.
"I'm looking forward to the time when you can pay your
fee in full."

Was she only deluding herself to think she heard desperation beneath the snarl? "This isn't you, Damien.
You're only saying that to push me away, aren't you?"

Tightening his jaw, he didn't answer. He drove in silence for another block.

"Damien?"

"What do you want from me? Lies? Sweet words?
False promises?"

"Of course not."

"Nothing has changed. I'll find Emily. We'll finish
what we started last night. Then I'll leave. That's the extent of our relationship, Jenna. There's no room in my life
for someone else, and I'm not about to risk what it took
me five years to build."

"What makes you think I'm asking to be a part of your
life? I know where we stand. You've made it perfectly
clear from the start."

"I don't want to get caught in your emotions."

He'd told her that, too. She slumped back against the
seat. Maybe he was right. Maybe she did want the lies and
the sweet words and the false promises. Maybe she didn't
want to believe that all they'd shared had been shallow,
meaningless sex.

Yet if shallow, meaningless sex was all it had been, he should be pleased. That's what he said he wanted, so why was he so miserable? "Damien, what's going on?"

His hands jerked on the wheel. "I don't want to hurt you, Jenna."

"Then why are you lashing out at me like an animal in pain?"

The car swerved suddenly. Swearing under his breath, Damien steered into the freshly plowed parking lot of a hamburger stand and braked to a stop. For a minute he sat without speaking, his jaw clenched, his frame vibrating with tension. Then he tipped back his head and exhaled harshly.

She lifted her hand and laid it gently on his sleeve. "Talk to me, Damien. After everything we've gone through, don't shut me out now."

The heater whirred quietly while the engine hummed. Keeping his movements carefully controlled, Damien unbuckled his seat belt and leaned his shoulders against the car door. "I'm sorry, Jenna. I've been acting like a real bastard all morning."

His apology was unexpected. She smiled. "Oh, your growls don't scare me that much anymore."

"You deserve better than this, but I'm not the man who can give it to you."

Love. The word was still unspoken, but it hung like a tangible force in the air between them. It had been there last night, too, hovering, taunting, tempting. Jenna firmed her jaw to keep it from trembling. "Damien, I—"

"I can't let myself get caught in your emotions, because my existence depends on isolation."

"Your gift has been the cause of so much pain and rejection, I understand why you'd prefer to live alone. I know why you sometimes act the way you do, and I don't blame you for it."

"You don't know all of it, Jenna. I didn't always live alone."

"From what you've told me about your childhood, you were essentially alone until you went to live with Rachel."

"I'm not talking about my childhood. I'm talking about my marriage."

Marriage? The word hit her like a blast of cold air. "You were married?"

"I moved to the cabin five years ago. After my wife died."

Jenna pulled back her hand and pressed it to her lips. His wife. Five years ago. Questions crowded her mind, yet now that he was finally opening up, she didn't want to push him. "I'm sorry. I didn't know. Rachel never told me."

"She should have. She's the only other person who understands my decision."

"Decision?"

His gaze steadied on hers. "I think you would understand, too. You loved your son. You know what losing that love did to you. You said you wanted to follow him, you said you didn't want to live."

She swallowed at the sudden lump that came to her throat. "Yes, that's how I felt."

"I loved my wife. When she died, I did follow her."

This was too much to take in all at once. Her perception of him was undergoing yet another shift. Had it been more than his family's and society's rejection that had driven him to isolate himself? Had it been grief?

"Claire and I met in Nome seven years ago, where we were both covering the Iditarod for different magazines," he said, his words as strained as his expression. "She helped me establish myself as a credible photographer, and by the time we were married the following summer, I'd pretty well retired from the psychic business. She had a small ranch near Santa Fe where we spent most of our time when we weren't traveling on assignment."

The suffering was there, in his words, in his eyes. She wanted to reach out to him, but she didn't know whether she should. "What happened?"

"Cancer. By the time she was diagnosed, they gave her three months. Six at most. She lasted almost a year."

"I'm sorry, Damien. I'm so sorry."

"I loved her. I felt her pain and tried to ease it by taking it on myself. I helped her for a while, but then she refused to let me. She was a strong woman." His mouth twisted into a tragic parody of a smile. "She had a mind of her own."

Jenna looked at the lines beside his eyes, the honed leanness of his features. He'd eased his dying wife's pain by taking it on himself? She thought of the awesome power of shared emotion, the way he'd experienced Emily's fear and loneliness, and she shuddered. "Oh, God."

"She'd wanted to spend the time she had left on the ranch she loved, but I was selfish. I didn't want to let her go. I took her to the cancer center in Houston. They'd already told us they could do nothing but make her more comfortable, but I couldn't accept that." His gaze clouded with memory, the brilliant blue glistening. "By that time she was too weak to fight me, so I hung on. I linked with her mind. I anchored myself in the bond between us and used every ounce of ability I had to keep death from taking her."

"And when you couldn't keep her, you followed her," Jenna said.

"Yes. I didn't want her to leave."

His gaze was growing distant, his breathing shallow. Although she wasn't touching him, Jenna felt his remembered agony close around her heart. "What happened?"

"She wanted peace. She wanted me to let her go." He swallowed, his throat working as he fought to retain control over his voice. "She pleaded with me to set her free, but I couldn't. I held on. The doctors shut down the machines and tried to pull me away, but I wouldn't let them. She grew cold, but it was only her body that was cold. I still felt her soul."

A sob shook her chest. So cold. Alex had been so cold, and she had tried to wake him up and tried—

"That's when I learned the limitations of my abilities. Learned that I was only human. Something snapped inside me. My mind lost its anchor. I disconnected from reality."

And Jenna had stayed in her room, and didn't want to get dressed, and didn't want to eat, and felt as if life was over because her son, her baby, was gone—

"Claire found peace. I found hell."

Reaching blindly, Jenna grasped his sleeve, needing the ordinary reassurance of the contact. "Oh, Damien. How did you survive?"

"Some outer shell of me managed to function. I took care of the funeral arrangements and settled our affairs. The only other person on this earth I had any bond with was my grandmother, so I said goodbye to her and made it as far as my cabin before the shell cracked."

"You broke down. Like me."

He covered her hand with his gloved fingers, the leather warm and heavy. "Yes. I don't know how long it took. Most of the summer I drifted in and out of reality, battling my way back to sanity. Then one day I was sitting under a pine tree on the ridge behind my cabin, and all of a sudden I smelled the needles, and felt the rough bark against my back, and heard the branches rattle, and tasted September on the breeze, and I knew I'd returned."

He'd been alone in his grief. She'd had the love and support of her family to help her through her breakdown, but Damien had been alone. She leaned toward him, pressing her forehead against his shoulder.

"I believed that my gift was gone," he said. "Burned out in my fight to save Claire. I didn't want it back. I grasped on to reality with the fervor of a drowning man and made sure I didn't put myself into a situation where I might learn my ability to transcend it wasn't really gone."

"And you cut yourself off from emotions," she murmured. "You cut yourself off from society and isolated yourself from the possibility of being caught in any human bond again. That's why you moved to the cabin. That's the decision you made."

"It was the only way I could guarantee my sanity. I won't risk losing it again." He squeezed her hand once, then gently eased her away and curled his fingers around the steering wheel. "Rachel shouldn't have sent you."

The enormity of what had happened to him gradually began to register. So did the consequences of her own stubborn determination. He had good reasons for those walls he'd built around his feelings. Valid reasons. Normal, human reasons. Yet she'd barged into his life and forced him to help her and never fully understood the impact of her actions. "Damien, I'm sorry."

He heard the genuine sympathy in her voice, the gentle understanding, and he wanted to bask in it. God, he wished that he could pull her into his arms once more, share her healing warmth, hold her until her trembling body ended the years of exile. He wanted to replay the wonder of their night together and pretend that he was like any other man, that he could accept more than her body.

But he couldn't hold her now, not with the power of those memories he had exhumed still churning around him. He couldn't touch her. His resolve was balancing on a knife edge of need. One nudge, one slip, and he risked losing his future.

He gripped the wheel harder, feeling the leather of his gloves curl damply against his palms and stretch tightly over his knuckles. A barrier against touch. A barrier against the world.

"I don't want your pity," he said. "I don't want anything from you except what I asked for."

Jenna pulled a tissue from her pocket and wiped her eyes.

If he was smart, if he had one ounce of sense, he would drive her to the nearest police station right now and let the cops complete the search for Emily. But he wanted to see this through to the end. No matter how much it would cost him, how reckless and self-destructive it would turn out to be, he didn't have the strength to leave Jenna yet.

Another car pulled into the parking lot. It passed them and drew up to the take-out window of the hamburger stand, but Damien still didn't move. Something seemed to tremble in the air between them.

As his silence continued, Jenna glanced at him. "Damien?"

He wasn't touching her, yet he could feel the swirls and eddies of her emotion. He braced himself as he felt something tug.

"Damien?" she repeated, concern sharpening her voice.

Shaking his head, he reached forward to put the car into gear. His gaze went automatically to the rearview mirror... and he stared. No. It couldn't be.

"What's wrong?"

The swirls steadied. "Check your map," he said.

Paper rustled as she did what he asked.

He looped his arm behind her seat and twisted to look out the back windshield. "Is there supposed to be a church near here?"

With her index finger she traced the street they had been on. "Nothing is marked for another six blocks east." She turned to follow his gaze.

He pointed through a gap in the row of brick buildings across the street. "What does that look like to you?"

"It's—" She paused, swallowing hard. "It's a cross."

The tires spun as Damien pulled back onto the street.

The church had been built out of pale brick, a mellow, weathered gold. The reason it hadn't been indicated on the map was clear—a rusty padlock hung from the front door and gray, graffiti-speckled boards covered the windows. The roof was bare of shingles in at least two places, but the steeple was intact. The narrow cross that topped it would be visible from an upper story window in any of the surrounding houses.

Damien circled the block, concentrating on the way the sunlight slanted past the buildings. Emily was close. She had to be. It was earlier in the afternoon than it had been when she'd held her paint-spattered hand against the sunlight a week ago, so the sun was higher in the sky, but somehow things looked…familiar. He turned into a side street that would bring them northeast of the church, driving slowly, following the path of the shadows, trying to judge how far away the window would have to be for him—for Emily—to glimpse that small cross.

Trying not to think about how close they had come to missing this scene, Damien eased the car to a stop near the entrance to an alley.

A dog barked from somewhere nearby. There was a whooshing clatter as a train passed over the elevated track a quarter mile away. But Emily wouldn't hear those things. Damien studied the row of modest frame houses. Although the storm of the previous night had knocked down most of the icicles, there were still a few long, twisted ones that clung to the eaves of several snow-draped roofs. But they all looked the same.

"Do you recognize anything?"

He shook his head, shielding his eyes with his hand as he checked the angle of the sunlight. "Not really. I just have this feeling." He caught a glimpse of movement at the other end of the alley. "Wait."

His pulse accelerated as he studied the figure who had come into view. It was a woman, a large woman. Although a scarf concealed the lower half of her face, as she came nearer he could see brassy blond hair sticking out from the edge of her knitted hat. She moved heavily, her boots slipping in the deep snow as she carried a brown paper grocery bag to the house on the opposite corner. She gave no more than a passing glance to the parked car, but it was enough. Even from a distance he felt the familiar, terrifying impact of those eyes.

Jenna turned toward him, her face shining with a transparent mixture of fear and hope. And faith.

Damien braced himself against the feelings that flowed from her so freely. He couldn't let himself accept them, because he'd never be able to give her what she wanted, what she deserved, in return.

But at least he could do this. He could fulfill the bargain they had struck, complete the deal.

He could give her Emily.

The raid was organized swiftly. Within minutes of Damien's phone call, two patrol cars silently converged on the quiet street, one taking up a position in front of the corner house, the other blocking the alley in the rear. Several minutes later, an unmarked car, red light flashing in the front windshield, pulled up at the curb and three plainclothes officers emerged.

To Jenna's surprise, she recognized one of them just as he entered the house. Evidently Frank Novacek had taken the information they had given him yesterday seriously enough to come to Chicago and follow up in person. Ignoring Damien's advice to wait until the police had moved in, Jenna flung open her car door and hurried across the street.

Events unfolded quickly after that. As Jenna and Damien waited on the sidewalk with one of the uniformed officers, Bernice Moss was led outside. Hatless, with her bleached blond hair straggling against her pudgy cheeks and her wrists handcuffed behind her back, she was deposited in the back seat of the nearest police car. Two men were brought out next, their shoulders hunched and heads down as they were shuffled to another car with the defeated posture of the habitual criminal.

Breathless minutes passed before Frank reappeared in the doorway of the house. He scowled when he saw Jenna and Damien, then impatiently motioned them inside.

The moment Jenna stepped over the threshold she heard a child's broken sobs from somewhere overhead. She brushed past Frank, breaking into a run as she followed the sounds up a narrow staircase to the second floor. She heard Frank call something and Damien's footsteps close behind her, but she didn't stop. She reached a dim hallway at the top of the stairs, her boots skidding on the tile floor as she turned toward the doorway on the left.

Cartoons danced across the screen of the small television near the opposite wall. Beside a fat radiator, a low shelf held a toy truck, a bucket of blocks and sheaves of crumpled paper. A package of cookies rested beside the brown paper grocery bag on the low table in the corner. The details of what she was seeing burst into her mind all at once, but her gaze was riveted on the figure that moved toward her.

Silhouetted against the sunlight that streamed through a long, narrow window, a policeman moved awkwardly, trying to soothe the crying child he cradled in his arms.

Jenna lunged forward, only to stop short when she was able to see the child's face.

It wasn't Emily.

"Tim Sorenson," Damien said, coming to a stop beside her. "That's the other child I saw."

Proof. It was all around them. The confirmation of everything he had said. But she didn't even pause to marvel at it. She had always believed him. "Where is she?" Jenna cried, pivoting to scan the room once more. "Where's Emily?"

Frank came through the doorway, followed by one of the other plainclothes officers. "We're still searching the house, Jenna," Frank said. "Please try to calm down. Mr. Reese, Lieutenant Strada here has a few questions for you."

Tim's sobs grew fainter as the officer who was holding him moved out of the room and down the stairs. A siren sounded from the street outside. Doors opened and closed and more footsteps filled the house.

Jenna looked around frantically. "Emily?"

"We've found Moss's phony adoption records," the other policeman said, moving forward. "We'll try to trace your niece through them if the search of the house doesn't turn her up, but for now it would be best if you and your friend—"

"But she was here two days ago. With the other boy." She turned to Damien. "We can't be too late. Please, after all this, we can't be too late. She was here. I know she was here. That's the truck she wanted, isn't it? And the window she looked through?"

"Yes, this is the place."

"But she's gone. Oh, God. She's gone again." Jenna knew she was on the brink of hysteria, but she was helpless to stop it. She felt as if she were in the center of a whirlpool. Everything was spinning by too fast, with no chance for her to regain control. After everything she had done, everything she had tried, to come so close and to lose her niece again...

In one smooth motion, too quickly for her to stop him, Damien pulled off his glove and clamped his hand over hers.

The shock of the sudden contact steadied her thoughts. Her gaze whipped to his. "No," she breathed. "You can't."

He clenched his jaw, his face set with determination. "I'll find her for you, Jenna."

She twisted her wrist, trying in vain to break his grip. She knew now what it was costing him, what the resurrection of his powers would mean to the life he had chosen. "No, Damien, you've done enough. I can't ask you to try—"

"We made a bargain," he gritted, tightening his grip, bringing his face close to hers. "Concentrate on Emily. Now. Emily."

She felt the tug. It was too fast, too intense to resist. A flash. A burst of cold. Then he released her and staggered backward.

"What the—"

"That's what I was telling you about, Strada."

Heedless of the policemen's stares, Jenna leapt to Damien's side and slid a supporting arm around his waist.

He pulled away and pivoted toward the hall, his back stiff, his steps uneven. He was halfway down the stairs before Jenna caught up with him. Shaking off her attempts to help him, he went down to the first floor, turned right and stopped beside the wall under the staircase. There was a sliver of darkness, a tiny gap...

A door.

Jenna found the knob and wrenched it open.

It was a small cupboard, crammed with old newspapers and pieces of cardboard and...

"Emily!" Jenna fell to her knees and reached for the child, who was huddled into a defensive ball. At the first touch of her hand, Emily raised a tear-streaked face, blinking at the light that streamed through the front door.

Baby-fine blond hair, longer than the last time Jenna had seen it, fell softly around a cherub's face. Gray eyes made luminous by tears widened in stunned recognition.

"Oh, Emily," Jenna cried, a smile breaking through two months of agony. Her fingers moved jerkily, signing while she spoke, the words tumbling in her eagerness. "Emily."

With a hoarse cry, the child pitched out of her hiding place and catapulted into her aunt's waiting arms.

Jenna's eyes misted as she felt her niece's arms lock in a stranglehold around her neck. She pressed her face to Emily's head, tightening her embrace to the point where they could barely breathe. Emily's narrow chest shook with muffled sobs as she burrowed closer. Jenna sat back on her heels, raining kisses on Emily's hair, her forehead, her cheeks, anything she could reach, closing her eyes and rocking back and forth in an age-old rhythm of comfort.

Damien moved behind her, far enough not to touch, yet close enough to see the tears of joy spill over her cheeks. He stood unflinching despite the activity that continued in the hall, deflecting the questions from Frank and his colleagues, keeping the police away, standing guard over the poignantly silent reunion of Jenna and her niece.

Emily rubbed her eyes against Jenna's shoulder, drying her tears without releasing her grip on her aunt's neck. Cautiously she raised her head and looked at Damien for the first time.

He'd been in this child's mind. He'd felt her humor, her fear, her loneliness. He'd felt the strength of her family's emotions. He understood how her difference would always isolate her in one way or another, no matter how much she might want to belong...

Her gaze focused on his face. A trembling smile of recognition touched the corners of her mouth.

For the space of a heartbeat he indulged himself, picturing what it would be like to kneel on the floor beside them, to wrap them both in the strength of his embrace and let himself be drawn into the circle of their love.

Emily thrust out her arm, spreading her fingers in an effort to reach him.

"Step over here for a moment, Mr. Reese." It was Frank's voice, impatient, official. "We need some more details."

"Lieutenant," someone called from outside. "A news crew just pulled up. What should I tell them?"

Jenna shifted, and Emily pulled back her hand to clutch her aunt's shoulder.

Tugging on his glove, Damien turned away.

Chapter Thirteen

Settling Emily securely on her hip, Jenna cradled the child's head against her shoulder to shelter her face from the barrage of camera flashes. Damien had pushed Frank to arrange transportation back to Minneapolis as quickly as possible to minimize the publicity that was bound to arise, but the airport terminal was already crowded with reporters. The cracking of the child-snatching ring was big news, and the recovery of Tim and Emily along with more than a dozen other missing children who had been listed in Bernice Moss's records was nothing short of miraculous.

But it wasn't merely news that this crowd was after.

"Mr. Reese! Over here, Mr. Reese," someone shouted. "Is it true that you used a medium to—"

"Hey, turn the kid this way, lady. Come on, honey, smile."

"Detective Novacek, can you give us more details of what led you—"

"How many people have been arrested so far?"

"Where's my uncle? He disappeared—"

"Is there any truth to the rumor that you conspired—"

"Please, won't you help me find my boyfriend—"

It was just as Damien had described. He had warned her this would happen, but it was so unfair. She had done this to him. She had forced him away from the safety of his anonymity. Was there no part of his nightmare that she hadn't resurrected?

Frank put his hand on the small of Jenna's back and steered her toward the security area. Damien moved in front, using his size and his forbidding demeanor to clear a path for them. The questions, the demands, the pleas mercifully faded. Jenna tightened her protective hold on Emily and wished she could somehow shelter Damien.

"Your family's waiting in the lounge at the end of the hall," Frank said as he led them through a set of double doors to a brightly lit corridor. "I thought your sister would prefer to have this reunion in private. I instructed the airport to inform her when your flight got—"

He didn't have the chance to finish his sentence before a door crashed open and Brigit raced toward them in a sprint that could have set a world record.

Jenna shifted Emily on her hip so she could see her mother, since at the first sight of Brigit's face, Jenna's eyes had filled with tears so quickly she couldn't see much of anything.

Brigit swept her daughter into her arms, clutching her with a fierceness that said more than words. For precious, endless seconds, they clung to each other, smiles trembling, eyes streaming, while their world finally righted itself.

Nora reached them next, followed closely by Jenna's father, Ian. They took turns holding their granddaughter, holding each other, crying and laughing as emotions overflowed. Frank ushered them back into the lounge, promising to arrange a more secure route for them to leave the airport. He rapped out orders into his radio with brisk efficiency, but behind his glasses his eyes were moist.

Jenna felt the love of her reunited family fill her with strength. Her mind was still reeling from the dizzying sequence of events that had occurred since noon, but the worry, the fear, the months of anxiety had finally collapsed. It was over. Emily was safe, she was home. And it was all because of Damien. Wiping her cheeks with her fingertips, she turned toward him.

He was standing beside their bags, his hands shoved into his pockets, his posture stiff as he watched the reunion. In a room that brimmed with happiness, he held himself aloof. Alone.

Something tilted inside her. No. This wasn't right. "Damien, come and join us."

"Mr. Reese," Jenna's father called. He strode across the room toward them and held out his hand. "I'm Ian Lawrence. And I'd like to express my gratitude for what you've done for all of us."

Damien stared at the outstretched hand, his jaw tightening.

"He can't shake hands, Ian," Nora said, hurrying forward. "It's not safe for him because of—"

"Oh, hell," Ian said. "I forgot." With a wide smile, he lifted his hand and gave Damien a hearty slap on the back. "Thank you. However you did it, I don't care. You brought our Em back to us."

"Yes, thank you." Nora dug into her purse for a tissue to wipe her eyes. "Thank you, from the bottom of my heart."

Damien took a step back.

"Frank told us that Moss woman confessed," Nora added. "You've been completely cleared of any suspicion, and I owe you an apology."

"We all owe you a debt we can never repay," Ian said.

Damien flinched. "You owe me nothing."

"You'll come to Brigit's place on Friday, won't you?" Nora asked. "We're giving Emily some time to settle in, but then we're having a celebration. Being with the people who love her is the best therapy there is. The whole family's coming." She looked at Jenna. "I'm going to bake every recipe in my chocolate book."

Ian grinned. "Your mom already bought up the local ice-cream supply."

"Ha! Grandpa cleaned out the stuffed animal section of the toy store."

Brigit, still clutching her daughter as if she had no intention of ever letting her go again, walked over to join them. "I heard the tape of what you went through, Mr. Reese, and I'm sorry I doubted you. Jenna was right. About everything. And I just want to say—" She blinked hard, struggling to get the words out.

A breathless silence fell over the group as she looked at Damien, her lips quivering too hard for her to speak.

The moment stretched on until Emily twisted in her mother's embrace to point at him. Interlocking her index fingers, she made a throaty sound.

Jenna choked back a sudden sob and raised her gaze to Damien's.

His eyes gleamed as he cleared his throat. "What did she say?"

"Friend," Nora said softly. "She called you friend."

The telephone started ringing the moment Jenna and Damien reached her apartment. She toed off her boots and raced across the living room to answer. It was a reporter who had heard her name on the evening news, looked up her number in the phone book and wanted to know how to reach Damien.

Shaking his head, Damien crossed the floor and pressed his finger down on the disconnect. "Better unplug the phone." He gestured toward the frantically blinking red light on her answering machine. "Now that the story's broken, you'll likely get more of this."

"You mean the reporters?"

"Frank said he'd hold a press conference, so that should satisfy most of them. The others are going to be harder to get rid of."

"Others?"

"Hear for yourself."

She glanced at the blinking light, then hit the message button. It was the airport all over again. People, complete strangers, asking for Damien, demanding his help. She ran a hand through her hair distractedly. "A week and a half ago I must have sounded just like them. I'm sorry, Damien. It's because of me that this is happening to you again."

"It'll blow over eventually."

The phone rang once more. She let the machine pick it up, then listened as a woman described her husband who had disappeared twenty years ago. Before the rambling tirade had finished, Jenna leaned over and disconnected the phone. "I'm sorry," she said again.

"It wasn't your fault. It was just bad luck that the woman in that news crew at Moss's house recognized me and decided to dredge up my past."

"We can try to minimize this." Belatedly realizing she was still wearing her coat, she walked back to the closet by the front door and hung it up beside Damien's. "None of us will substantiate the rumors that Chicago reporter started. We can say you're a friend of the family, that it was nothing more than good police work that led to Emily's rescue. I'm sure Frank would agree to that."

"He already did."

"That's good. You've been out of the spotlight for more than five years. If we don't feed the publicity, it should die out more quickly than it did in the past."

"It should. Eventually."

"I'm really sorry, Damien."

"My cabin doesn't have a telephone. I'll be leaving for Alberta in another week anyway."

"The assignment on those national parks, right?"

He nodded, then shoved his hands into the pockets of his jeans and walked to the table beside the couch. Silently, he studied the picture of Emily.

Jenna watched the way the lines of tension beside his mouth softened as he looked at the photograph, and she remembered that precious moment before they had left the airport. "It's not the harassment that bothers you the most, is it?" she asked. "It's the demands themselves. You have a hard time turning them down."

"Anyone would."

Anyone? No, just a sensitive, generous man like Damien. "That's another reason you used to court all that publicity when you were younger. You tried to make your special abilities reach as many people as possible, didn't you?"

"I used to try to help them all. Every single person who asked, no matter how slim the chances or how plausible the story." He smiled ruefully. "I suppose I felt morally obligated to share my gift in any way I could."

"That must have been terrible for you."

"Terrible. Exhilarating. Exhausting. But eventually I had to come to terms with the fact that it was impossible to keep up, no matter how the stories I heard moved me. I ended up disappointing more people than I helped."

"You deserved a life, too. No one could blame you."

"They often did, since they put their hopes on me and neglected the more conventional methods that could have solved their problems sooner. The number of cases that can't be solved without a psychic's assistance are very few."

Jenna thought about that for a while. Was it possible that the illegal adoption ring would have been discovered eventually without Damien's help?

He took his hand from his pocket and reached out to touch Emily's image. "She'll be all right, now. You don't need to worry about her anymore."

"Yes, she will. And I'm not worried. We all thank—"

"Don't," he said quietly.

She didn't need to hear him finish to know what he was thinking. He'd said it often enough. *Don't thank me. I'm not doing this for free.*

There it was. Their bargain. It hung in the air between them, the unspoken agreement to progress to the final stage of their relationship.

After I find your niece, when the intensity of your emotion drops, that's when we'll close the deal.

Although neither one of them had mentioned it since they'd found Emily, the awareness of what was going to happen had been there all along. That's why he had stayed with her and her niece instead of dropping out of sight at the first sign of the media. That's why he had accompanied her home.

Finally the end had come, and it was time to close the deal and deliver payment.

Suddenly nervous, Jenna picked up her bag, the one she'd taken with her to Chicago. The one that contained her crumpled corduroy skirt. "I think I'll unpack."

He withdrew his hand from the photograph and met her gaze. "All right."

"Would you like something to eat?" she asked.

"It's after midnight."

"I know it's late, but it won't take me long to go into the kitchen and pop something into the microwave...."

Another phrase Damien had once said tickled across her mind. *I want you in my bed, not in my kitchen.* She tightened her grip on the bag and took a step toward the hall. "I'll be right back."

He watched her closely, his expression inscrutable. "I'll wait."

Heat flared in her face as she left the room. Why did she suddenly feel so awkward? There was no reason for shyness, especially after what they had done last night.

But that had been unplanned. Wild. Passionate. Spontaneous. This was different. This time she couldn't use her anxiety as an excuse.

Yet why did she need an excuse?

They'd come a long, long way since that night in his cabin when his hostility and her desperation had led to their deal. They had joined their minds through her bond with her niece, had opened up the most traumatic memories of their pasts and understood each other more deeply than she would have imagined possible. Together they had experienced everything from pain to euphoria, and their knowledge of each other went far beyond the physical.

Jenna dropped her bag beside her dresser and turned to look at the bed. She remembered how Damien had traced the pattern of the bedspread with his fingertips. And how he had traced the curve of her waist with silk. She raised her hands to her burning cheeks. Tonight they wouldn't need the barrier of their clothing.

Deep inside, something clenched in anticipation. She'd already slept with him, but she hadn't yet seen him naked. Would the perfection of his face extend to the rest of him? How would his skin look in the lamplight? How would it feel? And taste?

He was still going to leave. He still wanted nothing from her but the use of her body. Yet the concept no longer shocked her. She understood him. Accepted him.

And as Jenna looked at the bed, she realized that the price Damien had demanded was something she was now willing, even eager to pay.

"I changed my mind."

At the voice from behind her she whirled around. "What?"

Damien was standing in the doorway to her bedroom, his arms crossed, his legs braced apart. He was watching her with the kind of predatory intensity that had always made her pulse race. As it did now. "I changed my mind," he repeated.

"About our deal?"

"No." He uncrossed his arms and stepped forward. "About waiting. I don't want to eat first, do you?"

"Maybe we should—"

"Later." Without any hesitation, he grasped the lower hem of his sweater and pulled it off, dropping it to the floor as he continued to walk toward her. Less than one stride later, he yanked off his thin black cotton turtleneck and flung it into the corner.

Jenna stared, incapable of saying anything coherent. She had felt the breadth, the solidity and the contours of that chest, had heard the raspy slide of cotton against the crisp black hair that spread over the taut skin, had explored the washboard ripples of that firm abdomen, but she had never imagined how... magnificent the reality would be.

Perfection? No, he was too human and too blatantly male to be described by a word that confining.

He reached for the elastic that held his hair back at his nape, and his biceps swelled into hard curves. "Are you hungry, Jenna?"

The note of teasing in his voice startled her. Teasing? *Damien?* He was discarding more than his clothing. He was shrugging off his wariness. The distance he was closing between them was more than physical.

"Ravenous," she replied.

"So am I." Stopping in front of her, he unsnapped the stud on the waistband of his jeans.

He still didn't touch her, even though he was standing close enough for her to feel the heat from his body. Or was it hers? Jenna fumbled behind her to grasp the edge of the dresser as she locked her knees to keep herself from trembling.

"Last night was just the appetizer," he said, placing his hands beside hers, holding her in place between his hard-muscled arms.

Desire was rapidly burning away the last of her nervousness. She looked at the pulse beating hard at the base of his throat, then raised her gaze to his mouth.

And she was shocked to realize that despite everything else they'd done together, they had never kissed.

His lips curved into a smile that sent tingles all the way to her toes. "What do you think, Jenna? Do you still want to wait?"

"No. Not one more second."

He brought his head closer, then veered to the side and pressed his lips to her shoulder. "I want to see you naked, Jenna. All the things we couldn't do before, all the things I told you about, I want to do now."

She thought of her blouse, and her pants, and his jeans, and impatience quivered through her. "I want to touch you, Damien. Really touch you."

Straightening up, he lifted his hand, splaying his fingers, holding his palm toward her. "Go ahead."

Jenna released her grip on the dresser, lifting her hand in a gesture that mirrored his. Time seemed to stop. She held her breath as the very air around them hummed with anticipation.

Before she could close the final distance between them, he twisted his wrist and caught her sleeve, then raised his other hand and touched her cheek.

Her breath escaped in a shuddering sigh. Through senses that were heightened by endless days of restraint,

Jenna felt his gentle caress send tendrils of contact reaching to her soul.

"Rose petals," he said softly. "Eyes the color of springtime. I've waited so long, Jenna."

She moved her head, rubbing her cheek against his palm, reveling in the sensation of his long, strong fingers on her skin. "This feels so...right. It was worth the wait."

Satisfaction spread over his face as he outlined the shape of her mouth with his fingertips. "There's no current carrying me away," he said, stroking her lower lip with his thumb. "I'm still here."

She swayed closer, pulling her wrist free from his light grasp to press her hands to his chest. Crisp hair curled against her fingers, taut skin slid beneath her palms. "I can feel your heart beating."

He traced her eyebrows, her temples, the delicate skin under her eyes with the reverence of a sculptor. "You're holding me. You're keeping me here."

They hadn't moved, yet Jenna was sure that the room began to revolve. She blinked, raising her gaze to his, and something more than desire sparked between them. "Damien?"

"You feel it too, don't you?"

The floor tilted, and Jenna grabbed his shoulders for support. "Damien, what's happening?"

"You do feel it." He cupped her chin, a smile of wonder melting away the last of his caution. Power crackled in the air as he focused on her lips.

Colors flashed behind her eyes. Sounds, scents, tastes flowed over her like the first rays of the rising sun. Life stretched and hummed through her bones. "I don't understand."

He lowered his head slowly until his mouth was a breath away from hers. "Do you feel the connection?"

Her palms tingled where they touched his skin. Her heart pounded in rhythm with his. "Connection? But—"

"It's strong. Stronger than any of the other bonds."

"But I'm not worried about Emily anymore," she said. Her voice sounded distant, as if she were drawing away, standing outside herself. But she had never felt more vividly... here.

"It's not your niece I've connected with." His words were no more than a puff of air across her lips.

Something pushed gently, coaxingly, inside her head. "What..."

"It's you, Jenna. I've connected with you."

Before the full implications of what he had said could register, he covered her lips with his.

Awareness blazed through her as his tongue slipped boldly between her lips. She received the pleasure of the moist caress at the same time she felt the satisfaction of giving it. She felt his arms go around her back, pulling her tightly to the front of his body, and she felt her own yielding softness. Her hands slid upward to grasp his face, and she felt the pressure of fingers on her cheeks.

The connection. He felt what she did. She experienced what he did. Yes, *yes!* She should have realized. She should have guessed. This was what it was like to make love with a telepath.

As if a strong wind blew open a door in her mind, impressions swept over her consciousness. Loneliness, seclusion... hope, need... fear. Desire. More than desire. Hunger. Craving.

His emotions poured into her, mixing with hers, building with a strength that didn't come from the mind. The kiss went on, an exploration of taste and texture, an exquisite sharing. He knew just the right pressure, just the right movements, precisely the place to flick with his tongue, exactly the moment to nip with his teeth. She felt an echo of her moan rise in Damien's throat as she cradled his cheeks in her palms and returned the emotion along with the kiss.

She was floating, swirling on a current of yearning, suffused with an energy that rose from some forgotten, instinctive level. Dizziness blurred her vision and she closed her eyes. Damien lifted his head, and she saw her face, cheeks flushed, lips swollen and parted. She felt his knuckles graze her neck as he fastened his hands on the edges of her blouse. She felt his urgency as he ripped the fabric open, shared his satisfaction as the buttons popped.

"Jenna," he whispered. She thought he whispered. "You're beautiful. More than I imagined. More than I dreamed."

There was no hesitancy, no question. She shrugged out of the remains of silk and lace, then looped her arms around Damien's neck, lifting herself for the caress she knew he wanted to give.

She felt his pleasure with her pleasure, enjoyed the tremors that followed his touch, helped him peel away the rest of their clothing before they staggered to the bed together and giddily wrapped each other in an embrace of naked skin. They rolled to the edge of the mattress, tangling their legs, trying to meld their bodies as closely as their minds.

The craving became yearning. Then necessity. Jenna didn't know whose fingers reached for the square packet in his wallet, whose hands smoothed the thin membrane into place, whose frustration over the reason for this final barrier flung the empty foil across the room. Her consciousness faded and twined with Damien's. They flowed into each other as naturally and inevitably as night flows into day.

The shaking began in her toes and the tips of her fingers. Jenna didn't even question it—her disbelief had been suspended long ago. The tremors spread inward, over every inch of her body, vibrating in a rhythm that ebbed and built, ebbed and built until she was riding the crest of a wave that was higher and faster and stronger and—

Jenna!

She felt Damien's cry and opened her eyes, her vision clearing enough for a glimpse of his face.

There was no word to describe the expression on his harsh, handsome features. He looked like a prisoner who had turned his face up to the sun after spending a lifetime in a dungeon, a lost sailor who had thought never to feel the firmness of the earth beneath his feet, a traveler coming home.

Jenna blinked back tears as she saw a joy so vast she felt humbled. "Damien."

His body convulsed, and the wave crashed over her. Wrapped in his arms, she gave herself up to the current, trusting his strength to bring them back.

For rich, sumptuous moments she drifted with him. She didn't want to return. She wanted to glory in the feelings that continued to tremble through their joined bodies, stay in this timeless embrace forever. But gradually, one by one, her senses untangled and steadied. She was lying on her back, her legs locked around Damien's waist, his face pressed against her throat. Shivers, brief aftershocks, whispered over her skin wherever it pressed against his. She lowered her legs, letting the soles of her feet skim lightly over the backs of his thighs, his knees, his calves, reveling in his masculine contours and textures. Her entire body was sated, suffused with contentment.

Bliss. That's what she felt. At last, the emptiness was filled. She'd wanted to make love, but what she and Damien had done was...incredible. It had been beyond what she had thought humanly possible. Nothing in her life could have prepared her for this. They had joined. Everything. Their bodies, their minds. Their hearts...

With a muffled curse, Damien withdrew and rolled to his back, flinging his forearm over his eyes.

She felt as if a part of her had been torn away. Turning on her side, she laid her hand on his chest. "Damien?"

At her touch, he flinched. "Don't," he said.

"Am I hurting you?"

"No."

She splayed her hand, tunneling her fingers through his springy mat of hair. He liked that. She knew he did—she'd felt the way he liked it. "What's wrong?"

He caught her hand and held it away from his chest. "This was a mistake."

Pain struck unexpectedly with his words. She steeled herself against it, trying to hold on to the happiness he had given her. "It was wonderful," she said. "I have no regrets."

His grip on her hand tightened. "I had no right to take what you gave me. This wasn't what I asked for."

"I was willing, Damien. More than willing."

"No, this wasn't part of our bargain."

If she hadn't been so attuned to his feelings, she might have heard only rejection in his voice. She might not have detected the desperation. She brushed a kiss over his shoulder, and another aftershock rippled through her as she tasted the musky tang of spent passion. "We'd agreed to do this."

"No, we didn't agree to this. What you gave me was more than sex, Jenna." He turned his head, meeting her gaze, finally letting her see the swirl of emotions that roiled in the depths of his eyes. "That's what I wanted, but that's not what this was."

"What..."

"I asked for your *body*. That was all. Nothing else."

"I know."

"Do you? Do you really understand what just happened between us?"

"How could I? I didn't know what to expect. You didn't tell me how a telepath—"

"It isn't always like that. Hell, I don't think it's ever been like that for me before. The connection was so strong."

The connection. With her. "But—"

"After all the times I've ridden the current, I should recognize it. I should have seen it coming, but I didn't want to."

"Damien, I—"

"This was love."

The word hung in the air between them. It seemed to echo in the sudden silence. An accusation. A confession. A curse.

Jenna's hand curled into a fist within his. "Love?"

"You love me," he stated. "I saw it. I felt it. You love me."

No. She already had too much to deal with. She was still trying to come to terms with the physical splendor of making love with Damien . . . making love . . . no. *No!*

He continued to look at her, his fingers enclosing hers in a grip that was bordering on painful. "Yes."

She was too vulnerable, too open, too . . . naked. She didn't want to face this possibility, didn't want to expose her feelings to the scrutiny she'd avoided until now. Yet the truth was so obvious, she should have realized it days ago. She hadn't let herself realize it. Her mind had shied away from the possibility in a futile attempt at self-protection, but—

She loved him. It had been growing inside her, hidden and stubborn, resisting her repeated attempts to stamp it out. But no matter how much she'd tried to prevent it, she'd had no choice. It just happened. She could no longer deny it.

The last of the sensual haze that had cocooned her perception finally melted away. She was completely, thoroughly, hopelessly in love with Damien Reese.

He released her hand and sat up, turning away, swinging his legs over the side of the bed so that he was out of her reach. His spine curved as he leaned forward and dropped his head into his hands. "I thought you understood," he said. "Love is the one thing that I can never accept from you, Jenna. I can never accept it from anyone."

Chapter Fourteen

The party to welcome Emily home passed in a blur for Jenna. The stuffed toys that Ian had bought overflowed every piece of Brigit's furniture that wasn't already groaning beneath the weight of Nora's baking. With the amazing resilience of the very young, Emily was on her way to recovering from her ordeal. So was Brigit. The family was reunited. Everything was as it should be. Yet even surrounded by celebration and happiness, Jenna nevertheless felt a sense of hollow loss inside.

In the days that followed, it grew deeper. She visited the real estate office to talk to her co-workers. Business was slow as it usually was during this time of the year, and there wasn't any need for her to cut short the vacation time she'd taken. She spent some evenings with her friends, but she found her thoughts drifting after only a few minutes. This morning she had gone to visit Rachel, but instead of drifting, Jenna's thoughts had been all too

sharply focused. Seeing Damien's grandmother, listening
to more details of his early years and his grief over his wife
had only made it all the more difficult for Jenna to accept the fact that he was gone.

Oh, yes. He was gone. Thoroughly, permanently gone.
He'd removed all traces of his presence from her home
and had left without a backward glance. She hadn't said
goodbye. She hadn't thought she'd be able to hold herself together long enough to pull on her clothes, so she'd
stayed where she was, huddled on the bed that still held
traces of the heat from his body, and she'd listened, unmoving, to the closing of the apartment door.

It had been five days. In her head she'd always known
that it would end this way. But in her heart . . .

Slumping into the corner of the couch, she let the magazine on her lap flip shut. She should have gone back to
work early, cleaned up her files, cleaned the windows,
anything. She shouldn't have decided to spend the rest of
her days off moping around this empty apartment, looking through back issues of these magazines, studying the
photographs that Damien had taken. It was a poor sub-
stitute for his presence, but at least it was some kind of
connection. She'd spent hours marveling at his talent and
his sensitivity, remembering . . .

Remembering.

The images crowded in, jostling across her mind. This
was where he had listened while she'd told him about
Alex. This was where he had held her while she'd cried. In
that chair at the table he had licked chocolate icing off his
fingers while he'd eaten half a pan of brownies. Four
hundred miles beyond that window, he had led her to her
niece. Through that doorway was the bed where he'd
whirled her to a plane of existence where senses blended
and emotions flowed and flared with a power that still

burned in her memory. He'd given her bliss, she'd given him love.

But he hadn't taken it. He didn't want it.

She stood up abruptly, tossing the magazine on top of the stack on the coffee table. This wasn't fair. It just wasn't fair. She knew all the reasons why he didn't want to risk establishing bonds with anyone. It was his gift, those telepathic abilities that had warped his childhood and made him an outcast. She might have been able to heal after the loss of her son, but Damien was different. He felt everything more intensely. His pain was so much worse.

He'd warned her, hadn't he? Right at the start, he'd told her that he recognized love but he didn't want any part of it. She'd warned herself, too. She'd known that falling in love with this man would be the worst possible thing she could do.

You love me, he'd said. *I saw it. I felt it. You love me.*

He had known before she had. She had deceived herself, but it was impossible to deceive a psychic. They had connected, spiritually and physically. Even though it had been five days since that wild, explosive joining, her body still quivered and tingled whenever she allowed herself to remember.

Was that the real reason she had gone against her upbringing and common sense and had agreed to the price he'd demanded for his help? Had she already been falling in love with him? Had her heart known all along that what he asked of her she was willing to give him freely?

She crossed her arms over her stomach, trying to keep her thoughts away from that painful loop. He was right. He'd only asked for her body, but she'd given him her heart and her love.

And he didn't want either one.

The tears were already scalding her cheeks before she realized that she was crying. She wiped them off impatiently. For someone who didn't normally give in to tears, she'd shed more in the past week than in the previous four years.

He didn't want her love. Or her family's gratitude, or anyone's friendship. No bonds. No emotions. He'd explained all that when he'd told her about his wife, and about his struggle to regain his grip on reality. He'd suffered so much. If she really loved him, she would accept his decision and let him go, wouldn't she?

Jenna walked to the window and gazed blankly at the buildings across the street. If she really loved him? *If?* She had it on the very best authority that she did. So why couldn't she come to terms with his decision? Why wasn't she over at Brigit's, visiting with Emily, enjoying the company of the child who had been the focus of all her love, getting on with her life the way Damien was getting on with his?

At least the media frenzy that had followed Emily's rescue had died down considerably in the past few days. Her family had closed ranks, refusing to give out any details. As he'd promised, Frank and the detective from Chicago had held press conferences where they'd credited their success to good, solid police work. When the Sorensons flew back to Des Moines with Tim, they told the press the same thing.

Hopefully the publicity wouldn't cause Damien any more problems. She didn't know how the town of Hemlock would react to people who might try to follow him home, but she suspected that inquisitive strangers wouldn't get a warm reception. And he used a different name for his work, so he'd always be able to escape through that if he needed to.

Yes, he would be able to get on with his life, exactly the life he wanted. She shouldn't try to interfere. She'd already brought him so much misery.

But she'd also brought him happiness. Joy. Understanding. Acceptance. She knew that, because they had connected. Damien had felt her love, and she had felt...

What had she felt? She was no telepath, and yet she'd felt the strength of the current that had swept through them. The connection had gone both ways. She'd seen herself through his eyes, felt his pleasure, felt a myriad of emotions. Those emotions hadn't been only hers.

Curling her hands into fists, she whirled around, looking at the empty apartment, looking at her empty future. The emotions *hadn't* been only hers. *She'd* felt the current. Could that have meant the love was...shared?

Did he love her? And was that the reason he had been so desperate to leave?

Suddenly, what had seemed so complex became glaringly simple. She loved him, and that wasn't going to change, no matter how much time or distance he tried to put between them. He would always have problems because of his gift, but they weren't insurmountable. If he really did love her...

If?

Knowing full well that it might turn out to be the most futile, self-destructive, painful thing she'd ever done, Jenna strode to her bedroom and yanked her suitcase out of her closet. She tossed it into the center of her bed and started throwing in her clothes. The lethargy that had held her here all week had finally been swept away, as if...as if a strong wind had blown open a door in her mind.

Yes. *Yes!* The connection had gone both ways.

She'd wasted five days. In two more he would be leaving for Alberta and it might be months before she could have the chance to see him again. By then it might be too

late. By then the walls around his feelings might be to
thick for anyone to break through. It might be too la
now.

But she had been willing to brave the toughest odds fo
the sake of her sister's child. Why the hell was she lettin,
the man she loved slip away without a fight?

Determination tingled through her body. Jenna Law
rence would not give up. Not this time. The stakes wer
too high, and she wasn't about to let pride or caution ge
in her way. Her heart might be battered, but it was sti
beating. Damien might be gone, but she knew where t
find him.

Damien saw the wolf tracks when he was half a mil
from the cabin. There were two sets, one a bit smaller tha
the other. The heavier, larger one had a distinctive, un
even pattern to the spacing of the paw prints. Shifting hi
camera to his back, he knelt down for a closer look. Yes
there was a jagged edge to the pad of the right forepaw
Evidently Smoke had finally decided to return and ha
brought company.

Straightening up quickly, he started forward, his snow
shoes swishing over the snow drift. This was the first sig
he'd seen of Smoke since he'd returned to the cabin si
days ago. For a while he'd thought the animal was gon
for good. Wait until he told Jenna about this. She'd bee
concerned that Smoke wouldn't be able to survive on hi
own, but not only had the wolf survived, he had found..

Oh, God, he was doing it again. Thinking about he
Wanting to show her things, tell her things. He'd left he
almost a week ago, but he had yet to truly leave.

But this was for the best. Making a swift, clean cut wa
the most painless way. For both of them. He knew h
shouldn't have taken what she'd offered, what she hadn'
even known she'd offered. It had been unforgivably self

sh. She deserved better than a bitter recluse of a man who wouldn't let himself love her. He'd seen how well she had fitted into the warmth of her family. Her grief over her son was almost healed. In time she would find another man who could give her love, and a future, and—

Swearing sharply, he pushed aside a spruce bough with enough force to make it snap. No matter how much discipline he tried to exert, he couldn't prevent the stab of primitive possessiveness that ripped through him each time he thought of Jenna with someone else.

And sometimes, in moments of weakness, he wanted to return to Minneapolis, kick down the apartment door that he'd so carefully closed, sling Jenna over his shoulder and carry her all the way back to his cabin. She was *his,* dammit. How could he face the empty bleakness of the years ahead now that he'd sampled her love?

Fool. Idiot. He'd thought he'd made the only decision possible. Six days without her and he didn't know what the hell he wanted.

The wolf tracks veered off to the right and disappeared into a spruce thicket, then reemerged on the other side, paralleling the path Damien's snowshoes had left this morning. He should have been making preparations for his trip to Alberta instead of doing this day-long hike through the woods. He'd taken the camera along, but he'd used it more as an excuse than as a tool. He was getting tired of looking at life through a viewfinder, weary of being an outsider. Especially now that he'd tasted the heady sense of belonging when Jenna had welcomed him into—

Damn! How far would he have to go to be rid of her?

He approached the cabin from the back, following the path beside the woodshed. He had almost reached the front yard when he heard a familiar growl.

Hackles raised, head lowered, Smoke moved out of the early-evening shadows and loped directly into his path.

Upper lip curled back in warning, the wolf fixed his gaze on Damien.

"You've been away too long, Smoke," he said calmly, continuing to move forward. "Jenna would have something to say about those manners of yours."

"I already did."

He'd been hearing her voice in his imagination so many times a day, it took him a beat to grasp the fact that it was real.

But it was. And so was she. As he came around the corner of the cabin, the scene struck him all at once. There was a truck parked at the end of a pair of snowy ruts behind his Jeep, a red pickup with a sign on the door from the Hemlock Garage. Steam rose from a bowl that had been set into the snowdrift at the foot of the porch steps. And at the top of the steps, with her neon pink ski jacket gleaming through the dusk like a smile, stood . . .

"Jenna," he breathed.

In a spray of snow, Smoke bounded toward the bowl. He gobbled down what was left, ran his tongue around the inside of the rim, then loped toward the trees at the edge of the clearing. Tail held high, he blended into the shadows. A moment later, a pale gray shape disappeared into the forest behind him.

Damien barely noticed. He squatted down to undo the bindings of his snowshoes, leaving them where they were as he walked to the edge of the porch. Heart pounding, he stood there and looked up at her.

Yes, she was real. His imagination had never been able to duplicate the springtime green of those eyes, or the defiant tilt of her chin. "Jenna," he said again. Had any sound ever felt this good on his tongue? "Jenna, what are you doing here?"

"Making dinner." She smiled hesitantly. "Do you want some before I feed it all to your wolf?"

That smile was dissolving six days of good intentions. Damien glanced behind him at the truck. "You'll be able to make it to the road before dark if you start—"

"Oh, no you don't. I didn't fly to Hemlock and wheedle the use of that truck out of your local mechanic and put up with your pet's antisocial idea of saying hello just to quit now."

"He wasn't antisocial. He was protecting his mate."

"His what?"

"Didn't you see the other wolf?"

She looked toward the trees, her hand going to her throat, but then she shook her head and raised her chin. "I'm glad he's no longer alone. But even if he'd brought an entire pack, I wouldn't have let that stop me."

Only once before had he heard such determination in her voice. He took a step closer. "Is it Emily? Is she all right?"

"She's fine. The whole family is fine." She paused. "Almost fine."

"What's wrong?"

For a while she didn't answer, her breath escaping in delicate puffs of vapor, her pale hair lifting in the cold breeze. When she finally spoke, her words slipped right past his crumbling defenses. "I miss you, Damien," she said softly.

How could she have come here after the way he had left her? And the things he'd said? Why did her eyes still shine as if she thought the world was full of wonder? He should let her go. Send her away. Remind himself of his resolve never again to let . . .

It might be stupid, crazy and thoroughly irresponsible, but he was powerless to prevent what happened next. He put one foot on the bottom step, vaulted up to the porch and did what he'd wanted to do in the first place. Despite his bulky parka and her fluffy jacket, he wrapped his arms around her in an embrace so tight he was sure he could feel her heart beating against his.

Her sigh spoke more clearly than words of the misery of the past six days. "Oh, Damien. I know you told me not to come, but I had to."

"I can't let you stay with me," he said, not loosening his hold in the slightest.

Snuggling against him, she locked her hands behind his neck. "You don't have to leave for your assignment until tomorrow. I'm staying until then. We have some things we need to talk about."

"I thought we'd said it all."

"We might have said it, but not aloud." She leaned back in the circle of his arms and her smile strengthened.

Looking down into her open, trusting face, drinking in her hopeful expression, he still couldn't end the embrace. He might be a fool, but for now he was a happy fool.

Damien moved his right arm to the small of her back, reached out with his left to open the cabin door, then lifted her off her feet and held her tightly to the front of his body as he walked inside. Kicking the door shut with his heel, he pressed his face to her hair and inhaled greedily. Just a little longer. Maybe for tonight. Or maybe he could delay his trip and—

With a muffled exclamation, she twisted out of his embrace. "No," she said shakily. "Wait. I have something I need to say."

He dropped his gloves to the floor. His boots and his parka followed. He reached for the zipper of her jacket.

She took a deep breath. "I love you, Damien."

His hands shook but he didn't stop. He eased off her jacket and tossed it to the floor on top of his. "Don't love me. I can't accept your love."

"It doesn't make any difference. I love you anyway."

"I didn't ask for your love."

"No. No one can ask for it. Or bargain for it. Or put a price on it." She stepped back. "For someone who is an expert when it comes to sensing emotions, you missed the most important thing about love."

"Don't do this, Jenna," he said, catching her shoulders to keep her from retreating further. "Please. It's so good to have you here. I don't want to—"

"I understand. Really I do. Because of your abilities you think you can't risk accepting what I'm offering. There's no denying that loving someone is a risk. That's the whole point."

"What do you mean?"

She pressed her palms to his chest. "Love is unconditional. It's given freely. If we're lucky enough to find it, we can't think about what it costs." Her gaze locked on his as she slid her hands upward. "Love, Damien, is a gift."

A gift. All his life he'd put another meaning on that word. In the space of a heartbeat, Jenna was turning everything around.

"It's a true gift," she went on. "Something that has no price. That's my love. And I'm giving it to you."

His pulse sped, his body quivered. "Jenna, I—"

"All right. As I said, it's a gift. With no strings, no cost. But before you send me away for good, I want you to consider something else. Because of your abilities, you feel emotions more deeply than other people, but they're still the same emotions. We all take risks, we all have to deal with them. It's part of being human." Tears glistened in her eyes. "You loved your wife. I loved my son. It hurt to lose them, and it will always hurt. I understand."

"Yes, you do. Only someone who loves deeply will hurt deeply."

She blinked hard, pressing her lips together until she regained control over her voice. "The stakes are high, but I still believe it's worth the risk."

Walls were shattering. The wonder he'd always sensed in her gaze was flowing into him. "Jenna, I've lived alone for so long. Even when I was married, we essentially lived in isolation. I don't know whether I could end that."

"Life is about change. The sun rising. Winter turning to spring. We've come so far together already, we'll be able to find a way if you want to. You're the one who's shown me that anything is possible."

Anything? If only... "You've seen what my life is like, the rejection, the demands, the harassment."

"And we handled it together, didn't we? You managed to function perfectly well around other people."

"That's because you were there beside me—" He drew in his breath. Of course. The strength of Jenna's emotions had helped keep his own abilities under control. Just as she had been his beacon back to reality each time he'd traveled the void.

Hell, why hadn't he seen it before? He'd believed that he needed to avoid strong emotion in order to live a normal life, but it was the other way around. The closer he'd grown to Jenna, the better he'd been able to cope. Was she right? Was it really possible?

He felt her faith tug at him, filling him with longing.

"It won't be easy," she said. "We'll both need to make compromises, but if you're willing to move to Minneapolis, we could find a house, maybe one like your grandmother used to have, and you could fix up a darkroom. Maybe set up a studio. I could arrange my schedule so I could accompany you on the assignments you took. And—"

"And I could see Rachel again," he said, the future that had once seemed so bleak now blossoming in front of him.

"Yes. She misses you. My family would welcome you, too. You won't have to keep fighting your battles alone."

"And I could learn sign language. For Emily."

"Oh, Damien, yes. Yes!"

The misery of the past six days dissolved like mist in the dawn wind. What he wanted—deep in his heart, really wanted—became perfectly clear.

She lifted her hand and placed it against his cheek with a touch as gentle as her smile and as strong as the promise of spring. "I love you, Damien. I always will. The bond is there for you anytime you're ready."

Closing his eyes, he leaned into her caress. And saw himself. Wild, black hair, lean cheeks, harsh lines beside a trembling mouth. Loneliness. Need. And something he thought he'd never see again. Hope.

She pressed closer, sliding her hand to the back of his head as she raised her face. "There. That's all I have to say. If you still want me to leave—"

"No."

"What?"

"I don't want you to leave me."

"Does that mean—"

He brought his lips down on hers, giving her his answer without words. The connection between them, that invisible, intangible bond that bound them more surely than a wedding ring, surged from his heart to hers. He tasted her surprise, heard her muffled cry of joy, and the room started to whirl around him. Yet he'd never felt more solidly anchored. He deepened the kiss, parting her lips, opening his mind, letting the emotion capture him. Yet he'd never felt more free.

I love you.

The words were formless. Soundless. They echoed in the air he breathed and vibrated through his bones. Smiling, he scooped Jenna into his arms and carried her to his bed, to the place where he'd first heard her. There would be time enough for talk later. There would be a lifetime of chances and risks they would face together.

But for now, Damien had a gift of his own he was eager to share.

Epilogue

It was in the hushed, reverent, breathless moment before dawn, when the world awaits the promise of renewal and the human soul reaches out for an affirmation of life, that Damien heard the child's cry.

Smiling lazily, he rolled over and fitted himself against Jenna's back, hooking her ankle with his to draw her more snugly to the front of his body. His hand skimmed over her hip to rest on her swollen abdomen.

She stirred sleepily. "Is he up again?"

He kissed her shoulder, splaying his fingers as he traced the movements of their unborn son. "He's restless."

"Waking me up just to get attention," she mumbled. "He's as demanding as his father."

"Uh-huh." He skimmed his hand upward to cup her breast, enjoying the heavy warmth in his palm the same way he enjoyed all the changes in her body. And the changes in his life during the past year. "I didn't hear any protests from you last night."

"Mmm. I suppose you didn't."

"As a matter of fact, you never said a word."

She wiggled her hips more securely into the cradle of his thighs. "Maybe not aloud."

He moved his hand back to her belly, feeling the outline of a tiny foot. No matter how many times he touched her, it was still a miracle. His wife. Their child. A new beginning, another chance.

And as the light from another dawn strengthened, he tightened his embrace, his heart filled with wonder at the life he held. And the blessings he'd been granted.

There would be no end to Damien's gifts.

*　*　*　*　*

Silhouette

SPECIAL EDITION

That SPECIAL *Woman!*

Do you take this man...?

A woman determined to stay single: Serena Fanon
A man with a proposal: Travis Holden

The last thing Serena Fanon expected on her return
home to Big Sky Country was an offer of marriage. Most
surprising was the man doing the asking—Travis Holden.
Serena thought she wasn't interested. But
how could she refuse Montana's best-lookin',
most heart-stoppin' man?

Made in MONTANA

Find out this September in
MONTANA PASSION
(SE #1051, 9/96)
by
Jackie Merritt

Look us up on-line at: http://www.romance.net

TSW996

MILLION DOLLAR SWEEPSTAKES
AND EXTRA BONUS PRIZE DRAWING

No purchase necessary. To enter the sweepstakes, follow the directions published and complete and mail your Official Entry Form. If your Official Entry Form is missing, or you wish to obtain an additional one (limit: one Official Entry Form per request, one request per outer mailing envelope) send a separate, stamped, self-addressed #10 envelope (4 1/8" x 9 1/2") via first class mail to: Million Dollar Sweepstakes and Extra Bonus Prize Drawing Entry Form, P.O. Box 1867, Buffalo, NY 14269-1867. Request must be received no later than January 15, 1998. For eligibility into the sweepstakes, entries must be received no later than March 31, 1998. No liability is assumed for printing errors, lost, late, non-delivered or misdirected entries. Odds of winning are determined by the number of eligible entries distributed and received.

Sweepstakes open to residents of the U.S. (except Puerto Rico), Canada and Europe who are 18 years of age or older. All applicable laws and regulations apply. Sweepstakes offer void wherever prohibited by law. Values of all prizes are in U.S. currency. This sweepstakes is presented by Torstar Corp., its subsidiaries and affiliates, in conjunction with book, merchandise and/or product offerings. For a copy of the Official Rules governing this sweepstakes, send a self-addressed, stamped envelope (WA residents need not affix return postage) to: MILLION DOLLAR SWEEPSTAKES AND EXTRA BONUS PRIZE DRAWING Rules, P.O. Box 4470, Blair, NE 68009-4470, USA.

SWP-ME96

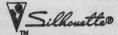

As seen on TV!
Free Gift Offer

With a Free Gift proof-of-purchase from any Silhouette® book,
you can receive a beautiful cubic zirconia pendant.

This gorgeous marquise-shaped stone is a genuine cubic
zirconia—accented by an 18" gold tone necklace.
(Approximate retail value $19.95)

Send for yours today...
compliments of ▼ *Silhouette*®
™

To receive your free gift, a cubic zirconia pendant, send us one original proof-of-
purchase, photocopies not accepted, from the back of any Silhouette Romance™,
Silhouette Desire®, Silhouette Special Edition®, Silhouette Intimate Moments®
or Silhouette Yours Truly™ title available in August, September or October at your favorite
retail outlet, together with the Free Gift Certificate, plus a check or money order for
$1.65 U.S./$2.15 CAN. (do not send cash) to cover postage and handling, payable
to Silhouette Free Gift Offer. We will send you the specified gift. Allow 6 to 8 weeks for
delivery. Offer good until October 31, 1996 or while quantities last. Offer valid in the
U.S. and Canada only.

Free Gift Certificate

Name: _____

Address: _____

City: _____ State/Province: _____ Zip/Postal Code: _____

Mail this certificate, one proof-of-purchase and a check or money order for postage
and handling to: SILHOUETTE FREE GIFT OFFER 1996. In the U.S.: 3010 Walden
Avenue, P.O. Box 9077, Buffalo NY 14269-9077. In Canada: P.O. Box 613, Fort Erie,
Ontario L2Z 5X3.

FREE GIFT OFFER
084-KMD

ONE PROOF-OF-PURCHASE

To collect your fabulous FREE GIFT, a cubic zirconia pendant, you must include this
original proof-of-purchase for each gift with the properly completed Free Gift Certificate.

084-KMD

There's nothing quite like a family

The new miniseries by
Pat Warren

Three siblings are about to be reunited.
And each finds love along the way....

HANNAH
Her life is about to change now that she's met
the irresistible Joel Merrick in HOME FOR HANNAH
(Special Edition #1048, August 1996).

MICHAEL
He's been on his own all his life. Now he's
going to take a risk on love...and
take part in the reunion he's been
waiting for in MICHAEL'S HOUSE
(Intimate Moments #737, September 1996).

KATE
A job as a nanny leads her to Aaron Carver,
his adorable baby daughter and the
fulfillment of her dreams in KEEPING KATE
(Special Edition #1060, October 1996).

Meet these three siblings from

Silhouette SPECIAL EDITION®
and

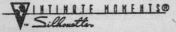

The exciting new cross-line continuity series about love,
marriage—and Daddy's unexpected need for a baby carriage!

You loved

THE BABY NOTION by Dixie Browning (Desire #1011 7/96)
and
BABY IN A BASKET by Helen R. Myers
(Romance #1169 8/96)

Now the series continues with...

MARRIED...WITH TWINS! by Jennifer Mikels
(Special Edition #1054 9/96)

The soon-to-be separated Kincaids just found out they're
about to be parents. Will their newfound family grant them a
second chance at marriage?

Don't miss the next books in this wonderful series:

HOW TO HOOK A HUSBAND (AND A BABY)
by Carolyn Zane (Yours Truly #29 10/96)

DISCOVERED: DADDY
by Marilyn Pappano (Intimate Moments #746 11/96)

DADDY KNOWS LAST continues each month...
only from

Silhouette®

Look us up on-line at: http://www.romance.net

DKL-SE

You're About to Become a *Privileged Woman*

Reap the rewards of fabulous free gifts and benefits with proofs-of-purchase from Silhouette and Harlequin books

Pages & Privileges™

It's our way of thanking you for buying our books at your favorite retail stores.

**Harlequin and Silhouette—
the most privileged readers in the world!**

For more information about Harlequin and Silhouette's **PAGES & PRIVILEGES** program call the Pages & Privileges Benefits Desk: **1-503-794-2499**

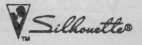

Silhouette®

SSE-PP175